ABOUT THE AUTHOR

Neil Grimmett was born in Birmingham. After being expelled from school at 14 years of age, he spent the next decade on the road and in recording studios playing the drums with various rock bands. He has also worked making high explosives at a top secret establishment for the Ministry of Defence; as a gamekeeper for minor aristocracy; and as a professional handler of show dogs.

For the last eight years Neil's short stories have appeared in leading literary magazines and web sites around the world: he has published over thirty-five so far with others pending. After travelling around the Greek Islands, Neil currently lives in Spain with his wife Lisa.

Neil Grimmett

THE BESTOWING SUN

FLAME
BOOKS

FLAME BOOKS

Published in 2004 by FLAME BOOKS

Flame Books Ltd, PO Box 11944, Birmingham, B14 7WF, UK

www.flamebooks.com

© Neil Grimmett, 2004
All rights reserved

The moral right of the author has been asserted

*This book is sold subject to the condition that it shall not,
by way of trade or otherwise, be lent, re-sold, or otherwise
circulated without the publisher's prior consent in any
form of binding or cover other than in which it is published
and without a similar condition including this condition
being imposed on the subsequent purchaser*

Printed in England by JRDigitial Print Services Ltd

Cover Artwork © Louise Yeandle, 2004

Design & Typesetting by REPUBLIKA D&MPB, Italy

ISBN 0-9545945-2-5

For

LISA: for everything

CHAPTER ONE

"Mommy." Richard snatched the sketch pad and ran from the room yelling: "Mommy, William's painted another picture of you, again – and you are *still* in the nudie!"

William stared down at his own long, thin legs. They were white – unlike his brother Richard's, that as well as being shorter and much thicker were already tanned - although the grass in their fields was only just beginning to grow - whispering and sweet-tasting in its rebirth.

He made no response to his brother's act and appeared as far away and dreamy as ever; yet it felt as if a layer of skin had been torn away. The reason – or the main one of many – that he was not bothering to chase was that he wanted to catch the exact shade of his blood as he visualized it flowing from this wound. Already, William was starting to understand that his own demise would need to be recorded with precision and honesty if all his other creations were to exist beyond this time and place; and be set free to expand from any constraints he might impose through his own ego.

"Oh, it's not me," William heard his mother say. Then the gentle rustle of paper, so that light – even the cold one in this dreary dead glimmer – might fill the shadows and illuminate his vision. William listened to the laughter: bubbling from her throat before she choked it back, as he imagined the picture crumbling in her mind. For that moment had been a young girl's laugh. She gave him the sketch pad back later that day just before his bedtime. He did not bother to ask if she'd shown this one to his father. Since the unveiling of the painting - the one commissioned by him - the subject was no longer mentionable. Not that William would have had anything to say if it were. He had a card, pinned to his wall with a quote from Matisse stating: 'That painters must begin by cutting out their tongues'.

The kitchen, particularly the kitchen table, was where the family spent most of their time together. The farmhouse was a three storey building, with high ceilings, five separate chimney blocks and fireplaces in every bedroom. Each of the many rooms was filled with its own share of antiques and oil paintings - gathering dust in the gloom of heavily draped windows. One small front room was used at Christmas: the artificial tree brought down – already decorated – from the attic, the jackdaws nest swept from the chimney and a fire lit. By Boxing Day they were all back in the kitchen with the coal-fired range smoking a little more than usual, and the rest of the indoors contracted to three small bedrooms and one, almost modernized, bathroom. Herbie, William's father, called everything in the house junk and would have sold it all and replaced it with the new and more functional, if it had not been for pressure from his wife, Madeline, and his own doubts about getting a proper price.

The kitchen table was oak. It could seat six along each side with a large carver chair at one end only. Herbie sat there, always. The matching chair from the other end was placed in front of a walnut roll-top desk – the only other place the man ever allowed himself to be seen sitting still. On its top, a dirt-encrusted, once pale green telephone balanced on a pile of Farmer's Weekly, Herbie's sole reading apart from the court news in the local paper

- which gave him a constant source of amusement; especially if he knew the name of the person fined or jailed. Herbie revelled in seeing someone's failure in print: then reading out undeniable evidence that his assessment - even if previously unstated - had once again turned out to be correct. The rest of the desk was stacked with catalogues, accounts and bills, wage packets waiting to be filled or, rarely, collected. Nobody had ever seen the wooden lathes closed for even one day: "The cows don't know it's Christmas: Pigs and chicken have never heard of a holiday" – Herbie's constant reminder if anyone suggested lowering that wooden curtain.

Shortly, during the coming haymaking, the table would be full of workers arriving in relays for breakfast, dinner and other snacks to keep them going until the light faded. Always, their mother would be seated at Herbie's left-hand side dealing out plates like some old lady at a whist drive, or spreading butter on the face of a loaf still warm from the nearby bakers, before slicing the bread thickly but perfectly even. A typical conversation at these times that William had to endure, sat, if not at the table then on the small chintz sofa by its side would be something like, "I can't abide unevenly cut bread," Roly Cart the tractor driver and farm labourer might break the silence by speaking to either Herbie, or to his usual employer, Herbie's distant relative and neighbouring farmer, Silas. Or as the boys had to call him 'Uncle Silas'.

"There is nothing worse," Clicker, a part-time worker, always dried-out and brought in for the harvest would agree. "Not that I know of anyway." He was driving in the trailers, balanced and swaying with the building bricks of hay moulting and peeling in the breeze. Madeline carried on spreading and buttering. Conversation over as the minutes ticked away, to the pendulum's dull steel sway: scything with a rhythm that would once have echoed to hand-wielded, curved blades as they left the grain for gleaning. The three hundred year old stone weights inside the clock chained to gravity and always falling except when, once in every seven days Herbie's stubby fingers wound them back to begin again – the clock probably in those centuries never allowed to miss a single beat.

William was allergic to the damp spores in the house and suffered from hay fever. His brother and father loved to sniff the pollen from the first may-blossom or elderflower and let their gold-dust nostrils flare at his tears. It was, according to the weather report a low pollen count at the moment; and yet this morning he'd sneezed himself into near exhaustion.

"Oak," Madeline assured him as the panic began to take control and he gasped in another clean breath from his inhaler: one he could easily believe was the last he might ever take. "The oak trees are blossoming, waking up from their old solid slumberings. You know they say that if every leaf fell from an oak tree in the winter, the Devil can have us all."

William held onto the edge of the table and tried to let that image of hope fill his mind; instead, he felt *its* life filling his lungs: rebirths: awakenings. Like some flower wine that years in the bottle suddenly re-ferments at the moment its children bloom: fighting inside the glass to become young and full of heady effervescence again. Or shattering its constraints and turning its bitterness into vinegar: a dark stain, and if left unnoticed, a powder among the shattered, crown-of-thorn glass remains. William let go of the table and sat opposite his brother, ignoring Herbie's look and latest comment about needing to get an oxygen tent erected on the lawn.

He'd already made two jokes at both of his sons' expense.

Richard carried on shovelling down his food as William tried to find the courage to block his throat with a first mouthful. He also sensed that something awful was coming. Jokes and flattery were two of Herbie's main weapons – and he never spent either cheaply. Aggression and bluster only ever followed if they failed and he was challenged; or, on the rare occasion *he* had to deliver something other than his usual 'good tidings'. William believed that his mother had been enchanted, caught and was still controlled by his father's apparent worship and constant praise of her. She never seemed to grow tired of it and was, as usual, being put off-guard.

"That idiot relative of mine," Herbie said, looking sadly down at his plate - the food gone long before anyone else hardly got started: "he went and forgot to spray the Far Fields."

The 'Far Fields' totalled over sixty acres of old pasture and marshland. Sometimes they grazed beef cattle there, always the grass was cut for hay. Silas and Herbie stopped raging their private war for a few weeks and joined forces at this time of year as it saved both men time and money.

"The trouble is the docks," Herbie told Madeline. "I am so worried about them and what to do for the best."

"They'll spoil the hay," Richard said, his mouth open, full of food, half masticated, the pink and grey of life and death mingling inside, but still making William want to paint even this and be free from what he sensed was coming next.

He thought back to the last time his father had played the flattery and humorous game. When Silas and Roly had joined the family at teatime to discuss the future work, "He takes after his mother," Herbie had assured the men as one of them passed some comment on the worthlessness of having an 'artist' in the family. "You go down to the school and see the wall of his classroom and the corridors: covered with his works: teachers say he is a prodigy. They know they are probably sitting on a gold mine."

Richard kicked him under the table and 'Uncle' Silas made a disparaging noise.

"I'll prove it," Herbie said. "William get your sketch block out. I'm commissioning you to do a painting. This family, with its *relation* and *friend* gathered at the table."

William had looked to his mother for help but saw instead her smiling, flicking at her hair. So William went and got his pad and began to make some of his usual speedy sketches, his blueprint in code, that had nothing to do with what anyone else saw. He began - despite the attempts of all the sitters to wriggle and pose, and the fact that the dust from their clothes filled the air and made him gasp so that he might as well have been at the top of a Dutch barn with them – to see more than he'd seen before. It was, he realized the strongest impression so far of his life and youth. And one instigated by his father's seeming nonsense - or was there, he questioned as he worked, something more to his actions ? "Cunning as a fox", he'd heard too many times about Herbie to ignore, but could still not believe it was anything more than a coincidence. William had carried on until the pencil felt as heavy as any bale dropping green and still moist from a dry conveyor belt into the dustiest loft space known.

William had worked solidly on the painting every day since. Nobody was allowed to invade the small corner of his bedroom. Even Herbie got tired of asking, when ? William knew when: the moment the sun reached the mark. It was Herbie's way of knowing when another winter was over and summer returned. A pencil line on the wall that in another family might have shown the progress of children. This one, Herbie explained, told him the exact height the sun needed to have climbed to have driven off that dead flat, expensive and unproductive time of year. To begin the cycle again. That was the moment, William decided, this painting would be completed.

It reached its spot. A short time after, William set up his easel, covered it with a cloth and just as the family sat down for breakfast, got ready for the unveiling. "I will hang this above my desk," Herbie announced, giving his wife's shoulder a squeeze.

Richard had grunted and struggled to his feet the moment the cloth uncovered the canvas, Madeline gave a small cry and clasped her hand over her face. Herbie took the painting without a word or a look at William and carried it off. William had not been able to find it since though, as now, he was still haunted by it.

"The docks will sweat," Richard added to his father's explanation: "if they are not taken out of the grass before it is baled they will sweat inside the barns and send it all bad and frowsty."

Herbie smiled at his usual ally, "What we need," he said, "is a couple of very keen-eyed lads to walk along the rows after the grass has been cut, just going along nice and slowly, and picking out any of the docks."

"My friend Timmy could help," Richard said quickly. "He's looking for some work during the holidays – I bet you his eyes are just as keen as..."

Herbie shut him up with a warning glower. This time he did not bother to repeat another of his well-proven adages: 'If you have a boy, you have a boy. If you have two boys, you have half a boy. And if you have three boys, you have no boy at all'. That was, unless, those two boys did not like each other and would prefer to walk either side of the rows of drying grass pulling out the weeds rather than having to speak, let alone fool around together.

"It will be very nice and picturesque out over the moors at the present," Herbie continued, "and later on, with the sun full up and all the flowers it will be a regular Constable scene. You," Herbie touched Madeline's arm, "could take a picnic out to them. Why I might even come and join in myself."

William knew there was no point arguing or bringing up their agreement that he no longer had to try and do anything on the farm. This, he could only conceive, was his father's revenge for the painting. Herbie was not a man that forgave or forgot anything, in William's judgment.

"But what about the pollen ?" Richard tried. "It will get terrible out there."

William could not recall how many years it was since he'd heard Richard show anything like concern over him. It made him realize how much his brother dreaded spending two weeks virtually alone in his company. Richard was just over a year older than William and had lost interest in his brother the day he refused to climb on the back of his toy tractor and be driven off to work. Now, with Richard in his teens and William about to join him at senior school after the break, there was still nothing obvious they had in common except a mutual dislike. William felt more bad about that briefly than the prospect of the mind-numbing toil, and the hours away from real work.

"William can wear one of my new dust masks, if it *is* bad." Herbie stated. He'd recently bought a consignment of them from some surplus sale to comply with another 'rule dreamt up in Europe'. William had noticed them in one of the sheds: their boxes open with the thin white gauze already stained by particles of dust from the oil-stained earth and rusting farm implements awaiting their recycling.

"A picnic," Madeline sighed dreamily. "I used to love picnics when I was a girl. Beautiful summer dresses. Men in blazers and straw hats. Punting on the river. One man fell in looking at me, even though his fiancée was sat at his feet. Of course, I was very slim then, my hair so long and golden," she reminded them all. "Not that anyone would think it now, but I was considered a beauty in my time."

"You still are. You still are," Herbie stated. "Isn't she boys ?"

"Yes," Richard agreed. "You are."

They all waited for William to speak as he felt himself struggling not to drown.

CHAPTER TWO

William watched as the bedroom door opened and a procession of heavy, brutal shapes, darker than the mist filling his eyes floated in. He assessed that his vision was still seeing double but that there had to be at least three real figures, one of them female: though definitely not his wife.

"Fuck me sideways it stinks like a brewery in here," one voice said.

William began to struggle and attempt to sit up.

"Come on Mr. Halliday," another male voice said, "wake yourself it's time to leave."

"Drunken bastard," the woman hissed.

The bed began to shake and a light seemed to explode above his head. William tried to recall what had happened and led to this. Something came rushing back. Another row. Lorna leaving, demanding that she be allowed to take their daughter with her, he not allowing it. His brother-in-law, Warwick, calling, sounding tired but still amused and pleased: 'Your wife, my little sis has been here and wants me to give you a warning. If you do not let her have her daughter, or get out of the house so that she can come back and look after her, she will call the police. And frankly, from what I've witnessed lately, I can't say that I blame her.'

"Come on now, Mr.William Robert Halliday: you are being arrested."

William was naked as the cover was thrown off him and policewoman Wills could not help noticing that he was erect and large. Both policemen made their own observations: the main one being, that though he was angry and clearly still drunk, he was at least two stone overweight and flabby: not likely to give them too much trouble if it came down to that.

"Fucking domestics," PC Rudd could not help thinking. He was just too jaded to get in time with this latest swing of the political pendulum. He even pitied the man and his chances. If he'd actually hit his wife or worse there would have been no sympathy, but even with the desk sergeant's gentle coaxing she'd been unable to envisage as much as an angry prod of the digit. He was just another silly bastard, who'd decided too late in life he was an artist, then refused to work at anything else, drank and she, they all, hated him.

William managed to get on a pair of baggy blue canvas trousers and a T-shirt, white once, and a smock, both now like the trousers: an abstract of hard-dried oil paints moving stiffly against the sagging of his body, as his mind registered somewhere in amongst the grids and a deep understanding that this was a necessary shedding of another skin, he slumped forward: unwilling still to let go of everything.

The two men helped him to his feet. WPC Wills stared with disgust at this mess,

"Do you ever actually get any paint on the picture," she asked, "or is it just yourself that you like to cover?"

"Actually, I'd just love to paint you, you shitty little dyke. In the nude with the veins in your clitoris swelling off the canvas."

PC Rudd could not stop the slight judder of laughter flowing from his body into the arm of their captive as they escorted him away: he must at least have an artist's eye, he decided, to have spotted that so quickly. The younger officer on the other side spilled anger through his grip mainly because he still hadn't and believed he may stand a chance. WPC Wills took out her notebook and wrote the offer down. 'Perfect,' she thought: 'better than any confession.'

On the landing, a smart-looking woman had William's daughter, Florence, awake, dressed and standing as rigid and offended as her mother had appeared before leaving earlier. Scowling at her father, waiting for him to be removed, for everything to be proper again. William heard the woman tell her that mommy would be brought home soon.

In the car he began to pull himself together slightly: "What exactly am I being arrested for ?" William demanded. He reached quickly into his smock pocket for his cigarettes and Policewoman Wills pounced. She grabbed his hand, then, making certain her nails dug into his wrist and left a scar first, twisted it into a finger lock, bending until something slipped and he cried out in pain.

"What was that for you bitch ?" William yelled as PC Rudd span round and the driver slowed.

"I thought he was going for something in his pocket," she explained to them all.

"My cigarettes, if that is okay."

"It is not," the younger officer stated: "smoking is *another* antisocial habit that others do not have to be subjected to."

"What am I being arrested for ?"

"You made verbal threats against your wife and child," PC Rudd explained. "It is now a criminal offence to do so, you are being taken to the police station to be questioned over the incident and possibly charged."

"And you invaded her *personal space*: which is another offence," WPC Wills added.

"And you've just invaded mine. That was my painting hand. I think you've damaged my favourite finger as well."

"I heard what you would like to paint, *Sir*, and both these officers have witnessed it."

"Have they," PC Rudd heard him say and, once again found it hard not to warm to the man: "both lucky bastards then."

"I saw a couple of your paintings," PC Rudd found himself needing to say as they pulled around the back of the police station and before they released William into the system, "if I had your talent I wouldn't give a fig for all of this." He hoped it would help. Instead he heard the man reply bitterly: "Talent is nothing; work is everything."

~

The cell was cold. William sat on the blue plastic mattress, his head and hand hurting. The cup of tea was tepid and greasy, his cigarette gone out with no lighters allowed. He was attempting to find some words to drown out the ones recently spoken and now echoing around the sterile, yet stained, detention cell. Then, they did not seem important and sprang up in panic and desperation, as the realization hit home that for the first time in his life he was not free. That his liberty had been so easily and inexorably snatched away and just exactly what that was worth. William grabbed the door: its blunted steel ribs, the unfinished exposed construction: no need for the niceties of any skin for those inside. He began to shake the heavy steel. William met the eye as the spy hole nictitated and confirmed he was still alive and closed. Footsteps retreated, bolts shot in other doors and other children of the night groaned or begged forgiveness.

William climbed back onto the bed and pulled the coarse blanket up to his chin. There were no words anyway to change those already said. So many, meant or unmeant. Now, recorded, signed and witnessed. Waiting for tomorrow's court appearance and all that followed. He saw himself: middle-aged, homeless and loveless. And all because something he'd believed long buried had been germinating instead. Waiting for its time to come around again; a curse not a blessing. He felt alone and lost and full of self pity, but could still find enough pride to wish he'd not just made the most ridiculous mistake so far.

After the interrogation William was allowed to use the phone, and, with everything seeming to speed just out of control, he chose to call his brother, Richard. He could not even begin to count the number of years since they had last spoken as the phone rang, the dialing call shared with the desk sergeant. They'd both listened, but with only one picturing that it was trembling into a pale green phone on a roll-top desk. And though Richard and his wife had taken over the farmhouse – William knew that his parents were semi-retired and had converted some barns for their home – in his mind's eye, nothing else would have changed much in that house.

Annie, Richard's wife he guessed, finally answered the phone. In the background he imagined the three children being woken up, all of them still young, all of them completely unknown to him. He listened as Annie explained to his brother, "Your brother is on the phone, he has been arrested and a policeman is listening to the call."

"Billy Bob" – Richard was still the only person to have made this connection out of Herbie's attempt to give his son a fine English name – "after all these years brother: finally went and did it this time my son by the sounds of it."

"Richard, I'm sorry to disturb you but things must have gotten out of hand a bit. I need someone to pick me up and then give me an address or something or I may not be given bail tomorrow."

"We can't do anything tonight," Richard said too quickly, "both of us took a late night drink and would be over the limit to drive."

William heard the sergeant clear his throat at this. He could not imagine his brother drinking anything with the morning's work waiting.

"Then I'll have to spend the rest of the night locked up here." William knew he sounded pathetic but was too shaken to care.

"That won't do you much harm, Billy Bob," Richard said, sounding pleased and uncaring: "probably get a decent fry-up in the morning."

"What about a bail address, Richard, can I give *yours*?"

"A what?"

"Look Richard, Lorna has claimed that I threatened her and Florence. She's even gone as far as saying that I made a threat to kill them both. It looks like until I can sort things out I will have a restraint order stopping me going back to my own house. Also, until I can prove my innocence, I will probably be on bail. If I can't give a suitable address I may have to go and stay on remand or in a bail hostel."

"You sure know all the words Billy Bob."

"You can get a crash course in them here, Richard. They are simple but carry a lot of power."

"So do threats, brother: so do threats to kill."

"I did not mean anything: just some words spoken in anger."

A sigh of frustration breathed from somewhere into both of the brothers' ears. The desk sergeant knew where this was leading and he wanted to try and get back to sleep and not listen to one more domestic squabble tonight.

"So you are telling me no ?" William still needed to ask.

"Look William, my wife has three young children to look after and runs a B&B from here. I have the farm to work mostly by myself now. The one you squandered your share of away a long time ago. Nothing has changed for me. Or ever will. I can't see what you expect me to do about your mess, sorry."

William could still not believe he'd been desperate enough to have rung. Now, beginning to feel the dull reality finding its way through another hangover, that call felt more vile than the memory that he *had* threatened to kill his wife and daughter. 'We all kill the one we love," he recalled. Only he did not love either of them, never had. And that was the real crime.

A pale light washed through the thick opalescence of the cell window, bathing, through its insect-eye fragments, everything in a wash of softness for one moment. A tempera impression before the electric lights again dominated, revealing the cut sharp lines, the stains of bodily fluids upon the walls, graffiti and clawed messages, even one of what he had just confessed to never having: 'Alf Luvs Jane'.

And that light made him think: in a way it had been a tray of child's paints that led back to this – more than any lack of love. Art again. A world viewed again through shape and color. His vision that had obviously, 'Seriously intended to stay'. A simple gift given to a child that he was now going probably to never have anything to do with again. In a way a mirror to his own family's experience of him. He could almost hear his wife, unburdening herself to the policemen earlier. Telling them how it all began. Without really knowing how it had.

~

Lorna's mother bought her granddaughter a small pad of paper and the paints to get her started. No more than a stocking filler lost amongst so much. Florence found it several days later, or rather, Lorna desperate not to cause her mother anymore upset after her first Christmas alone, made certain she did,

"Look Florence," Lorna said, "what else your nanny bought you." At least her mother made an effort. Not like her father and his *young* woman: a cheque gummed inside a card – two days before Christmas from somewhere in Southern France and written in a hand Lorna did not want to recognize. Or the usual, 'winter scene' sent surreptitiously by Madeline to a son who never replied and a daughter-in-law she could probably not even recall having met, and a grandchild still unseen. "Come and see if you have any of your nanny's artistic flair."

Her mother who'd always been a member of the local art club was spending more time than ever painting since she had been deserted. "It was one thing I loved before I met him: loved all the way through our marriage and is still mine, and so important."

"Please Florence, it would be so kind to give nanny a picture to say thank you for all these wonderful gifts."

Lorna saw her daughter glance up from the electronic game beeping its incessant demands: fascinating, compared to the pile of books William had insisted on buying her again; alive and sparkling against the dry paint blocks and stark white of paper. Florence dropped her gaze back as a crystallized explosion called her back too late, and, for the briefest moment there was an expression on her face that made Lorna shudder. It was one that had nothing to do with her or any members of her side of the family and everything to do with what she most disliked about William; and the man whom she'd met a couple of times and was now her father-in-law. A look that seemed at first kind, then, just as you were prepared to accept that gift, became far off and dismissive, and as interested in your real needs as any light glinting on the edge of a scalpel. The noise of an axe falling outside was suddenly comforting with its irregular brutality. Lorna dismissed what she'd witnessed, for now. And left her daughter to the game.

William pushed open the back door carrying in a wicker basket full of logs. He was sweating though a fine powdering of snow covered the ground, "Warm you twice those logs: once when you cut them and again when they burn: now that's what I call value."

Probably, Lorna guessed, another of Herbie's sayings, delivered as unconsciously as the rest of his traits,

"Maybe," Lorna said angrily, "you could manage to persuade your daughter to put down the only toy that seems of any interest to her and paint a picture for her nanny."

"Or pick up a book maybe," William said. Yesterday he'd tried to read her the opening pages of, 'Where the North Wind Blows', ignoring at first the electronic interruptions, but giving up when Lorna arrived and switched on a Christmas special episode of drivel from another hospital or pub – William never watched television and would not have known the difference.

"Thank you," Lorna said, knowing that he would have been waiting his chance for a small revenge.

By late afternoon, after much effort and determination from Lorna, Florence managed to produce three paintings. At one time, she actually appeared genuinely interested. Each time she added another wash of paint or made some unexpected shape, Florence moved back wanting to let her mother see and then get some reaction from William. He was trying to read *another* book that she knew no one normal would have heard of and was clearly disinterested in both of them. Each, 'Oh Brilliant' or, 'Just like Nanny' from her had started to make the work heavier and frantic. Then suddenly the picture became a mass of dark furious waves, swirling and exploding, with the brush pushing holes in the tray of paints. Finally, the liquid oozed through the paper and flowed down her daughter's bare legs and seeped into Lorna's new white ski pants.

They both moved back from the pad, the tintinnabulation of the brush falling and then drowning in the jar, a relief, before their eyes met with something like a shared shame and guilt passing between them.

"That's better," a voice broke into their puzzled reaction: "you are even beginning to feel what an artist feels."

"Oh," Lorna said, "hark at Picasso there. Do you remember what happened when I let him try and paint your bedroom !" And mother and daughter where laughing, relieved, even, it felt to Lorna, rescued from some terrible beginning of a nightmare.

William went back to his book. He'd lied about his past from the start. There was no reason, or way, to change anything now. Lorna came from out of the area - which meant more than five miles away from his village. She had gone to a different school and apart, from being a friend of a friend had no real contact with any of his family. When they were first together, Lorna must have heard some rumors and tried to find out. "I went away, to escape my family and discover myself," he told her, "that was all. Nothing else." She'd never asked again.

Later that night, after Florence had gone to bed and only the keenest hearing would have heard the steady stream of electrons juxtaposing their song against the screech owls swirling over the nearby lake, William walked in and took down Madeline's card. Lorna had just watched him carry in a jar full of water, and nearly worked up the enthusiasm to make some comment about wasn't his wine glass big enough anymore. Lorna did not like drink. Her mother claimed to be allergic to its fumes and had banned her father for years. She was convinced that William was drinking way too much though he denied it. He sat at the dining table, opened her mother's gift of paints, then, after licking the brush as if it were the first cigarette after one of his habitual attempts to quit, began painting on the back of the card.

Lorna waited for the joke. And waited. She saw the litre bottle of Italian Barola remain untouched on the table, the wood fire dancing through its green lens every time she looked over, then become a glow beginning to crumble into cooling ash as she left for bed. Still without a word passing between them.

She felt him climb in next to her later. Not heavy or drunk, not for the first time this holiday attempting to force his hand between her firmly closed thighs or even find a way in from behind as she feigned sleep. But cold and tired – asleep before she was. Lorna dismissed any puzzlement with a relief at being left alone.

The next morning she'd forgotten about it. There was no sign of anything to remind her. William had left early for work. The insurance company was opening for a couple of days before closing again for the New Year break, and though Lorna knew William could easily have taken the whole time off and got one of the junior members to have covered, it was typical of him to go in and do the work himself. Lorna knew also that he would be home late rather than early. That was one thing she would admit about her husband: he was a good provider.

Her mother arrived. They kissed and Lorna hid her surprise at just how old and haggard the woman was beginning to look – as if her father had stolen everything before leaving. She made a mental note that in the New Year to take her in hand: a decent haircut, some new clothes, beauty treatments, and, why not: a boyfriend – just for going places, a bit of fun. Lorna liked the idea so much she suggested it.

"Never, not me again," her mother replied. "I have had my fill of men forever. In fact, it seems now, that sat with my easel out in a field full of flowers, with a breeze in my hair and leaves whispering without complaint is where I am at my happiest. And in reality always was."

"Talking about painting," Lorna said eager to distract her mother from where she knew she was heading, "Florence has got something to show you - *haven't* you darling."

Florence squatted down between the two of them and daintily placed the pad on her lap.

"Oh," her mother said looking down at the first, "such nice colours."

Lorna knew her mother was not impressed.

"And what is this one ?" She asked seeing the second.

Florence sniffed in an angry breath: "This is daddy chopping logs and mommy trying on her nurse's uniform while he's not looking."

Lorna shuddered, "William bought me one for Christmas," she said quickly - "it's his idea of a joke."

"And mommy won't wear it," Florence giggled. "Not for him anyway."

"I should hope not," her nanny told her. "And why would William want a nurse anyway, Lorna ?"

Lorna felt herself glowing red.

"I know," she said suddenly recalling, "let's all have a laugh, because I know something that even Miss Big Ears doesn't know."

Lorna hurried over to the fireplace and snatched the card. As her hand touched it and she carried it over to them, an even worse picture came into her mind than the one implied by her daughter, and before she could show it she had to stop and take a look herself. Luckily, just as she'd imagined it was just a load of illegible rubbish.

"And here is what your brilliant father can manage," she announced, breathing a deep sigh of relief.

"Oh my God it *is* brilliant." Lorna's mother sounded shocked and vibrant. She grabbed the card and sped across to the window. Florence skimmed her pad across the floor like some crippled bird released too soon. Lorna joined her mother. "I cannot believe that he did this. He has done more on this shiny little card with those child's paints than I have got close to in fifty years of painting. The members of my club would die to be able to do this."

"But what is it ? What on earth are you going on about ?" Lorna asked feeling an anger and fear swelling inside, both for her mother's sanity and some hidden threat to herself.

"It is just the tone and movement. There is too much to take in at once. Can't you feel its energy ? Look, these are lines of cut grass, slightly serpentine across the earth and there is something out of place lying in it. These two shapes are boys working in the field, above them these black things are buzzards or birds or something like that. I'm not certain what they mean, but something, everything is here for a reason, I know that. The light, shading, texture, everything. Your husband, I promise you darling, is a very gifted artist. You should encourage him in any way you can."

And as Lorna tried to explain to the councilor at the shelter, then to the police and later to anyone that would listen: those words were a portent as black as any shapes hovering in the sky of that little painting.

People were being herded into the corridors: funneled from open van doors straight into the cold gape of the detention cells. The slamming and opening of each door, the footsteps, the voices, all had an automaton, resigned quality that William could not associate with any other experience in his life. He imagined trying to catch them in a painting. Drifting away from his own situation as easily as if he was in the most spectacular landscape: free again, more free in fact than he'd felt for years.

A short while before, his door opened and the police guard placed a brown, veined tray with a plastic knife and fork, a cup of tea, a paper plate with one sausage, some beans and an egg on his lap. William did not feel its weight or smell any aroma, but noticed the man's knuckles were bruised, in one place had burst and were a dark purple with ripples of cerise pooling into the softness.

"If you want to wash and brush up," he said, "I should look sharp. This place will have filled up by ten." William gave no response. "It's the magistrate's court next door. It is sitting today." Still nothing. The officer left. There was nothing that he could recognize – or want to – in that man's face. Twice during the night when he'd checked he felt the same thing. And the way those blue eyes – a blue with a clarity that demanded you looked away - had flicked over him was worse than any gob of spit or fist crashing into his steel eye.

The duty solicitor arrived, and the guard felt a sadistic pleasure at assuring him the prisoner was safe and very quiet. He opened the door and almost shoved him in before there was any chance to ask for an escort.

"I believe you asked for a duty solicitor last night and met my colleague," Mr. Thorpe stated, then, tossing his calling card, a packet of cigarettes on the mattress, wanting to keep things quick and simple: no chance of any glory here. This was just another hubby getting it all wrong, heading for the park bench. In fact, it looked as if this one had already been trying it out for size.

"As you were probably informed last night when you were charged, we will need to give a bail address, just a formality."

"I've got an address," William said feeling angry at being disturbed from his thoughts at painting this scene: "it's called my home."

"You will not be granted bail if you do not have a place where the magistrates are happy to release you to. It is only until your case is heard. Believe you me, a person like you would not like to end up in a bail hostel or be held on remand."

"Case ? Remand ? We just had a silly row. She probably regrets this already and wants me home." William tried.

The solicitor could hear the lack of conviction in his client's voice. He would have to school him on that before the first hearing,

"I don't think so Mr. Halliday. She's made the police take out an exclusion order and has agreed to press charges. There will be a real effort made by them to see that she does, so she's not wasting police time or endangering the cause of all battered wives."

"I'll just have a word with her then. There is no point in all of this. And I've never battered anyone," William said angrily.

Paul Thorpe felt some tension but decided to be brutal, "An exclusion order and undoubtedly, your future bail conditions, will be in place just to make certain you do not have a word. You will probably be excluded from going within five miles of the place, phoning or writing until the trial is over."

The duty solicitor liked to wear a tracksuit and trainers for these early morning calls – it usually met the requirements adequately and allowed him to take a jog and sometimes pop in for a swim at the nearby pool: to wash off the feel of this place. Now he was glad for another reason: the reaction of his placid client at the mention of five miles. He leapt up and spilled the tray of food over Paul's thighs. Paul joined him on his feet and made for the emergency summons button.

"My paintings and work. All my equipment. No way is anyone keeping me away from that." William raved.

Paul felt his finger reach the button and he pressed it while trying to keep speaking. "Mr. Halliday, calm down. I am sure something will be arranged. Some of the remand centres probably even run art courses."

"I need my work you wanker. Not a lesson in painting. What do you think this has all been about ? Tell that fucking judge I have to have my paints."

Paul could hear the bell ringing and at least the laughter of two of the morons that were supposed to be in charge. "Of course I will do my best, but usually all properties have to remain in situ until the divorce settlement is decided."

The door opened and he fell out in his hurry to escape. His hope that the news about divorce might have shocked the man into a more reasonable acceptance of his situation having obviously failed.

"You get my canvases you parasitic little tosser," William shouted through the quickly closing door.

"Enjoyed a spot of breakfast with your client did you sir ?" One of the policemen joked. Laughter filling the throat of the tunnels as he left from those he knew, with some satisfaction that he could follow. But knowing also that he would be back, and back again.

Though not for William. Any remaining laughter died out quickly as Mr. Oscar Whitting QC was escorted into the cells. The two officers saw their desk sergeant - the captain of this ship - cleaning the floor with his tongue, watched Paul Thorpe jump out of his way and attempt to hide. All of the solicitors and junior counsels stopped their bargaining or coaching and just stared. Most of their clients knew who this was even if as yet their crimes had not reached his level of involvement.

"Open the door," the sergeant snapped as he reached his two dumb, glaring officers. Mr. Whitting allowed the desk sergeant to pass him back the folded carrier bag of clothes and dismissed the man with a flare of his heavy, black-haired nostrils.

"Yes," the sergeant said to himself with a little relief, "you are not used to this stink are you ? Not for a long time now, I'll bet." Then he came back to earth with a terrible thought: "I hope to all the stars above that everything has been done by the book, or I'll have somebody's balls before he has mine."

"Good morning William," Oscar said softly, making sure the door was closed.

William looked up and for a moment did not know whether to weep or laugh.

"I hope you appreciate that I may well be late for a very interesting murder case, and a rather titillating brief on a alleged gang rape, by coming here at your father's request. I want you to get showered and then put these on – I imagine they will have cleared a place for you by now to do so. Incidentally William, though it has been a very long time, I do not like to see you looking quite so corpulent. I am going to go now and make certain that we are first in. Your father will also be in court to take you back home as soon as I get you out. He wanted you to know that they are getting the barn next to theirs ready for you and it can be your home and   studio."

For some reason William could not find a way of speaking. A

question filled his mind: was this liberation or the worst prison on offer ? He was unsure and too shocked to even wonder how his father could have known – or who might have told him. Then he felt an incredible lightness filling him: freedom *was* suddenly the most precious thing. William got up and shook his savior's hand.

"The only trouble with these magistrate's courts," Oscar continued trying to cast his mind back many many years, "is that they are usually presided over by two carrots and a swede, but I doubt if they'll want me to make a stew out of them."

Oscar went to get ready. Another murder case was one thing: but in truth he was delighted to be able to do something for the first time ever for his very dear friend Herbie. Even if he had once stolen the prettiest girl they'd all known. Then hidden her away like some ogre with a treasure and left them all heartbroken. Something, if the rumours were true, that the eldest son had once tried to emulate and failed.

CHAPTER THREE

Selina was here because of the project, Richard reminded himself again. Selina, the most beautiful girl in his class at school, the whole school, the village, probably the world, had just walked through their farm gate. It was their final year at school and although they lived along the same narrow road, caught the bus a few stops apart, went to school discos, village fetes and harvest homes, this was the only time she had ever been in *his* company or spoken to *him*. And all because of a collection of ancient farm implements.

For the first time in his life Richard suddenly found the farmyard chaotic and shabby. He noticed that a couple of barn doors no longer hung straight and needed repainting. The bantams spurring and strutting in the chaff appeared ill-bred and pretentious. He was glad that Madeline's peacocks were off in one of the orchards, shaking their dull eyes awake in dusty feathers, yelling their stupid 'Mee-yon mee-yon ! Eee-e-yoy ee-e-yoy' as if it were the only thing worth hearing all night.

Richard watched her trying to walk evenly across the cobbles that quickly lost their 'character' as her long thin legs struggled to cope with them. The longest, shapeliest legs he'd ever seen: prettier legs than even Maddy's were claimed to have been; and pointed out many times in old photographs that still *did* not do them justice. Selina was wearing white knee length boots and a maxi-skirt, but that did not hide what Richard could see. And not, he assured himself, with what his brother often accused both he and his father of having: 'a market eye for everything'. He watched as one of her long, pointed heels sank and then came back up from between the powder-red cobbles with something green smearing the white hide: a brown green that he waded through daily. Richard heard her gasp then sigh in frustration as she tried to hop clear. He felt a shock pass through him as she grabbed his shoulder for balance. One day he vowed, as she let go and walked angrily toward his back door, those cobbles would be torn up and a clean, hygienic driveway laid.

Madeline sat her down as soon as Selina got in and began to sponge her boot off. Richard knew she'd been spying out on them. He tried not to let his gaze burn over his mother's shoulder onto the leg being revealed as Selina stretched backward in the chair and giggled as if she could feel every stroke through the leather – like a real princess, he thought, feeling that pea through a thousand mattresses.

"What beautiful legs you have," Madeline said, "such fine fine ankles. You'll not believe this, but I once had beautiful legs myself."

Selina carried on giggling as if the idea was more humorous than any feather between the toes.

"One day," Madeline said, "when Richard brings you round for tea, we'll get some of the photographs out and I will show you."

Selina stopped laughing and was about to say something in reply to his mother's presumptions that Richard knew he did not want to hear.

"Maddy," he said quickly, "we have got to go and make our notes. We are doing a project for our school exams. Nothing else, okay ?" He hoped it would at least slow her down.

Richard had already guessed his mother would imagine, or hope, that this was his girlfriend – or even better, his quest. It would be perfect for her. And an answer, maybe, to the question she loved to pose. "How did he do it ? I told him, no. I even ran away to stay with some friends in London. But he managed to find me. The crafty sneak got my address out of my mother – conned her like some fairground hustler – then chugged his way up on that old Buffs Superior and pulled up outside as if he'd been invited. What is the point in running ? I thought. May as well accept the inevitable now and get it over with." How many times Richard had heard the tale he could not count, always with Herbie sat   listening, never contradicting, letting her enjoy the flight of imagination if that is what it was; showing no pain at any of the words. Even when she finished off with, 'Of course I told him I never loved him. He knew that then and I've been reminding him ever since'. Sometimes Richard heard his father sneak off later to one of the barns where that old bike still waited and usually started with the first kick as if it was kept ready and waiting.

Richard tried now to picture himself listening to such a tale. The wealthy landowner in pursuit of the unobtainable, like a character out of one of those romantic novels Maddy was always reading. Then he had the horrible thought of Selina's reaction to the story the first time she got to hear it and how it would make any attention from him appear. He was glad when he heard her get to her feet and begin to move along the corridor after him. At least Herbie was out for the morning, he thought, that was one small blessing. Herbie loved nothing better it seemed to Richard than to charm ladies: young or old alike.

"Well I would never," he heard Selina reply to whatever his

mother must have just said and he'd missed.

"That is just what I said, exactly how I started." Madeline told her.

Richard felt a relief when he heard the phone start ringing and the two of them were able to escape into the front parlour where the items she'd come to see waited.

Selina stood in the room without speaking, she ran her fingers over the pitted iron of a curved blade as if she were smoothing some living creature, then the old harnesses – oiled and soaped but still a cracked ancient skin: worn out and discarded. According to Herbie: all rubbish. Richard collected and hoarded everything. Now watching her delicate unblemished hand contaminating itself, he began to question why.

Selina was noticing that the plough blade felt warmer, more alive than the leather: a strange tingling from its still sharp edge: the strap, limp and impotent. "My father," Selina said, "told me that very old metal like this has an energy that does not exist anymore. Not since the first atomic bombs: it is all contaminated. But this is still pure and very precious."

Richard wondered what Herbie would say to that and then how valuable it might be, "I saved it," he told her, "cleaned it up and painted it. I've a load more, older ones even. I am going to renovate them all in bright colors and some time in the future I will put them on my lawn for a display."

"I hate people doing things like that," Selina said, tossing her head like some young shire suddenly feeling the weight of the reins. She crushed the dry leather in her hand and let it fall against her thigh. "Making twee and kitsch objects out of something ancient and powerful really turns me off. It is only real art that ever moves me."

"You like art do you ?" Richard asked. Sensing, while fearing, a slight chance to alter how he felt she was now viewing him.

"I love it more than anything. My father is always taking me to all the art galleries, even the Louvre. I actually won a prize for one of my own paintings." Selina felt like bragging a little and didn't add that it was when she was seven and Tony Hart had awarded it to her on television and that if her mother ever played the tape again she was going to kill herself.

"We are a very artistic family ourselves," Richard dared, though of course we don't all get the time to go traipsing around galleries."

Selina made a noise that Richard knew was dismissive and challenging him. She was holding an old, wickedly pointed and sharp pair of sheep shears. He heard the whisper of them opening and closing, snipping the air, it felt, into separate breaths now. Richard grabbed her wrist. There was a moment when he wished for the courage to put his mouth over hers, then say: You'll share more than a roomful of breath with me before I'm through with you. Instead, he pulled her out of the room.

"I'll show you then," he said, leading her out and down another long corridor toward his brother's studio.

Since William had won a scholarship and, still to Richard's amazement, Herbie's blessing to leave the 'normal' school and have his *artistic* ability nurtured, this room - the only one in the house with any real space and light had been out-of-bounds: to them all. Richard felt the round, blue porcelain door knob veined now with threads of dried paint. A picture of the chaos that would lay beyond, almost, more than any real fear of possible retribution, nearly stopped him. "One day," he told himself as the heavy door scraped open, "this will be my main room. Every night the work clothes will get changed and I will sit in here with my family: not huddled away in the kitchen waiting for the next day to begin."

Richard was just about to breath a sigh of relief in surprise at seeing how tidy and organised the room initially appeared, when Selina cried out loudly and pushed him aside in her rush to get inside. Then Richard saw the paintings and wanted desperately to get her back out.

"My God," Selina was almost yelling at him: "they are wonderful, stunning." She could not contain herself. She knew at that precise instant that so much was suddenly being made clear. In four large canvases hanging in a sloping line, all in various stages of progress, Selina saw clearly a figure escaping from the constraints she herself was surrounded by; evolving into the woman she had often dreamt one day of becoming. Selina could not believe it. She had come with this crude, always staring and leering, farmer's boy to this smelly ugly farm and hidden away amongst all the dark brutal clutter was this, this light: she stood there breathing heavily: caught like a moth in its glow.

Richard saw only what he'd always suspected his brother was painting: filth. Naked women, familiar in some way, and yet transformed into some liquid formulation. Women distended and exposed it seemed to him: like one of their cows birthing or being forced to take the bull for the first time; or some multi-breasted sow suckling or slabbed into a piece of hanging meat. And now, the girl he knew he wanted to be with was standing in front of them paying homage. Richard wanted to look away and, more than any other image, lose this one forever. He looked around and saw the jars of brushes, hundreds of them, bristling – a coat of some wild beast in anger or fear at this cornering. Stacks of canvases piled against the walls: their pure white backs and skeletons of planed wood, a moment of relief. Then, worst of all, above the pinned sketches, photographs, and paint charts, a row of self-portraits of his brother. All of them staring, not at them, not at the nudes: but at each other. Eye to eye, smile to smile: as if only they could see and understand.

Richard span round to escape and met the biggest shock of the day so far. His real brother. Glaring and wild. Lately they hardly ever met or spoke. He knew that his brother was drinking. Cider with the old men in barns. Bottles of moonshine carried home and left around for his parents to see. And though he did not fear him, he'd come to recognize something unpredictable in his movements and moods.

"What the fuck are you doing in here you bastard," William hissed thickly in his face.

Richard stepped back into the room, placing himself between William and Selina. He could see a bottle of spirit or wine in his brother's one hand, a thick heavy-looking one still full and unopened. In the other hand he had some new brushes, long and pointed. He tried to make a judgment as to which weapon he would use,

"I was showing Selina around," Richard said, "she is very interested in art." He moved as he spoke, slowly and slyly. Moved, as Herbie had taught and coached him, up onto the balls of his feet. William did not even bother to acknowledge the presence of the girl.

"*You* never come in here," William shouted. "You stink of shit. I don't want you looking at my work." William felt violated and furious. There had been so many times when he wanted just this: but now behind his back. He could hardly control himself.

Richard made a slight move closer to his brother. Time for talking was, he knew, over.

"Do you think you would ever paint me ?" A sweet gentle voice asked. Both brothers looked at where it had come from.

Richard did not want to believe what he had just heard. He would have much preferred the splintering shards of glass and the flow of blood and liquor to even the vaguest thought of her being transformed into any of this.

William glanced past his brother at what he'd easily dismissed as being another of the thick, coarse girls that moved around this area: a herd of grazing beasts - feeding and waiting their time to breed. The glance became a look, became a stare, then something transfixed. William stripped her clothes away in seconds to reveal the most beautiful body he'd ever seen; then he started to probe through the next layer and began to see the secrets of her form. Their eyes locked and he met something impenetrable even to his vivisector's gaze.

Selina could feel his look. She felt as if she was being opened out like some rare, night blooming orchid that no one would ever see, petal by petal until the hidden treasure could be witnessed for the first time. Then a shadow fell.

"You leave her alone," Richard shouted and moved on his brother.

William brought the bottle up and Selina gave a scream – though not out of fear for what they may do to each other, but for what she knew had just been torn away from her.

"Now then boys," a steady calming voice said. Nothing ever phased Herbie. Especially in front of a pretty face. "Young bucks fighting over a startled-looking doe. Tut tut tut. Not enough to occupy you, that's the trouble. Now, young lady, you come and have a cup of tea and bit of cake and tell me how my friend Miles is getting on. Richard, the electric fence in six acres is down. And William.." Herbie looked and shook his head. "William ahh William." He led Selina away.

William barged in leaving Richard standing at the door.

"I swear," Richard said, "if you ever try to paint that girl I will break both your arms and burn your eyes out. I swear that now and forever."

He stamped along the corridor. The cellars underneath caught and returned the echoes of his heavy footsteps: clod-like against the dismissive, musical laughter of his brother.

CHAPTER FOUR

Great Aunt Flo had always, in secret, loved the men. At least according to her brother, Sorley, Herbie's father: a man that liked to pull a cork, chain-smoke and bet on anything that moved. He enjoyed teasing her constantly about the fact, when the horse, or horse and trap managed to return him home from another long session in the local shebeen. Back to her house, where he'd come with a six month old son and a heartbreak that stayed unmended and would help drive him to a premature grave, "My God Flo," he'd say, "you're the only virgin left alive in this village but you've got the eye for it alright – you can't fool me with your starch and stays."

And she would humour and spoil him right until the end; then carry on in exactly the same fashion with the ten year old Herbie: indulging and pandering to his every whim. Helping to nurture what was already nature, until he became so self contained and mysterious that no one could get close to understanding his motives or desires. All his friends really knew for sure was that each time he vanished, something wonderful and new was sure to follow: a bigger motorbike, sportier car, or more attractive girlfriend. " 'Flash' will go to the Devil," their fathers assured them to assuage their jealousy. "Put a beggar on a horse and he'll ride it to hell," their mothers adding.

None of them realizing – not even his doting aunt – that this side of Herbie's character was no more than a calculated and steeled reaction to every charming weakness he'd recorded from his father. The 'flash' mere illusions dancing off his surface for others to be dazzled and held by until there was no longer any need, in Aunt Flo's estimation, to keep up the pretence. She dated that exactly to the time when Madeline *allowed* herself to be blinded and caught. Then everything faded and changed - including, and especially, all the fawning and flattery she'd grown accustomed to. It filled her with resentment and hatred and she began her campaign of revenge; and some way of bringing Herbie back to his proper place. Firstly, through the toil of the farm, garden and home. Then, when that failed completely, by taking to her bed. More than 'taking': clinging to it, as if it were a piece of wreckage left over from a voyage she'd laboured all her life to enjoy and suddenly found ended by something, she considered, colder and harder than any iceberg.

After the two boys were born, and Aunt Flo recognized her greatest weapon was at hand, it was too late to change the rules and take full advantage. She'd played the game so well and thoroughly that her real body could not be shown to recover; and bedridden she would have to remain, nearly. Both of the boys learned quickly that this fragile old lady, propped-up in her massive bed, smelling of lavender and a melange of bitter sweetness, would dole out candies and pocket-money in return for allowing the chalice of their ears to be filled with the slow drip of poison about their mother.

Richard took a lot more than William; and then would sit listening and agreeing with every grievance that his mother loved, or needed, to voice night after night to Herbie. William took his share but said nothing, except once, very near to the end. They were all seated as usual at the kitchen table, when Madeline became more unhappy than ever:

"I'm being worn out by that woman, *your* aunt. Lifting her up and down now, cleaning her. I am not a nurse. And do you know what I get in return ? She hates me and tries to turn my children against me. Of course you, Hawkeye, can't see a thing wrong can you ? Right from the start you've left me to her mercy. Sat there like some old bird with her head darting around looking and listening for anything to use against me."

Herbie sat in silence. He'd grown tired of saying it would not be for much longer; and that part of the farm *was* still hers.

"She's like a scrawny old fowl," Richard added , "one that's had all the feathers pecked off its head and neck: all red and bristly. Cluck cluck cluck."

"She cannot help being ill," Herbie risked. "Try and think how terrible it must be for a person once used to being so active to find themselves like this. Not able to use their legs anymore."

William was eight years old and already obsessed with his sketch pad and pastels. He appeared to be paying no interest to any of this, then, stopping sketching for a second, looked at them and said slowly and deliberately,

"Actually, she is much more like a vulture. A greedy old one that still likes nothing better than a bone to gnaw on before dropping and watching the jelly ooze from the cracks. And she *can* walk. I've watched her loads of times: dancing around the room as light as one of the feathers in her pillow when she thinks everyone is busy on the farm. And those envelopes she keeps giving to me and Richard to take to the post-box are stuffed full of money. I opened one to see. Money for everyone but you."

Madeline was on her feet in an instant and moving to the old lady's section of the farmhouse. Herbie paused for a moment and looked as if he would like to have given his precocious son a battering before running to try and part what was about to happen. Richard stared at his brother, already back to melding colours on his pad and as distant to this scene as they were to each other. Richard thought of the day his brother had refused to go to work with him on that toy tractor and imagined him instead hiding outside his aunt's window, or sneakily opening envelopes. At that moment he was glad for the first time, he was the one without a 'gift'.

A month later the snows came. An event unusual in itself for this area. "It is a sort of temperate valley," Herbie liked to brag. "The Mendips one side, the Brendons and Quantock hills the other: sucking all the bad weather away. Giving us our very own Shangri-la."

Richard flattened a snowball against his great-aunt's French window, then another. He sneaked up to see the look of surprise on her face and then to collect his cough candy, humbug and half-a-crown. Instead, he saw the rictus dead grin of an old virgin: her hands clutching the counterpane as if something was still too precious to be revealed.

Because of the snow Aunt Flo would end up lying in state for over one week before the roads were cleared, giving all of the family time for their mourning, reflection or relief. Madeline cried. She could not help it, though, as she laid the old lady out, the picture of her sons strolling off to the postbox giving away the money that was hers and Herbie's by right stayed firmly in her vision. Madeline had noticed things going on before William's revelations. Every time some obscure relative or one of the neighbouring farmers turned up, something went. An antique in return for some flattery or half-a-dozen duck eggs, a painting for some tall story or a dollop of cream. Still Madeline cried and made sure the old lady looked respectable. She placed two florins on her hooded eyes, coins kept for just such a closing; and tried to let the artificial lilies next to the bed make her think of her own upbringing and what true glory really was claimed to be: not any illusion of beauty: nor the wasted life she'd spent on this woman.

Richard could not help feeling that she looked somehow reptilian in death. He was well used to seeing dead animals. One of Herbie's helpful aphorisms: 'Where you have livestock, son: one day you will have dead stock.' A few days later, Richard had a better lesson about the meaning of life and death. Also, for the first time, something he did not want to see, about the strange mix his parents had concocted: a glimpse of something he vaguely knew he was striving to deny and leave behind.

He was walking in the snow along one of the rhine-lined lanes, the normal, slow green water hidden under a blanket of whiteness. He found himself thinking about once when he was younger and had been given the task of herding the cows along this route to the temporary milking parlour for the first time alone. One of their best cows had stepped too close to the edge of the rhine. Just a small narrow ditch, seemingly shallow and almost dry. Just a trickle, heading seaward from the reclaimed marshland this place had once been. But a trap that suddenly betrayed its treacherous secret. A secret that had claimed, and would continue to claim the lives of many poor, reckless or unlucky motorists. It was deep, the clear water a thin ice above layers of silt and black, stinking bog.

The cow went under and came back up, throwing slime and a foul stench off its head as if some wolf had sprang on its back and only some triggered instinct could save it from this. It began a wild kicking charge along the ditch, constantly attempting to climb up on the next solid-looking patch of crust. Going under each time it proved another illusion and getting more furious in its panic.

Richard slipped down one of the sloping banks as near as he dared to the water. He was covered with silt and narrowly missed being brained by a flaying hoof. The rest of the cattle carried on along the road, oblivious to the death struggles of their sister: the atavism of predator and prey, Richard saw, too ingrained, even after all the centuries, to risk any involvement. He began to yell and then to scream. The cow reached one of the many low bridges that crossed the rhines for entry into the adjoining fields. It stopped knowing that it could not get under it or scale its side. It attempted to turn round in what looked like an explosion of water and sediment. The cow actually managed to flip itself upside-down in a heave, and then go under the water again feet upward and kicking. Richard cried out, knowing that it would not come up this time. It did though, spinning like a log and facing back the way it had just come. It began its journey again, only slower as if it already knew its eventual fate but did not want to hurry to meet it.

Suddenly, Herbie arrived on his bike. Richard knew his father did have eyes like a hawk. All of the farm labourers – already becoming something of a rarity – nicknamed him 'Hawkeye' for how many times he caught them out skiving. Always, it seemed he'd seen or sensed exactly what was happening in his own domain; while equally never appearing to want to see a thing beyond it.

Herbie ran back to the little bridge then over it into the field. On his way he picked up an old twisted post of bog oak that must have been dredged up the last time the rhine was cleared. He reached the swimming cow, braced himself and smashed the club down between the animal's ears. The cow bobbed under and Richard knew that his father was putting it out of its misery before dealing with him. The cow stopped moving along the rhine and tried to turn away from Herbie. He waited for it to turn, then moved so he was in front of it again, and this time hit it even harder and across the soft part of its snout. Blood flecked into the massing of froth beginning to drool from the animal's mouth. It tried to turn again. Before it had got half way round, Herbie began to batter it repeatedly on either side of its face so there was nowhere left to escape the attack – or only one place: back up the bank it had slid down. The hoofs began a sideways scarring of the dry bank as it began to get a grip. Two more blows on its butt and the cow hauled itself to freedom.

Herbie stood and watched as the animal slithered from the last embrace of fluid, as if witnessing the moment of its birth again. Then he seemed to become more interested in the piece of wood, balancing it in his hands, weighing it, sighting and examining its petrified form, trying, it almost felt to Richard as he kept half an eye on the filthy cow charging back to the rest of the herd, to recall or imagine what it may have once been. Herbie carried the object to his bike, "We'll not get a full quota of milk out of her today." His only words before peddling off. The uneven sound of the worn crank, a-rhythmical and strained - sawing its diminishing noise like cuts across Richard's still racing heart.

Near the spot where it had happened, Richard now found something. A patch of snow had melted, or been dissolved by something seeping up from the earth. The grass remained flattened and was stained by what appeared to be a deposit of rusted iron filings. But it was what was poking its way through the crust that held him: three flowers. Already upright and in full bloom. Their colours, against the background of snow, iridescent. Richard loved wild flowers. And always shared his excitement - and slight unease over his feelings about them, with only one person.

Herbie and Madeline held no interest in them whatsoever. Madeline having only time for what she cultivated in the greenhouse and Herbie, the lawn which he manicured in straight-line formality; and moaned constantly about having to tend. William appeared to believe they warranted no more than a glance or flick of a brush to fulfil any role in his vision. But Great Aunt Flo understood his passion completely. And she knew them all. Their different names from the matter-of-fact cataloguing, to their magical country ones. More: its role in life: glamour or curse. She knew what they could cure or induce. Which ones brought luck into a home; or should never be invited in.

Richard carefully removed one and, placing it inside his shirt against his flesh hurried back. He could not wait to learn about this flower that waited under the snow for any moment to take its chance. Richard had never seen anything close to it and knew this was something special.

The excitement carried him as far as her door. He actually stepped inside and drew the flower out before the shock of the truth all came instantly back. Her skin looked duller, going, he saw, grey to greenish like some pheasant left to hang too long. Only the coins gleamed: open-eyed in frozen horror at his intrusion. And Richard began to sob. Already the hardest boy in his school, Herbie's son, struggling in determined strides to lose the other side of his nature, let it weep for one last time. He understood now what he had lost and was losing. Richard took the flower and positioned it gently in her fine hair just behind one ear. Something no other man had done to Flo before. And though there were still others to visit her – both personally and professionally – it would remain there and go into the ground with her. Its secrets buried along with Richard's desire to ever have them explained again.

Herbie came one last time alone. He'd paid his respects already, but with a litany of recriminations from the now unforgiving Madeline clouding his thoughts and any memories, he still felt some need. At that time the snow had gotten deeper and the undertaker had phoned to suggest that maybe they could bring the body out on a tractor. Luckily, even Maddy would not go for that so he'd still the chance. Now the thaw was beginning. Tomorrow, Herbie judged, they would be able to get through. So this would be his aunt's last night in the house after eighty or more years. Madeline was already planning on what they would do when Flo's part was no longer partitioned off. Herbie had not noticed before how strange it was that, by merely passing through a heavy velvet drape – ringed and merry sounding - in a corridor it was possible to step back in time. The continuation of the corridor and the few rooms she insisted on keeping separate, unchanged since his father first brought him here.

Years later, when the small alterations were made, it would still seem to him that an invisible barrier existed. Now, as he slipped through the curtain, having made certain that Madeline was sleeping, Herbie felt the overwhelming intensity of the different dimension. Even sound changed to a heavy more ponderous thing. The beat of the grandfather clock suddenly touchable, it's pendulum brushing the case and wearing away a dust of walnut, the ship, a galleon, or according to his father 'The Flying Dutchman' moved as if in a thickening ocean. "Think," he heard Sorley say again, "how many times that ghost ship has sailed around the world since we set him off."

Then the smell filled his lungs with a damp thickness making breathing a more considered, precious act. Two candles, lemon scented, burnt either side of her bed and offered some relief as

Herbie sat down. And, without any warning, saw the snake rise again from in front of the rosewood livery cabinet – no longer full of cold food as it would have been at that time but holding drinks and medicine instead. Its polish a little deeper, its top more warped and split. Only the snake's appearance unchanged.

Herbie recalled that he would have been around eight. Not yet eight, he could, unusually for him, date it accurately because, on his eighth birthday his portrait was done. A photographic one which was then hand-coloured. It still hung in this room. A handsome boy with dazzling blue eyes and a quizzical expression as he stared down at something on the couch with him. Herbie's explanation to all of the family, "The photographer gave me this book to read while the plate was being exposed. It was full of pictures of ladies in bathing suits and I was thinking why has this stupid man given me this to look at ? What a waste of time: pictures of women without their clothes on when I could have been looking at motorcars or better still aeroplanes."

"Huh !" Madeline always adding if she were present, "so you can see that it is not only the colour of his eyes that has changed since then."

There was no portrait on the wall the day of the snake. No bed-ridden aunt. Just a boy doing as he always did after school: rushing through the house to get out of his school uniform and help on the farm, or go into one of the barns and tinker around. Something slithered in the corner of his vision making the hairs on the back of his shaven neck remember they had once been there and attempt to stand up. He turned and the serpent stopped and rose up on its tail. As tall as the boy and letting his scent and fear pass over a flicking tongue as Herbie was frozen to the spot. The thing collapsed like some rope trick and appeared to be dragged in reverse under the low shelf of the cabinet just inches off the floor. Herbie began screaming for his father:

"Sorley. Sorley." He'd never called him by anything other than his Christian name. The same as his children would one day do with him. Though Herbie claimed that in his case it was because they were more like brothers than father and son - and he the more mature and responsible one at that. But not at this time.

"Sorley, a snake," he yelled as the back door into the room had flown open and his father, already immaculately dressed for the evening ahead, brushed him aside and stood directly before the livery cabinet as if he already knew.

"Where ? What ?" Sorley panted sounding out of breath as he always did after any quick movement.

Herbie stared at his father's usual silver-tipped cane that on this day of magic turned suddenly into a sword.

"Under the low shelf. A snake. A big one, glistening like a rainbow. It reared up on me."

The blade flashed a sweeping arc from one barley twist leg to the other, shaving the unworn carpet beneath. Next it was thrust in snicker-snack like the magician they had recently watched at the country circus. But now, like then: no blood: no death.

Sorley got down onto his pin-striped knees and peered underneath, the pink gold of his watch chain gently swaying and dancing hypnotic waves over the wicked blade of the sword cane. "There is nothing, Herbie. And no way up or out that I can see."

Aunt Flo came in from the garden carrying a trug full of cut flowers, fruit from the orchard and a marrow veined in green and gold.

"What on earth is going on now ?" she asked. "Half the farm workers are stood around staring."

"Herbie saw a snake," Sorley said getting to his feet and slipping the blade quickly and expertly back into the stick.

"A grass snake I expect," Flo offered. "It'll stink the house out if you've frightened it."

"No it wasn't," Herbie knew them well enough.

"An adder then," his aunt said looking more concerned. "You were not bit ?"

"It was not an adder." Herbie could catch them easily.

He would still do it now for a party trick. Letting them dangle limp, as if dead in his large, muscled grasp, and explaining to any shocked guests or bods from the ministry of agriculture: "See when I move it: side to side, up and down, or round and round, how its eyes always stay focused on mine ? I know that it is not really dead. It is just feigning – waiting for its moment to strike." They, more hypnotized by Herbie than any snake. No one doubting the truth of what he said.

No more than his word was doubted that day. He was not a boy to make up or believe in stories. They'd searched the room and beyond for hours. Sorley only opened his watch case once – about the time, Herbie judged, that the local pub would have let its well-greased bolt slide open. Aunt Flo still had eggs to collect, workers to chase. Herbie knew that they both loved him more than enough to stay searching all night.

"It must have gone back the way that it came," he offered.

They agreed.

"I'll bet you," Sorley said, "that it escaped from that circus we saw. There will be some exotic dancer looking all over for her snake." Then whispering to his son. "A bit like old Flo." A wink from the red-rimmed but still bright blue eye.

Herbie blinked his own eye and saw his father bow out of the room again and the mirage of that long-forgotten snake vanish forever from his vision. Then as his vision cleared he saw that the coins had been stolen from his aunt's dead eyes. And heard another little snake wriggle from behind the sofa.

"Get out from behind there," Herbie said, feeling the momentary fear turn into anger.

A flutter of paper fanned the still air of the room, cool against his burning skin. Herbie watched the pages of the sketch pad cascade over the back of the velvet seat as his son's white hands appeared, as dead this moment to him as those on the bed clasped next to his knees, and saw for an instant, without understanding, those pages animate like some flick book his aunt back into life.

" Give me that money you little thief," Herbie spat out those words. He saw his son's grasping, frail fingers drop the coins into his own shaking hand. He closed his fist and struggled not to raise it against the boy. "Now those drawings."

William backed off instantly the pad whirled behind him and his eyes going so wild and afraid that Herbie wished the warm coins were over them. "Give them here," he tried again. "If your mother knew that you'd sneaked in here and was stealing money from the dead it would destroy her. I can hardly bear to look at you anymore."

"I needed to see her eyes again." William said, sounding older than Herbie could believe. "I could not get them right. I was not stealing your precious money. Artists steal everything but that. It is farmers that take money from the dead."

William walked arrogantly out. Ignoring the feeble voice that whispered for him to come back. Herbie called again, he was desperate to apologize, sit his son next to him and tell him about the snake and how his father would never have doubted him. Try to explain that it was just a mistake. But one that *he'd* made too easily. And in a way he was glad that the boy refused to return and listen.

Shortly after the funeral, the family solicitor, a relative with the same name and one-time employer of the rising star Oscar Whitting, read out her will. Flo still officially owned the farmhouse and about three quarters of the total land. All of the land, in fact that Herbie had not acquired through his own efforts: the best land and the two major barns. Herbie had talked to his aunt about it each time he made an improvement. "Of course it will go to you," she always assured him without ever letting him see her will. A family likeness for being crafty and secretive that he could hardly complain about.

Aunt Flo left Herbie the farmhouse, and the few acres of land surrounding it. Also, all of the remaining antiques - including, and specified: the grandfather clock; the 'snake' livery; and *his* portrait. She left nothing personally - not even a message of thanks - to Madeline which appeared to give her more delight than anything. Richard - who as the eldest son in the normal tradition, would have expected most of the remaining property - got a small legacy. Everything else went to William. To be set up in a trust, Oscar's uncle explained to all the shocked faces, until he came of age and could make his own decisions.

Nearly ten years later they would gather again – minus the solicitor – for another announcement about the will. This time from William. It was just after his seventeenth birthday. All of the family knew that he had not been attending his college. And that what he did was becoming more and more removed from their control or influence.

"I've quit college," William stated after his request to speak to them. "And I want to go to Italy. There is an artist who wants me to go and study with him."

Don Welland, a visiting American artist, who normally lived and worked in the Marche region of Italy, had invited William minutes after seeing his portfolio. "You must come and work in my studio. Get out of this gloom before you go totally blind," he'd said half jokingly.

"I also want to set up my own studio over there," William continued very business-like, "so I will need some money."

Madeline tried to speak and was silenced by Herbie's warning finger.

"I am willing to sell you all of the land and property on it for two-thirds of its value. If not I will go without a penny and leave instructions to sell it to the highest bidder the day I'm officially old enough."

This time Richard tried to get to his feet, his fists already clenched. He'd left school without a single qualification and, apart from a couple of days at the local agricultural college, had thought of nothing in life but what his wretched brother was just about to sell. Herbie crushed his shoulder back into the chair, and then left a kinder hand remain reassuringly on him.

"You have a deal," Herbie said quickly as if he'd known what was coming. "I'll instruct the bank tomorrow. We won't be the only farm that needs to pay of a bigger mortgage to survive. But I'll tell you one thing before you go: changing where you are doesn't change who you are. Whatever gifts you have came from here; and you owe the place something in return. There was work to do here that probably only you could have done. I saw it clearly in that early painting you did of us. So run away without having the guts to see it through: but you will never be free of its call. I know that much."

"Great. Thanks for the artistic opinion," William said: "and sudden concern over my work. Oh, and one other thing: I want those two coins. You remember, the ones I stole once."

Herbie's other hand came up from below the table, fast as if he was about to strike. Instead the fingers flared open and two golden florins span out of his grasp making everyone look up and then down. Their sound: two cymbals vibrating either side of the family: a spinning crescendo in reverse, contracting and diminishing as it held them here together for this final time in its embrace.

CHAPTER FIVE

Silvanus, Richard's 'Uncle Silas' owned a vicious tongue and a temper to match. Also, he took a sadistic delight in anyone else's humiliation or personal destruction: nothing was ever allowed to fade or be forgotten: from the smallest flaw that he could work on, to the largest crack that was already ruining some reputation, marriage or life. Girls or women who strayed were his speciality, "I hear she always was a bit of a shagger," his usual opening line, before delivering to some husband or boyfriend the full history: every name and blemish revealed.

Last week, as the first of the hay bales began to be brought in and carpet the base of the vast barn: intricately laid building blocks that would rise up into the arched roof above until the last person forced his way out of that space: closing it behind him like some slave escaping the stones of this green, sweet-scented pyramid, Silas had began the undermining of his own children.

'Making mow', some of the older farmers and their workers called the gathering and stacking of hay. Some still ritualised it with the likes of corn dollies, or tales of the green man and wicker men – or other beliefs: all nonsense according to Herbie, and now Richard. Silas, though, insisted on the barrel. A large red or brown plastic keg, filled from the large oak vat in one of Silas's tin sheds that Clicker used to brew his scrumpy. The same tin shed that was a notorious shebeen where cider drinkers still gathered and put the world to rights by paraffin light. Silas had the keg placed on its side between the first two bales to come off the first trailer. They would be the last ones to go up and by then, the barrel better be emptied or every bit of bad luck imagined would descend on the coming year.

Herbie did not drink the stuff. In fact the only drink that he ever took outside his own home was half-a-shandy at the bar of the local pub. Never in the lounge, always stood at the bar with the heavy drinkers who might snigger about it, but quietly, very quietly. Herbie still had a chest measurement half as large again as the most brutal of them, and reactions and eyesight that were claimed to have been a fraction away from being good enough for pilot training and night bombing missions during the war. A gentleman who was never seen out without a necktie and jacket yet could, and would often just for some challenge, work most men to death. His own strange blend that none of them still got close to unravelling.

One time, Herbie had come in with a guest and ordered the man his double whiskey and his own shandy asking, as always, for there to be more lemonade than beer. A large, recently-arrived pig breeder had made some comment. Then when no one laughed, tried another. Herbie hit him in the ribs, a short stabbing punch that dropped the man flat between the red-topped bar stools. Herbie explained to the visitor how once he spent hours punching a rough Hessian sack filled with wet sand and swinging slowly from a meat hook in a barn. And how a short straight punch was often the most damaging. All of the time the man lay on the floor and had not taken a breath as Herbie counted off the seconds in slow-motion and tried to bluster his way out of what he'd so easily been goaded into. Finally the man breathed, his broken ribs a reminder that would fade long before the story did.

Richard heard it many times. He'd been punching that same bag from its first telling. And had learnt to leave cider alone from his first experience of that. It was filthy stuff as far as Richard was concerned. A small amount could suddenly take your legs away - 'Knee Cracker' one of its many names, a bit more and it could turn you inside out and squeeze your head with a hangover harder than the press used to extract the original juice. Too much for too long and it fermented your brain - turning cider alcoholics in to the most violent and unpredictable of drinkers. Richard knew that Clicker and his cronies spent every night standing like ghosts in their grey smock coats, mumbling and snarling, while drowning slowly in a lake of this forbidden fruit.

Silas and Roly Cart liked a drop – so did the Clay brothers who arrived each evening after their long day's work in the local sawmill to help as their father had always done. But still it would be hard to empty the barrel in time. So that was why, Silas later claimed, he let his children take a little. Richard knew it was a lie. He saw them first and should have stopped it: he knew that before Herbie told him.

Silas's two sons were half the age of Richard and William. Everyone said that Silas had waited so long because he did not want any pressure put on him to retire too soon. Others said it was so that he could work Roly to death before he might expect to retire in the tied cottage for a few years of ease or ask for a redundancy payment when the boys stole his job. Whatever, Richard watched as the younger one took up the two-handled, straw-brown cider mug and half-filled it from the keg. He drank some and passed it gently to his brother. Richard momentarily thought of William for the first time since he'd left, and tasted his own anger as bitter as any vinegar fly could create. He left them to it and did not bother to attract the attention of Silas until they had refilled the mug several times. But he had already known and gestured for Richard to keep quiet. Silas whispered to Clicker and Roly and they joined in with his surreptitious game.

Richard was disgusted by their degeneration. He began to wish that Herbie was not out loading trailers. He would never have allowed either of his sons to behave or be ridiculed in this way and would have stopped this quickly. When Madeline brought out some sandwiches and soft drinks and did bring it to a close, it was too late. By the time Silas's wife arrived to collect the boys they were both semi-unconscious and covered in streaks of their own vomit.

"The little buggers," Silas kept shouting down from the barn: "if only I'd seen 'em."

"Tell the missis," Richard heard Clicker call out, "to put plastic sheets on the bed tonight. There is a touch of sweet in that cider. A bit of Morgan went in with the Kingston Blacks. Go through you like a dose of salts if you're not used to it."

Richard felt himself beginning to despise these people and the way they carried on. He heard their laughter and continuing crudities: worse than animals, he told himself. Soon, he knew, with all the new technology beginning to arrive, this would all be over. A curiosity for some story book, or - it came to him without warning - a painting.

~

Now the bales were near the top and an elevator was being used to off-load each trailer. It was hot in the remaining roof space and Richard, Silas, Clicker and Roly were forced to work close – sometimes even having to share the lifting and jamming into place of another bale. The Clay brothers were standing below on the trailer loading a regular stream of hay onto the chattering wooden lath and steel chain-driven belt. They were both over six-foot-five tall, flaxen-headed and handsome enough to turn heads. Richard could not recall having heard either of them manage to complete a full sentence that meant anything. Their father who often arrived and 'liked' to make mow when his job as cattle drover and collector for the abattoir allowed him, made them both appear small and garrulous.

"I hear she's been getting a pork chop that young filly," Silas started, moving to one side of the elevator and swinging bales to Clicker. "You must know her from your schooling days Richard. What's her name ? Slackie ? Slapper ? or Supplier ? I can't quite recall."

Richard had heard all of the gossip. Even Annie, his normally easy-going girlfriend, recently joining in. "Selina," Richard told Silas and the other two men, paying attention and ready for Silas to expound in his usual style, "her name is Selina, okay ?"

"Spread 'em wider, more like, from what I heard the other day. And she'll be getting more than a pork chop when his wife finds out," Roly Cart said, catching a bale and letting its own motion swing it away. An effortless action with no step or movement made that was not essential to the rhythm of the task. He saw the orange strings that tied the bale, bow taught and cruel, but not making the slightest indent on the calloused flesh of the man's hands. Richard looked at the permanent stoop and simian shape that work had stretched and crushed into the labourer's form. In a recent magazine there was a feature on a machine that could spin and wrap grass into large bales, sealed inside black plastic, everything done by a skilled driver and technology. How, he wondered, pleased to imagine the answer, would that appeal to this man who had known stooks and rows of men whispering their scythe blades across the earth?

"More hay," Richard yelled down to the brothers, ordering them to speed up and not wanting to hear anymore what this, soon to be, impotent latter-day Luddite might have to say. Usually, this near to the top of the barn, work was allowed to slow a little. The brothers looked at each other and shared a slightly more confused frown than usual before doing as ordered.

"Go on Roly," Silas said, picking up the new beat and reddening slightly in the face: "tell us what you heard then."

"Well, I was out the back doing a bit on the patch," Roly said.

Roly's tied cottage with its very large vegetable garden (the only large thing connected with the place) was near where the village butcher, Winston and his wife, Mavis, had constructed their modern luxury home.

"Right at the end of my seed bed, near to where they have their posh lawn," he continued, catching the bales off Richard: "and I heard them at it."

For some reason Richard found himself thinking of the only piece of advice Roly had ever given him. A few weeks ago when he was first officially noticed with Annie, "A young man should go out when he first gets married and buy all of his vegetable seeds. Just the once. Not a luxury: but the proper start. From then on though, you should always gather the next year's from your own plants. I'm still eating what I planted the day after I was wed." At that moment Richard felt he understood something of these lives. Their expectation and acceptance. Now he felt a growing anger at what else seemed to demand attention or fill some void.

"I'd just seen 'poor' Mavis go out with the young ones and that young tart slip in through the back gate. She must have been waiting, hiding I suppose. It could have only been about five minutes later and she starts moaning and groaning like some cow that's lost its calf."

Then, with Silas goading him on and taking his share of the hay, Richard watched the old farm worker giving a parody of what he'd *imagined* was happening, along with his accompanying vocal imitation.

"More hay," Richard called again and both the Clays, smiling now and enjoying the challenge, responded gladly. The stream became a green torrent, the slaps of bales on the belt and the judders and groaning of the elevator giving a strange harmony to Roly's continuing performance.

"How long do you reckon it went on for ?" Silas shouted above the squeals of his worker.

"Must have been a good hour boss, at least."

"No good for a premature little boy then that one. Spoiled already," Silas said stumbling as he attempted to clear another bale.

"Needs the full bull," Roly said, giving a final long howl. "And one other thing: when she came out, she was all red-faced with her hair matted. Also she had something in her hand that looked to me like her panties. I saw the wife coming down the front just as she reached the back gate. 'That was close,' I said: 'nearly didn't make it !' Of course she looked down her nose at I, like some fine lady that has just trodden in something."

That image brought back the day when Selina came for the first and only time into their farmyard and with it, his fantasy, that had come to nothing.

Herbie climbed off the tractor with the final load brought in. He stood with his hands on his hips watching with a puzzled look the speed the brothers were working and trying to guess what exactly was going on. Madeline and Annie arrived with some drinks and stood with him watching. Richard and Silas appeared to be almost fighting to get the bales from the belt quicker than each other. Roly stood still, looking drained and uncertain as to what was actually being decided. Clicker was being buried under a storm of hay, beads of sweat bursting from his face. Richard could smell stale rotting apples seeping from his pores - acrid among the sweet sweet scent of fresh cut grass.

Then Silas fell.

He went sideways out of the top of the barn. Richard had watched as the bright-red face slowly looked at him, then the eyes glaze over and roll back into his head as if he were searching himself for something forgotten. His hand reached out across the belt toward Richard and actually was caught for a second before the motion of his falling body saved him from probably having it torn off. Silas hit the elevator on the way down, and then the corner of the trailer, the sharp metal edge with his head, before rolling under the grease and oil- dripping axel. Annie screamed as Herbie rushed over. The brothers looked uncertain as to whether they were supposed to stop and help.

"I expect he just wants a sup o' cider," Richard called down as his father lifted the limp head off the rock-hard ground. "More hay you pair, what do you think you are being paid for? And you," he turned and stared through Roly: "if you are not too worn out with all that passion maybe you might like to start doing something to earn your keep."

Roly Cart had buried his wife a dozen years before. All of his children had fled the countryside and never bothered to visit or write to their father. Roly suddenly felt the cold loneliness of his life as his employer lay unconscious below. He understood that if Silas *was* getting weak or became too ill to continue and this family, as they surely would, managed to buy them out, things would get a lot colder and lonelier for him. Richard let their eyes meet and hold, assuring him, as if he could read his thought easily, that they certainly would. The last bale from the trailer arrived and, as Roly began to lift it, Richard tore it easily from his grasp. He jammed it into place so hard that momentarily, the whole mow moved, as if it too understood what was coming and shuddered at the prospect.

~

Selina laid her head on Miles's shoulder. He felt the first tear roll warm down over his neck, before her sobbing and heaving rocked the same worn leather chair in his library that she used to squeeze on next to him as a child, always wanting another story. All those pages of Hardy and Dickens, Turgenev and Checkov felt as if they were being washed away by this: the smallest print on the thinnest rice paper dissolving into nothing but useless tissue. He heard an older version of the crying coming from his wife in the kitchen. Miles looked at the rows of books and felt a wash of guilt touch him. Had he brought his daughter to this ? Encouraged her to step into his safe vicarious existence and find there was a different reality waiting outside ?

Even now, he found himself searching the shelves for some neat line or stanza to quote. Instead, he saw the bruises beginning to darken on the white parchment of his daughter's cheek, could follow the uneven lines and wails of red, clawed down her long neck and spine, see the full stops of blood starting to coagulate on her perfect knees as she must have fallen trying to escape. He wanted to say, "you were always scuffing those knees when you were a little girl," but with that went her mother's warning that if she did not stop being such a hoyden, her legs would be ruined and *no man* would ever look twice at her.

Miles fought back a tear of his own at how far off the mark that statement had turned out to be. He tried to smooth her long, raven hair and saw where a handful was torn from her scalp. For years in his role as architect and surveyor the people in this village and beyond always came to him for cheap plans and help; then ran him in circles over each inch of land they felt they owned or should own; involved him in border disputes or litigations if someone dared to stroll, cast a shadow or breath on their wretched soil. Now the same 'neighbours' must have stood by and calmly watched his child being torn to bits. Was it any wonder that he preferred his books? he asked himself feeling Selina begin to shake, probably going into shock.

Selina kept asking herself the one question over and over: Why did she go to the church? She was not even christened. Her father had refused apparently, telling her later, she could do it for herself if she so chose but to bear in mind that it was the most terrible edifice to hypocrisy and servitude dreamt up by the most corrupt of men. So she decided to go like some lamb and confirm it for herself. And it was all Winston's fault. He told her not to go to the harvest home dance. People, he warned her, were beginning to gossip about their relationship. Also, Mavis, his fat, ugly bitch of a wife, suddenly wanted a night out. So, Selina decided, if she could not go dancing, she would go to the special Thanksgiving service. She was certain the little cream dress, with matching hat and veil, black gloves and high heels was appropriate though she felt plenty of hostile or jealous looks on her entry.

Then it was over and they all went out. Selina followed close on the heels of Winston and Mavis – along with her mother, father and two sisters: butchers all: and the only reason Winston had allowed himself to become involved in the trade: or so he told her the day she found dried blood on his back and nearly gagged. Selina raised her delicate, thin-wristed hand to shake the vicar's as she'd seen everyone else do and he turned his back on her. The baby-faced, podgy little man in his white frock, who'd been apparently, driven from his last parish for being caught up in a scandal involving a gamekeeper and some teenage au pair girl, was refusing to contaminate himself with her. Selina tried to out-wait him, then, as she sensed everyone looking, brushed it aside and walked confidently along the path. She saw him turn and smile as the women attacked, first verbally, then physically.

"You bloody little whore," Mavis squealed the moment Selina was a few steps clear of the vicar and was just beginning, despite her efforts, to feel her cheeks burning from his action. The wooden, arched gate was blocked by her lover and the rest of his family. Selina tossed her head and started to move by her and then through them. As she got close, Mavis's sister slapped her. She did it so hard Selina's hat flew off and landed among the gravestones. Then the mother grasped her hair and dragged her off the path with her daughters following. As the punches, kicks, slaps, scratches and spit began to fly, she saw Winston and his father-in-law staring and could see that they would love to have joined in. Her clothes began to be torn open and she felt one of her small white breasts exposed as she turned and saw lots of faces frozen in delight. She knew most of their names. The same ones cut in the stone all around them, dissolving and melding in the earth below. Selina's head hit one of those stones as she fell. The name and date worn beyond recognition, she managed to notice.

Then she was lifted softly and without effort. Selina was in Herbie's arms and saw his sad smile as he hurried her to the gate, sweeping the two men out of his way as if they were lighter than her. Richard swung the gate open and let his father through. The two of them stood blocking it as she fled. One shoe on, one shoe off, staggering and not able to stop sobbing all along the slow road home, seeing curtains twitch and cars drive past with hard-eyed drivers and grinning, smirking children making lurid faces out of the back windows.

A car stopped. She had not seen or heard its approach. Miles got out and grabbed her as she began to struggle to get away before recognizing him. "Herbie called from the vicarage," he told her: "we know what happened."

It felt much later to both Selina and Miles when she could finally stop heaving and speak. "I will never be able to hold my head up in this village again will I ?" she asked.

Miles wanted to say , "Why should you care about that ?" Instead he tried to assure that she would.

"Nobody will even want to speak to me again, never." Selina said.

He was about to tell her that these scandals were all part of village life. The world in a microcosm. Emotions intensified not shrunken. Why, he was going to ask do you think so much great literature came from rural, seemingly simple countryside settings? When something stopped him and made him wish silently that her words were true.

Richard was walking straight up their drive. He had her hat and a shoe in one hand and, as if this Cinderella was already his for claiming, the largest bouquet of red roses in the other.

CHAPTER SIX

William paused as the flames took hold slowly, too slowly, as if they did not at first accept this task; knew better than this tottering fire-starter; or worse, that they chose to protract the event. William was beyond the gift or torture. He dropped his next load of canvases onto the hillside and began fumbling through a box of bottles and jars. He found what he was searching for, opened the lid on some fine chemical and began whipping the smouldering mass into obedience. He dropped the bottle with a dull scream as invisible flames fired back along the tendrils and ignited in a flash, luckily, the small amount of remaining liquid. His hand carried on burning as he attempted to shake it out. The sound of the fanned swirling flames silencing the chant of the cicadas, briefly.

"That crazy English boy is off again," Angelia told her husband, Antonio. She was spying on him, watching closely since his return. "So where is his bitch ?" she'd asked earlier when Antonio brought him back, "and all of his *'artist friends'* now ?" Both questions getting no more than a shrug for an answer. She stood watching the fire growing into a blaze, saw the 'painter' William, dancing in its glow – drunk as usual by the wildness of his movements – before collapsing and crawling around their property like some beast.

"I will tell you something," Angelia turned on her husband

again – seemingly oblivious, as normal to the antics of this tenant: "he will burn our villa to the ground, start a forest fire, turn thousand year old olives to ash. Then call it art !" Still she failed to get any response. "At least someone will know what this work means without anyone needing to explain it: 'Drunkard destroys property'."

Antonio thought back to the humiliation and shame of the young man earlier in the night when he went to collect him. The look and smell of it even as he struggled to keep some pride and manners intact. Antonio took to William from the start and sensed that he came from a good family. He'd wanted so many times to reach out and warn him. It was like watching one of his own children become too wild at some game, tearing down a slope until the slope is a cliff. But there always needed to be a time for building scar tissue, that was Antonio's philosophy – the amount according to each person's soul and destiny. He judged that his young friend had built enough and soon, he guessed he would be driving him to the airport or ferry, and alone. The villa would be empty again: its marble floors cold and polished by his wife's nagging tongue.

"He will not burn anything of ours," Antonio told her, and because he was desperate to make sure William was safe, added: "I guarantee that. It is his heart that he is burning tonight. Leave him to it. I will go and watch though, to make *you* happy - as is my fate in this life."

The fire grew cold before William began to sit up and Antonio slipped silently away into the olive and citrus groves. Maybe, he thought, there might be a wild rabbit to shoot this new day. That would make the vigil worthwhile, trying to discard his own feelings of satisfaction at making certain the young fool had not burnt himself completely or choked on a throatful of regurgitated red wine – wine from Antonio's own barrels. "A nice thyme and olive-fed rabbit," he whispered to Faunus, in payment for the oil and herbs rubbed gently into the boy's hand. He smiled to know that the treatment would go unrecognised but have the same effect all the same. Like so many things, he decided, giving a shrug and accepting already that there would be no gift from any god - ancient or new.

William could taste metal and ash and worst of all, paint. The bitter remnants of the work in progress or completed in this country that made even the recent events sweet in comparison. His humiliation at the exhibition, the betrayal by his so-called friends, and the parting from Karla: all nothing by the side of this waste. He stood up and looked at the circle of white ash: "Funny," William could not help thinking, "how often a fire ends up making such a perfect round shape out of so much chaos." And in the briefest flicker of light he wanted to draw it. He quickly dowsed that glow of false hope and stamped coldly back to the villa, trying not to see the small sacks of water undulating on his hand like glistening dewdrops in the cold dawn. William dragged himself onto the bed. Karla had been next to him the last time he'd lain here, untouched, he recalled with some regret. He put his injured hand softly on the pillow where the indent made by her head still existed, let it lay there until he felt the first blister burst and send its water flowing over what should have been her face. William closed his eyes and forced them to try and make an image of her appear. Unable, already to see her as she really was, and afraid that without a single sketch or painting left he ever would again. Or, the unknown, unforming faces whispered, that he ever really had or truly wanted to.

~

William had inherited enough of Herbie's horse sense to know he was being used. Don Welland was a vampire: "An artistic vampire," Karla would tell him later, "but not one that takes blood: one that seeks to inject his victim with his own."

This was some time after William's ceremonial burning of his portfolio: the pale flamed – though painless - rehearsal for the future immolation. The rest of Don Welland's 'assistants' clapped and cheered as the sketches and a few paintings from the college that led to this invitation – disappeared. William watched their hands and mouths move and hid the deep satisfaction he felt from knowing that, even if he did not see them again, all of his important beginnings were safe.

"Now we will seek to set *you* free," Don told him.

After months of sticking or daubing spots and squares on Don's huge 'coverings', William was *encouraged* to start using his 'gift' to help in the creation of a light chamber for a very wealthy Italian couple. It took him less than a week working with the rest of his assistants to realize that they really were without any vision of their own. Their main attributes appeared to be equally rich parents and a blind devotion to Don. It was also at this time that he understood Don Welland's greatest creations were those he forced into the minds of any potential clients or disciples. Along with the ability to crush any opinion other than his own.

"Do none of you understand," Don yelled at them the first day his patrons came to view the progress of their chamber, "the difference between a faint mist that will burn off with the sun like some early morning curtain to reveal the clarity of true light and the brumous weight you are coating this space with ? What *can* I trust you with ?" Don began tugging at staging, then moving and refocusing some of the lenses. All of his tribe stood with their heads bowed except William,

"You have got the position of this building wrong," he said. "I've been making some early morning and late evening sketches. I've seen the way the mountains reflect and steal the light. This place will never get the better of them but it could work in harmony if.."

"Ah," Don Welland raised a hand to silence him, "the *boy* from darkest Somerset. The *laddie* from the Levels: home of fog and gloom is now going to tell the *man* from New Mexico about light. The artist who wants to paint pictures of himself, glaring at what he would like some idealized woman to be; or some lost arcadian landscape, now shows the artist who once covered and gave rebirth to a dead volcano about sun and mountains. Bravo ! Pray continue young maestro."

William left them to their laughter and took himself again to a café near a converted olive mill where a group of artists shared studios and worked. One of the assistants told him about them in disgust at the communal meal they shared in the apartment above Don's studio each night. The group once attacked one of Don's projects. A cave coated in modern materials fixed to strands of white titanium. It made William think briefly of the Witch of Wookey Hole that Herbie had taken them all to see. Only, instead of her petrified drip by limestone drip of growth, her sin was hidden and shrinking in a plastic mac under an umbrella. Any levity it gave him was quickly lost as the thought conjured up his parents and the letters from Madeline that he hardly bothered to read or consider replying to.

"Sprayed the whole place with their juvenile attempts at art," the assistant sobbed. "Destroyed a masterpiece out of jealousy."

William met them a couple of times and heard how painting was dead and Don Welland even worse. And how their various projects were the only real thing happening. Two of the young men were working on creating a new body for dead animals found on roads: "Slaughtered by greed and reborn by art." They explained. "We wanted to use some of the poor farm beasts but we got shot at when we tried to collect some. What could be worse than the exploitation of animals by farmers ?" William said nothing but felt they were all staring through him as if they knew all about his background. Another member was a huge girl called Jojo who was living on a stage like the front of an open doll's house and filming every action with a bank of video cameras. "You can come to the premier," she offered: "though it will not be completed for another ten years." Other members were just sitting around drinking the closest thing to Absinth they could find while denying colour and form by creating what they called 'amorphous moments'. They made William laugh and think of the cider drinkers back home and what Herbie would have paid for any of it.

One thing William did recognize though that his father would have seen, was their obsession with Don Welland's prices and, strangely, his mistress, Karla. William had seen her a few times sauntering around. Once he even thought she was staring at him before Don hurried her off. "Who," he asked Jack - one of the 'Frankenstein' boys – "is she: and why so important ?"

His partner slapped his forehead. "Contact, you fool. Contact Supreme."

"Ms Shagged-her-way through the whole art establishment," Jojo told him. "Knows them all already; knows them all."

"Get her on your side and you are home and dry."

William heard Herbie intoning his own version of 'It's not what you know, it's who you know that counts. Art for art's sake, my arse !'

The rest of the group began to fill in the details of her life from model to art gallery assistant, gallery owner's mistress to art dealer's. On and on until Don Welland.

William was more fascinated by their expressions and how he could unmask them than by the antics of some art groupie. Art, it seemed to him, like love to so many people in this world was no more than a game: a greedy one that had no room for any purity in its rules.

Then Karla arrived at the perfect moment for William to join the dance.

~

William felt devastated. He read part of the letter again. It was among the pages of the regular Madeline news. Always she sent her love, and included that of his father's. He doubted at first if Herbie even knew she was writing; then recalled better and pictured him counting every comma without his mother knowing.

"Oh, and this is some other news," the letter suddenly stated among the cows and crops, the terrible fall his 'uncle' Silas had taken and his now black mood shifts, new tractors and machinery: "Richard has got himself engaged ! I do not know if you will remember the girl. It is not Annie as we all expected, and were waiting for the day. She is heartbroken. I have her round here every evening just about, sobbing, and hoping to catch Richard's eye. But he is too distracted to even notice her – and, I suppose, too much in love. Dear William, it reminds me so much of your father chasing me. The same eye for beauty, I imagine. The girl trying – I recognized that too well – to escape the inevitable. Now she has been caught and Richard, like his father before him is like the proverbial dog with two tales. Only I have the feeling with these changing times we all live in, she may be able to achieve her freedom too easily if she wants, unlike me, yet.

Oh, yes, the girl, Selina."

William was unable to read any more. Remember her? In his mind, he'd already painted her a hundred times since that day in his room. In every pose and in colour that would lift and set the deep spirit he'd sensed and briefly touched, free.

"Remember her!" he wanted to scream back into that cesspit as he saw his brother laying down with her. "Remember her?"

There were simply no words to describe what he felt. Not even a tone or brush stroke to express it. Nothing that could exist in the sudden vacuum created between his heart and mind. Its numbness was spreading, coating everything as if in a mist from the Somerset Levels. Olive trees were transforming outside on the hills into the stumped pollarded withies, citrus groves were damp and deformed cider orchards. William felt himself slipping into the ooze of some peat black bog, slowly but irrevocably drawn into its embrace, not to drown but to return to its source.

Then the door opened slowly and a young woman whispered in like a ghost. She had a striking, if, William noted straight away, slightly overweight figure. That though, gave her a voluptuous softness making her great bone structure seem inviting rather than threatening. Her hair was a shade of magenta and cut in a very asymmetrical bob. William thought her eyes a little too startled and round with too much white in them, also her mouth was too full and large. It was still easily, he saw: a beauty that could be adapted until it grew on a person and then just as easily leave nothing but pain when it was taken away. She was wearing a thin, almost diaphanous short purple dress and high, heavy brown leather boots.

"Help me," she said, closing the door softly. "I should not really be here"

"You must be Karla," William said, trying to sound casual as if stunning women were always coming into his room asking for assistance.

"And you the brilliant painter," Karla said, "that poor Donald is struggling to keep under his wings and hold onto as another of his possessions."

"Ditto, from what I've been told," William replied.

"Touché," Karla said and recognized a mixture of arrogance and sadness in his reply. The first she guessed was down to her presence, the other, already being hidden from her, made her pause in this latest quest. Still she sat on the edge of his bed. Karla had wanted to meet this young man when Don first mentioned him: his genius just waiting to be discovered; or in Karla's mind, inspired by the right partner. Now she was here and her attempts to explain or justify her actions to herself no longer mattered. Muse or cheap model. Karla wanted, for once, to be part of something more than the usual mediocrity with its greed and envy; a need to prove *her* worth this time. And Don Welland was already boring her to death with his jealousies and desperation. Any danger warnings she perceived were lost behind the intensity of this desire.

"How can I help you ?" William asked, slipping the letter under his sheets and crushing it tightly: squeezing any moisture from it: letting it become dry and barren. He concentrated with all his effort to look at her legs. They were so long, shapely and inviting. He felt himself growing hard and felt his breath come back and begin to deepen. William saw a light flicker in her pale, almost violet eyes as she smiled and looked down at the pulse moving his canvas trousers,

"I wanted to come and meet you and see some of your work," Karla said; but Don strictly forbade it." She felt herself growing light and easy in William's presence. "Donald was bragging about you at an exhibition. Telling everyone there about the great untapped talent you were. I made the mistake of saying that I would love to meet you and he went mad. Now I *am* here and one of his babies has already spotted me and shot off to tell him I imagine."

William gave her a sceptical look.

"Don't let them fool you that they are not under his control," she warned him. "He sponsors all of their work and uses them. He even got them to destroy that cave so it gave publicity to a dead project. He undoubtedly got them to take you in for some reason."

William judged that she was over crediting Don's power because of her own inability to break away.

"He's gone for the rest of the day," William told her. "a phone call about how the light was not hitting the spot or something made him rush off earlier to set the sun straight."

They both laughed.

"And incidentally: talent is nothing; work is everything," William stated. Making her feel that he already wanted her to understand and be part of his world.

"Donald," Karla said, "is an artistic vampire. I will tell you all about him one day. But I will tell you this for now: he has the eye. Forget all of his work: that's bullshit for the market. Find out what he likes, what he tries to fill with his own blood. The dealers and critics follow his offspring like vultures even if they are contaminated heavily with his disease. You must divest yourself of his influence soon. Do not leave it too late. Please show me something you have done on your own. I feel that you must be working. I sense it in fact."

William was not really listening. Instead, he was imagining what Don must have filled Karla with, and understanding that whatever it was, its flavour must have been more acid than honey.

He pictured the elderly, fat and slack-skinned man crawling over this young lady. It made him, against his will, think of the farm when he had once witnessed a young cow put to the bull. An aged beast with just enough pedigree and seed left to be worth trying a few more times before the knacker man arrived. William saw its eyes, behind a craquelure of blood, roll back into its massive skull in pain as it delivered one more wave of life and the young creature below rippled hungrily for more. William knew his own eyes were beginning to glaze over now as he could not stop lusting after Karla. A pain in his balls felt like he'd been kicked in them and he was desperate to empty them, and not into a sink or towel with the image of someone now lost in his mind, but into a woman for the first time. And it was going to be this woman: he suddenly knew that.

"Have you ?" Karla asked grinning, hearing in his breathing now what he desired.

"What ?"

"Something to show me."

"Donald does not want me to do any more figurative work. He's insisted that I concentrate on his stuff. So..."

Karla made a snort of contempt. She very slowly crossed her legs letting him see more of her thighs and put a hand on his shoulder: "Please," she said, "show me. I *know* you must be working."

William reached under the bed and brought up his sketch pad and three boards. He handed the whole lot over, guiltily, as if having it confiscated. Karla swung herself fully on the bed next to him and squeezed close to him. She lay the pad and boards so that they bridged both their laps, covering the top of her legs deliberately now, then began leafing through the pages cautiously and in silence. William saw as she leant forward that

Karla did not have a bra on and that he could, if he wanted, take in slowly their firm shape, and that she was inviting him to enjoy and study the sensual way her nipples pointed proudly upwards from their perfect aureoles. William saw as much as he wanted with a glance and did not feel Karla's disappointment as he concentrated instead on his drawings and colour codes: the blueprints and sketches for planned larger works.

"These are wonderful." Karla said truthfully. "The colours you are creating. The way you have made even these ugly people appear. You have caught Donald perfectly. You did not need me to tell you anything about him, did you ?" And she knew that he did not, and had seen more than her by far.

"Yes I did," William replied, feeling her warmth. The first female ever to be on a bed next to him apart from his mother. "I was full of doubts about what I was trying to do. Until you just said what you did - now I know I am right."

"William," Karla said lifting the work so that it was cradled against her like a child, "you must get away from all of these people. It is time you stopped having doubts or letting these hangers-on take control of you. I know a great villa you could rent. A sculptor once worked there and it has a fantastic studio space. I will take you and show you if you are interested and ready to break free."

"Will you come ?" William asked, blurting it out. Knowing it was a stupid request and that she was with someone rich and important, but still unable to stop himself.

"I just said that I would take you," Karla told him, playing with him, knowing now that she could get easily what she wanted. But still, for a change, desperately wanting it.

"I meant," William said determined to push the matter to its end, "that if I went and rented this studio and began working, I would be alone."

"All artists are alone," Karla snapped at him, and shoved his work back angrily.

"Would you come and let me paint you ?" William tried. "Model for me sometimes ?"

"Is that *all* that you would want ?" Karla stared at him. "Well ?"

"No," William admitted lowering his head. "No it is not."

Karla laughed, then suddenly stopped, "I've just heard footsteps," she said. "They are coming for me. All of them. Don will have ordered them to come and see what's going on. They'll run back and tell him on the phone that we are alone in your room; invent things that are not true; we must not make enemies."

"I know," William said, "take your clothes off quickly."

"What !" Karla said, "Can't you even wait until we get to our villa ?"

"No I can't, but what I meant was take your clothes off and I'll start painting you. That ought to confuse our *enemies*, or buy us some time at least."

Karla started giggling as she stood up and slipped the dress off, followed by her boots and finally a small intricately embroidered pair of panties that she'd bought especially for this moment. William did not notice and was starting to paint her even as she'd struggled and wriggled around pulling off her boots. He let the paint bleed into the fibers of the pad - forcing this image to override all the other thoughts about anyone or anything else. Karla felt the intensity of his gaze and furious concentration growing stronger than anything she'd felt next to him on the bed. She still kept sensing that it would be some time before he could share any other passion with her.

'Villa Mirenda' or as it was still called locally, 'The Sculpture's House', was for William a lessening of nearly everything he'd brought with him. For the first eight months there were just long undisturbed days of work and making love, with everything else a celebration of living. The joy of bread baked nearly black in an olive-wood oven, a jug of red wine carried home at the same time from its slow dripping barrel, browning and sharp as it oxidized – 'an acquired taste', they said, and William was pleased to be acquiring it. A few tomatoes, some olives and cheese made up a feast. Every time they laid a table on the terrace and shared another meal, William was filled with the pleasure of how good life could be made to feel. He pictured his family seated at their table: the mounds of boiled stodge, slabs of tasteless bread and pots of stewed tea. The rush to get clear with that feeling that there was something guilty about actually savouring or enjoying any mouthful.

William was thrilled by the way these people treated their children, families, guests, and work. It did not matter how early he got up to sketch, one of the workers would be in a vineyard or moving goats, a builder on a roof or covered already in plaster or whitewash. If Karla and he took a stroll, as they often did in the late evening, the same or different people would be there carrying out similar tasks. But always with a lightness and ease, as if the length of days and warmth gave them time and space for a larger spirit and liberty from any enforced work ethic. It made England seem to William to be a prison of souls.

"I will never go back to that place," he told Karla one morning. She had never been to England. Her mother was from Italy, her father from Boston. "You cannot imagine what that place does to a person who wishes to live."

Karla was making him read the latest of his mother's letters to her – now being delivered by Antonio who kept offering to post *anything* William wanted to send in reply.

"You mean you will not be taking me to your brother's wedding ?" Karla teased. She knew there was something more than some falling out behind this, something that had touched even the way he painted and looked at her naked body earlier.

"I will not be going," William stated: "there is too much work to do. And I will not waste this light for some sham of a marriage."

Karla kept silent and dismissed the matter. She was far too proud and delighted with the way William was working. Since their arrival he'd painted or sketched every day and often into the night. A lot of the paintings were of her and she loved them. Also the ones of the surrounding landscape and villagers. All, she believed, inspired and liberated by their being together.

"I have set your body free," Karla said to him later that day as she wrapped her long legs around his back and held him inside her. She felt - even as William swelled, then struggled to hold on for her to come - a desire to leave her and get to his studio. All day it was there: some vision behind his eyes that had nothing to do with her, or the here and now. Karla clung on as he finished ejaculating, letting him feel her contracting and pulsing through his body as he grew limp and gave up his struggle to pull free. "Now you must not escape until you grow hard and come again. And tell me where your mind was the first time."

"It was you that told me to think of other things," William reminded her, feeling the sweat on his back chill as the swirling colours inside his head were dulled by her intrusion.

Karla recalled that. She was thrilled that after the first weeks of constant rushed and wild passion William had asked her to teach him how to satisfy her. Karla was seven years older than William. She could still count - and sometimes did – her many lovers. William, though he claimed some rushed encounters in the hay, had been a virgin. He did not fool her, and Karla wished he had not tried. He was patient and willing to learn. Now it was most unusual that he did not make her reach one or sometimes many orgasms. If he failed, he sulked all day, offering small gifts and spending time seducing her until he got another chance, though recently, she'd noticed, not so often. Also, he was adventurous, and becoming more so. Karla recalled the first time she took him into her mouth. The look on his face was, she later told him, priceless. Karla nearly choked trying to swallow as he jetted down her throat. There was so much and such a pressure in his release that semen actually bubbled back down her nose. And they had held each other and laughed. Since then Karla longed to be able to make him come like that again but could not.

A short while ago he asked if she liked being tied up and buggered. Then, after she refused him that - beginning to understand she needed to hold some things back - if she'd let *all* her other lovers have anal sex. Karla was hurt and responded by saying yes, but that still did not mean she was going to let him. It was their first small row and William reacted by painting for the next three nights and refusing to mention it again.

William was also reading a lot now. Karla was surprised at how little William knew about literature and been pleased to turn him onto some great writing. Now he was never without a pile of books on the go and was leaving her behind with the voraciousness of another appetite. She was thrilled to be part of his transformation and imagined them together always, learning and sharing. Then they met a couple over from England. A writer and his wife that were travelling for their honeymoon after years of struggling to be together. The girl, Daniella was an artist who'd exhibited in a lot of top galleries both in Italy and the rest of the world. Her husband, Simon's, first novel was just breaking. Everybody in their space was caught up in the electricity of their love for each other. Karla placed her hand on William's as they sat at the table with them. He was telling Daniella about his art and plans. "Me me me, I I I" Karla wanted to say and join in, instead he snatched his hand away and she saw a look flick across Simon's eyes – as quick as a lizard and accurate as any X-ray plate - and wanted to deny what he'd just so easily recorded. Assure him, as she'd began to do to herself, that it was a lie. Now, as she felt William growing hard inside her again and beginning to circle slowly above her, Karla thought back to that look and wondered what it would read like, in that writer's next or future book. 'Catch as you can', he'd described his work as being. What would he catch if he saw them now ? she asked.

She heard William's slow moan and felt his lips brush her ears and waited for him to say, for the first time what he had never said. Instead, Karla heard goat bells rolling as he lifted her legs around his neck, and saw his brilliant blue eyes glancing sideways out of the open shutter catching and darkening with the shadow of some raptor, becoming large enough as she watched, to be a golden eagle, soaring and floating softly on the thermals.

~

Some months after that day, and beyond the time of his brother's marriage, which William appeared to have let pass unnoticed, they had their first major row. He'd started allowing other people to intrude into their space. At first it was some of the locals and Antonio: whom they both adored and sat outside with them drinking wine and his own distilled Grappa late into the night. He responded always to their hospitality and one day took them to a family wedding. They were seated at a long table after the ceremony drinking and eating. "You are the first English man to sit at that table," the head of the family told William: "and it is over two hundred years old."

"I am honoured," William replied and Antonio translated.

"Tell your young friend," the man said, "that he will always be welcome to sit with us."

Karla watched the men clink their glasses together as if something was agreed and understood that lay beyond the need of language. She wanted to stay close to William that night, then, as the bride and groom got ready to leave and everything swirled in a chaos of toasts and wishes, Antonio clasped their hands together. "Maybe you will be next," he said in drunken Italian, "and we will have a big feast here for you."

William's Italian was still not good enough to understand. "What did he say?" William asked her.

"Oh," Karla said, "he hopes we are enjoying ourselves."

"Si," William told him loudly, drunk himself, "Si. Si. Si."

Antonio closed their hands even tighter and called out to the rest of the guests who cheered and clapped.

And that, Karla could mark as the beginning of their end.

Soon the locals stopped coming and Antonio was left to her the few times he came. Karla tried to accept it and understand how William must need the company of other artists. But she soon saw through them and what *they* all wanted.

"Do you have any idea how much this has, and will cost?" Karla demanded, looking at the damage and mess left behind after another 'gathering'- this one beginning some time Thursday, and petering out in the early hours of this Monday morning. She could see from the paleness of William's skin and bloodshot eyes that he would not be working today, again.

"What?" William replied crossly – he was still smarting over something said the previous night when stupidly he'd shown off his work-in-progress. "Fucking cats now," somebody said: "soon it will be a washing line full of nappies blowing over her head."

A procession of different people kept turning up. Some of them staying for weeks. At the moment she knew there was a poet called 'The Bass' and his girlfriend 'Opus 22', as well as others - some that she did not even know. Karla did not want to argue: especially within the hearing or view of strangers: but it seemed they were never alone now.

"I asked you," Karla said: "if you have any idea how much money all these *artists* are costing *us* ? And don't you find it strange how the jugs of wine, fresh bread and olives are suddenly left to rot as Champagne and truffles disappear ?"

"There is plenty of money," William said. Recently he'd been reading 'The History of Mr Polly' and come to the part where the eponymous hero suddenly realizes his inheritance has dwindled alarmingly. William's - though he was struggling to dismiss them - last three bank statements were more proof of Wells's powers of prophecy. Karla had read the last two and was not as easily fooled as any shopkeeper's bride.

"I may have to go back to work, in one of the galleries I expect," she said.

"You work for me," William snapped at her. "You are my model. I need you for my work."

"Oh I see. I am your employee now. Should I start calling you Mr. Halliday or shall we keep it informal still ?"

"Karla," William said softly, "I'm sorry. You know I did not mean that. I would love to go and do some painting - will you come and pose, please ?"

"Now that would make a change," Karla did not feel able or willing to stop. "Do you know as well as that couple upstairs there are still two men walking around that I have never seen before. One of them asked me if I would like to pose for him when he burst into my bath last night. On the toilet I think he suggested. And that last night you offered a room to some writer that is under the 24 hour supervision of two guards because he wants to mutilate himself so badly. He is not even allowed to have paper as he uses its sharp edge to slash himself or rolls it up into balls and tries to choke on it. He has to write on a special machine made of rubber and you have said that they can bring him here to work. When are you going to grow up ?"

William could not recall any of it – only what had been said about his painting. All he wanted now was some peace to go and start work on maybe painting out the two black cats.

"I am going out," Karla shouted. She stamped off to her car and heard one of the shutters creak open in a dry pleasure at her leaving.

William lay alone in their bed that night. He was tired out from working: the cats remained in the painting: they were perfect. Everyone else was gone. And he had told them no more parties: just work from now on. He found the name of the writer and let his custodians know he was not welcome. Then he cleaned and scrubbed the whole villa and cooked a meal for Karla's homecoming. A few hours later, he guessed she was not returning and tried to make himself feel some stronger emotion than he did but could not. All of his thoughts kept returning to the desert of white canvas daring him to enter again and find the way back to where he'd been; and to ignore the never-ending, nagging voice that whispered or screamed it was the wrong place. He was in front of the easel before the sun even touched the mist. William was still painting at midday when he vaguely heard the sound of the car, its tyres crumbling the dry earth and stone like cartwheels on ice or an old steam tractor on cobbles. That association came from nowhere and made him look up from the bright orange, yellow and flame reds blazing on the canvas more than any interest in who was arriving.

Karla saw the table still laid with both meals untouched. She knew from the immaculate gleam of marble and smell of oil and wood polish what William had done for her. She stood as one of the cats, Ruskin, rubbed himself against her bare legs trying to scent mark her and reclaim possession. Karla tried to shut out the thought of the way, men especially, tried to mark and then lay claim to a body. She hurried into William's studio.

William glanced at her, stepping away from the canvas, staring into it, she thought, almost as if he did not recognize who'd created it. She'd often seen that look before but found it frightening for the first time. Karla began to struggle to find some way of speaking and breaking back into his world. She sat on the edge of the chaise-longue. The one she'd lain on so many times, naked, open as a flower. Even the idea suddenly felt a million miles away. William was already dabbing a brush on the painting: the canvas as taught as a skin on a drum: its pulse beginning to race.

"I've got some great news for you," Karla said. "I went to see one of my girlfriends after our silly row yesterday. We went out for a meal so that I could weep on her shoulder, and I bumped into Lorenzo. He is a very well known art dealer."

"I remember," William interrupted her. "Was he the one before Don or the one before him ? Or another before ?"

"He was just one," Karla said, pleased to have got some reaction – wishing it was stronger though as the bounce of the canvas did not miss a beat.

"Anyway, he is very keen on exhibiting some of your work.

Don had shown him some sketches and he was going to contact you. In fact he wants to put on a show of your paintings soon. Your first exhibition in one of his main galleries. A solo show. He will make sure there are some collectors and critics there."

"Great," William said coldly: "maybe it will bring some money in."

Karla waited. She was willing him to get angry. To ask the inevitable question. Then she would tell exactly what it had cost her to get him this break – all of the details as slowly and detached as the strokes of the brush still whispering but not speaking. "Ask you bastard," she pleaded silently. Instead, Karla knew he was drifting away: slipping into that trance-like state: genuinely lost inside his creating. Once, she had loved to be there waiting for his return: to be able to believe she was part of the journey, or the reason for his safe homecoming. Now she just felt alone and abandoned.

For the rest of the week William worked solidly, both painting and framing the pictures *he* chose for the show. He was either crawling into their bed exhausted or sleeping in his studio. The painting he was working on did not include her and the couple of times she went into the studio he deliberately ignored her. So far William still had not touched her and refused to respond when she tried to arouse him in bed. "It's because I stayed out with my girlfriend that night isn't it ?" Karla asked.

"I'm just tired," William assured her. "I am trying to keep working and make sure that I get things right for *your* exhibition."

"It is your exhibition, William. Anyway, you once told me it improved your eye." She heard him sigh and then pretend to be quickly asleep. Karla felt at that moment that he would never be inside her again. Maybe, she tried to convince herself, it was just nerves. When it was over, and the show was the success it was bound to be, this would all be behind them. She curled against his back and held him tightly.

~

William left very early on the day of the exhibition with Antonio. All of the paintings loaded in the back of his small van. Karla pleaded to be allowed to go with them and to help him with the hanging. "There is no room in the front of the van," William told her.

"I could sit on your lap and we could talk about the first thing that comes up," Karla tried one of their early jokes.

"Come later," William said, matter-of-factly. "I will have everything ready by then and you will be able to give me a proper reaction to it. That will be more helpful."

Karla spent the rest of the day deciding what she would wear. Finally, she chose the purple dress and boots that she wore on their first meeting. He could guess if she was the same underneath and find out after the excitement of his big day. She thought she would wait until late before turning up: let him be looking for her when she arrived.

Karla parked some way from the gallery and strolled as calmly as she could through the early evening though her excitement was making her shake. She pushed open the gallery door and saw herself and their lives all round the walls. The light and radiance of the colours hid everyone else for a few moments. But not for long enough. She quickly saw Lorenzo with some young girl clinging to his arm and sneering at her. Then Don and all of his followers. Lots of other people she vaguely recognized, but none of the friendly faces she expected. A cold fear crept into her. She recalled telling William that time about making enemies and how easily they'd dismissed it afterwards.

"Ah Bella," Lorenzo announced hurrying over to her. He bowed graciously to kiss her cheek and then spat gasping in her ear: "Now bitch, we will see who leaves who. And what your quim buys in the world of art." He turned to the rest of the gallery. "Art lovers," he said, "in case there is somebody who does not recognize her from the wonderful paintings, allow me to introduce..."

Karla heard their laughter: cold rain falling on the burning flesh his verbal slap had caused. She saw them all looking at her and understood what they thought they were seeing. But there was nothing to say. No way of explaining what was real. It was too late. She heard the door open and turned to see William come in. He was dressed in a new suit and his hair was cut, and, she could not help realizing, for the first time since they'd been together, not by her.

Lorenzo brushed by her,

"Ah maestro," he cooed. "are you ready for your big night?"

She heard William reply and thought how nervous and trusting he sounded. Karla bit her swollen bottom lip and began to chew – a habit she thought was long over.

Then it began.

Karla wished that someone would actually say something rude or devastating. An opinion that was based on easily recognized and dealt with jealousies or personal dislike. Some giveaway that this was a set-up. But instead the game was played out with a velvet glove and she had to watch it smoothing and brushing softly until its victim was helpless in its charming but destroying grip. Twice Karla tried to get close to William as he stood with another small group, offering encouragement and uttering that most damning of all curses, "Promising." Always it seemed backs closed on her and she was left like some simulacrum shadowed or dripped from the paintings on the wall.

Only once did she get the chance to say something. Donald was standing next to Lorenzo, both grinning in front of one of her paintings, "I think *our* Karla has put on a little weight, since I last used her – as a model, I mean," Don said loudly.

"Ah well, I had a sneak preview very recently, so it is not so obvious tonight for me," Lorenzo replied making certain William turned and was listening.

"Neither of you *men* got close, not once," she answered, weakly. Karla wanted to get a whip and drive these people, all of them out of here: out of the temple she still believed his art and their love was.

"If only the boy had stayed a little longer," she heard Donald say to a couple of collectors that were dissecting one of William's paintings: "not been so easily distracted. But you can see the potential. The potential I spotted, as usual. Anyway, it was worth giving him this chance: if only to make him see more clearly one day."

On and on it went, until at the end, when William stood watching everyone file out, receiving pats on the shoulder and shakes of the hand as if they were the greatest gifts. Karla stood and waited for him to come to her. Lorenzo and the new girl along with a couple of the gallery assistants were obviously keen to close up. William walked past her,

"I want to take my paintings out of here tonight," she heard him say to them.

"Don't be silly," Lorenzo told him. "they can rest here until tomorrow. I do not mind giving them that long."

"I've already called someone," William said, "he's on his way right now. So if you do not mind."

Karla watched him unhook his first canvas. "William," she tried. "Can I help?"

His sad smile above the painting of her was worse than any cruel remark, she felt, he could have voiced. But then the words came and destroyed that belief:

"Karla you don't see; you don't understand. You never have; you never will. I don't give a damn what these tossers in this shitty little gallery think. Except for one thing: they are right. I ran away from the work I had to do. My father told me that before I left: his blessing instead of a curse. I can't go back and ever catch what and who I lost. And I can't carry on without that person or completing that stage. This has all been a game. A pretentious, worthless struggle to escape from the truth and reality. All of it. Including you."

Karla fled out into the street. She sat in her car and waited for what felt like hours before driving closer to the gallery and parking in the shadows. William was sat on a step next to the dark windows, two stacks of paintings either side of him like small pillars, his head bowed lower than the invisible roof they held aloft. "Eyeless in Gaza," came into Karla's mind and with it the memory of William sat in their garden reading that book, dressed in a pair of light green shorts and a new – birthday present from her – Panama hat. So happy and proud. From that to this, she thought, and me a big part of it, whatever he needs to say tonight.

Antonio pulled up. She watched him brush her lover's hair and hand him a flagon of wine. He began gently and carefully loading the paintings in the back of his van while William tipped the white jug and took a long drink.

Karla watched the tail-lights of the vehicle drive out of the town toward the distant village and hills. She sat thinking long after they faded and continued to follow them in her mind's eye.

"A week, two at the most," she decided, "and I will go home to him. He will not leave. He will see in the light the true value of his work, and us. Not what he imagines he left behind. And what person ? I know I was his first."

Karla carried on sitting well into the night, long after she judged William safely indoors. She tried to focus on the exact location of the villa. And knew, as she saw a distant beacon flicker into light, that it was a sign. A signal calling her back to him. She sat still and basked in its imagined warmth. Then felt herself burn.

CHAPTER SEVEN

Richard came in for his breakfast. The smell of the milking parlour clung to him: a melange of contradictory layers: disinfectants and iodine struggling to mask the splatterings of ordure and urea: all floating and swirling in a cloud of milk: as tangible, fresh and warm as if her child had never left the nipple. Madeline watched him struggling to lever his boot off against the worn sneer of the foot scraper – it too this morning, appearing to her to mock his tired eyes and the flecks of dung, wiped green across his brow. She saw her son's thick coarse fingers clinging to the door frame, knowing how soft they would feel from the lanoline used to balm every milk-drained teat. She longed to be able to take one of those hands in hers, wipe his face clean, do anything; or really, to be able to say something.

Madeline knew why Richard was so tired. Selina would have let him take her to another party, dance, or dinner last night with some of her friends from the office. All laying in their beds now building up for another session after their few hours gossiping and painting nails, or whatever secretaries, or 'personal assistants' did these days. While Richard made a fool of himself trying to keep up. She slammed the two plates on the counter next to the Rayburn and began slopping out breakfasts - recalling the last time Selina came for Sunday dinner and delighted in telling them how his falling asleep was now a regular feature of their nights out, and at one recent show in particular:

"I only have to leave him and go and have a dance with someone else and he's off. Sat in some chair with his head thrown back and mouth wide open for everyone to see, and snoring. So the other night, Lew..." (Madeline saw Herbie note that it was the third time this man's name had been mentioned since dinner began - a slight frown crossing his face as he continued to shovel down his dinner – though nothing could slow that hunger, and she'd long given up complaining) "gets a length of string and ties Richard's hair to the back of the chair. I tied his shoe laces to the legs of the chair and everyone counted to three, then Lew punched him hard in the stomach." Selina burst out laughing as she told her tale and Madeline watched Richard matching Herbie's pace without missing a mouthful, his long hair – grown despite the ridiculing of his father and other workers for her – dangling so that it brushed the edges of the white plate and hid his face.

"By the time he got himself free," Selina had continued leaving her dinner to go cold before being fed to the chicken as usual, "and was prowling around looking for someone to beat up on, we were all so well hidden he sulked off home without me and bolted the door so that I could not get in. You should have seen the look on his face when that punch landed."

Now Richard walked in and for the first time in over a month Madeline noticed that he was smiling, or smirking,

"Well," Richard said, "have I got some news or HAVE I GOT SOME NEWS."

Madeline waited, her breath held, for what she knew her son most desired and she dreaded: "Selina is with child." She heard it put in that old fashioned way - as this room must have heard the announcement so many times before. Instead she heard something much worse:

"Billy Bob is back." Richard announced.

Herbie stared over from the desk, but not at his son in surprise at the news – nothing ever seemed to goad that reaction from him – or in anger at what Richard still did with his brother's name, but straight at his wife. She though, would not meet his look or share any emotion with him. And that for Herbie was still the worst and emptiest place he could find himself banished.

"Been back over six months," Richard continued still not in a hurry to get to the table.

Madeline knew that William was travelling back. Her last letter – the one enclosing photographs of Richard's wedding was returned by someone who must have been a fine friend to her son. He'd written that 'William – of whom they should all be proud – was on his way home. Though he may' (strange, Madeline could recall thinking at the time, the way foreigners use our language) 'have a much longer journey than he yet understands.'

"And here is the best bit," Richard reached what was once his brother's chair and pulled it out: "he's got married. Billy Bob is selling insurance, door to door like some tallyman. His wife, and apparently no one at his office, knows anything about his daubings or adventures. And Selina's friend says his wife is up the spout."

Madeline imagined that bit of news must have marred this somewhat for Richard – though not much by the look of triumph on his face. Sometimes, she could even despise her eldest son for his continued dislike of his brother. Now though she just felt numb.

"And where exactly have you gleaned all this blether and gossip from boy ?" Herbie demanded. It stopped Richard's chortling with, unusual for these days, a snap of the old authority in its tone. Madeline was not impressed. Too little, too late, she nearly found the strength to say.

"One of Selina's friends, Trisha Greenway, knows the girl Lorna, slightly. She is younger than us and went to a private school but did turn up at a few young farmers do's. And apparently knows us slightly. In fact I think I can remember her meeting you two at one of the small shows when she was riding. When Selina and me announced our engagement. Anyway, they have bought a little cottage in the countryside: roses up the garden wall; and a bun in the oven."

"You just sound jealous, boy, that's all," Herbie snapped at him, still trying to gain some approval from his wife.

Selina had insisted that she would never live on a farm or in any old cottage. Richard took a joint mortgage out with her to buy a modern house on one of the nearby developments. Richard hated it, and the fact it was built on a small piece of land once owned by them and only sold, in his mind, because of his brother. He was delighted William was back and had failed. Jealous, he was not - even if Selina had refused to believe her friend's story just to annoy him - and he ignored Herbie's comment,

"Ha ha ha," Richard sat down in his brother's old place: "you remember the girl Maddy, I know you do, because I remember you said, at the time, that she looked like a horse. A plain one."

Madeline did have some vague memory of a group of girls surrounding her future daughter-in-law as she showed off her ring. Selina would have made them all look plain anyway. And then there was a recalled image of one of them with a long face, sad eyes and drooping lips. That, she knew, would never be a choice for William. That could not be the girl: "I don't think so," Madeline said. "She may have met your father. No doubt *she* would have found him charming and memorable."

"Oh yes you did," Richard carried on – he knew who the girl was and could recall her and his mother's comments clearly now: " 'A horse', you said: 'Horsey. A horsey-looking creature: probably desperate for its oats', I can hear it exactly as if it was yesterday. You'd got tipsy and were in fine form. No wonder he doesn't want her to know he used to paint: she might want to pose for him - saddle and all !"

Madeline ignored him and tried to visualize why her son would have returned home and married in such a hurry. And how badly things must have gone wrong that he needed to hide his past, even from his wife. But mostly, that *he* still felt enough loathing to keep away from his family. She shut out the querulous nagging, that whispered he was just as cunning as his father, and feared contact with them might reveal too many secrets about him - so that made them all expendable. She knew there was more to it - the same for both of her very different sons - a reason that she did not want, or dare, to think too much about.

Richard took himself home for dinner. Madeline often cooked the main meal early these days and invited him to stay - today, he knew there would be no such comfort for him or Herbie. He imagined his mother attacking her husband now - relentlessly and without pity - stretching this event back and back until it was as thin and taught as a flayed hide - with the real protagonists lost as the layers of flesh were peeled away. His house was quiet, cold and spotless. He saw Selina's coffee cup: clean and drying alone on the drainer. Richard picked it up and placed it against his lips. There was more warmth from the thin, almost translucent bone china rim - still carrying a faint orange stain from Selina's lipstick - than any kiss that had passed between them for some months now. Richard sensed that the silence between them was far more destructive than all the sound and fury entering his father's ears at the moment. But how to voice what was beyond words.

The phone rang. He rushed to it hoping it was Selina, intuiting that he was home and wanting to apologize for how cold she'd treated him again last night. Instead, it cut off the moment he spoke. Suddenly, Richard felt desolate and unhappy in this house and life. It was not a mood he understood and, for a brief moment it made him think of his brother and how simple his life now sounded, and content. An unthinkable thought drove him to the door. Work was the answer – it always was. Hard physical labour that left no space for any nonsense. Herbie had taught him that. And though most of the work was done with machines these days, there was always something.

Herbie heard the tractor start up and begin driving the saw bench across their yard, biting its way through, by the sound of it, a large dry piece of willow. He looked up at the clock and noted what time Richard was back and how many logs were beginning to pile up in the woodshed. Herbie knew exactly where Madeline was all through the second part of his hungry dinner break, and would remain. He came to a decision and moved quickly before anything could change his mind.

"If Selina's friend can get William's address or phone number, I will call or write and ask them both over to dinner," Herbie told his wife as she knelt in what was once William's studio leafing through one of his sketch books. He also noticed that the piles of paintings were not in their normal resting places.

"William will never come back to this place. Or to me. I will never see my son again." Madeline let her tired breath disturb and touch with its moisture a pastel sketch of another old lady lying on a bed: her eyes, dry deep hollows; then, in a moment before it faded, fresh and reborn.

"He will, I promise you he will. Some time he will come back, I know it," Herbie assured his wife. Madeline stayed silent and he heard the saw blade change tone as it fell into the empty core of the willow's heart: a moment of softness before it began to slice its way back out.

~

"Minos," Selina said the day that they brought him home from the sale. "You should have called him Minos, not Jester." As usual Richard was not exactly sure what she was going on about.

"Minos was the ruler of Crete," Selina explained slowly, "he was given a magnificent white bull by Poseidon to sacrifice. He admired it so much he could not do it and killed another in its place even though it then went on to ravage the island." Selina did not add to Richard's knowledge of Greek mythology by telling him that it paid back the kindness by mating with the king's wife who later gave birth to the Minotaur. Richard's jealousy was getting so intense she could imagine him following her every time she took a walk near one of the fields, if she did. That or trying to fulfil his other main preoccupation by getting the local blacksmith to make a hollow cow for her to climb into and see if that worked. "I just thought that a name should be in keeping with such a beautiful creature. Jester !"

The huge young Charolais bull had blown his steamy breath between them, the ring through its nose catching a mist of condensation and allowing a single drop to fall down onto one of Selina's high black leather boots. Richard stared down at his own dung-caked Wellingtons and felt angry and foolish that he'd dragged her to come and see what filled him with so much pride:

"He is cream and not white," Richard told her. "His origins

are French and not Greek. And *we* always call our bulls, Jester."

"He is as near to white as anything is ever likely to be, or remain, in this dull, dreary place," Selina had replied, having the last word and leaving Richard standing in the pen holding the bull which he could sense wanted to follow her.

Now he watched the animal shouldering its way through the herd of cows. "Lift a calf every day, and one day you will be carrying a cow." Herbie's explanation for the unpercievably slow growth of something you saw daily. But not Jester. He grew in slabs of unliftable, unmissable muscle, almost hour by hour it seemed. Human greed or need modifying his shape until now, paradoxically, he most resembled a cave drawing. Some idealized dream of plenty, tottering tamely on thin matchstick legs. The cows desperate to get their bribe of cow cake – or just be relieved of their burdens of milk – were pooling into the yard ready to force their ways into the portable milking parlour. The hardest thing was keeping them out to wait their turns. Jester towered above them. His wives: some pregnant for the first time; others, old whores or still virgins.

Richard looked at the creature's balls, swinging and tumescent, his dick looked as if he had been planting cabbages with it. Some young heifer must have gone through it, he thought, trying to see if the strange fire that glowed and faded according to the bull's mood was alight or quelled. It made him think of how long it was since he'd been willing to play Selina's stud. That was exactly how she made him feel; and he could not help it.

"I will never have a child," she told him from the start. "The idea of giving birth, of being cut, or some nappy changing food machine is the most repellent thing I can imagine for myself. And always has been." Richard put that down, at first, to being just talk. Then three months ago her contraceptive pill began to give her unbearable migraines and she said she was going to have a break. Richard felt a twinkle come into his eye, a fire in his loins begging to burn, knowing this was their big chance. Her way, he thought, of not admitting that she was wrong and really wanted to change her mind. Selina arrived home the first day after her period was over with enough condoms to fill a carrier bag. He pictured her, as she tipped them on the kitchen table as if they were his dinner, in the chemists buying up the shop: ribbed ones, fruit flavoured varieties, even an extra-large black skinned one. They nearly all lay in the bottom of his wardrobe, unopened. And would stay there.

Richard walked dreamily around the periphery of the concrete yard, though still with enough consciousness not to place himself between Jester and the wall. He turned as a heron broke its frozen prayers of camouflage and toppled into the sky.

Then Richard was flying with it.

Or diving after it, into a sky which must have become as liquid as the rhine it was fishing because he could not breathe. Everything started to slow as he gained height, then stopped completely as he paused in his ascent, turned and for a moment observed the world below. The cows were shrunken, and the bull definitely did look white, and magnificent. Then Richard began to follow another character from Greek mythology and plummet to earth. He landed sideways on top of the enclosing wall and luckily rolled off it outwards onto the soft soft grass. Richard knew he must be alive again because he managed a breath – though it did not sound right and felt worse. He lay there, unwilling and scared to risk moving.

Jester had flicked him like some annoying insect into the air. Richard knew of a lady, named Beryl, from their village who, when she was a 'pretty young maid' had been tossed by a bull.

One side of her body had become frozen, but subject to sudden spasms and attempts at rebirth: a tic so violent the village children, according to Herbie, used to follow her around just to witness the transformation, until some man took pity, married her and hid her away on some private estate. A distant cousin of Herbie's was recently gored to death and everyone said that it was his own fault for being a stupid bugger. Richard knew that if Jester was not dehorned he would be another dead silly bugger and not lying on the ground searching his mind for the consequences of what may be going to happen to him.

He moved and felt his legs respond and felt sure that his back or neck could not be broken. A month ago one of their neighbours tipped a tractor with no protective roll-bar over its cab. He'd lain there for over twenty hours until his wife found him. Now the only thing he was going to be driving was a wheelchair and then only if someone placed him in it and pushed. None of their tractors were fitted with roll-bars and Richard kept seeing and imagining every time he climbed on one what could happen. The image of Selina becoming his nurse was more frightening than any fear of injury and, one day as 'Ruby Don't Take your Love to Town' blurted out over the tractor radio, he came very close to running Herbie over. There was a terrible row and for once, Richard *was* going to get his own way on something connected with modernizing the farm. He did not even want to imagine what would be said - after all the lectures about farm safety he'd recently been delivering - when news of this incident got around.

Richard leant on the top of the wall. The cows ignored him and kept their eyes firmly and hopefully on the unopened, blue door to the parlour, their minds full of cow cake and the growing weight of milk. Jester's head was lowered as if scenting the earth for deeper concerns. The muscles on his back rippled and twitched. He gave no obvious sign of having just smashed a thirteen and a half stone man, who was feared on the football pitch for the weight of his tackles, over twenty feet into the air. Richard judged that he might have done it out of annoyance at him getting between a cow that was ready or close to being mated. Or perhaps a horsefly made him flick his massive head and neck in anger and Richard was just too close. Whatever, it was not a major attack of any madness; the bull could definitely stay and do its job.

Richard drew a sigh of relief at that. He needed to urinate. The stream started normal then went slightly pink and deepened until he looked away from its red to near-black colour. He felt everything begin to sway and tip and clung to the wall with both hands as his trembling penis dribbled blood down onto his feet. By the time everything stopped moving he felt a little more positive and tried to concentrate on the best thing to do. The idea of getting onto his bike and cycling back to the farm was out – he could hardly bear to shuffle his way slowly on the peat-soft earth. Richard knew if he just waited long enough Herbie would come to see what was taking so long, but that was likely to be hours away. A car may even come. Occasionally tourists did risk the rhine-lined lanes to come out this far: sometimes they touched the soft banks and slid sideways into the perfect jaws of the trap. Then they drowned: slowly and thickly in the silt-disturbed water. Recently it had been three naval ratings on leave from the Ark Royal. All of the world's oceans to choose and they ended-up in a ford car and a rhine a short way from where Richard once watched his father beat a cow out of that same embrace. It made him realize that he was even less likely to see a car with those deaths still on everyone's lips. So there was only one thing for it if he did not want to wait the hours for Herbie's arrival. Besides, the cows still needed milking.

Richard began to trudge gently over the fields. If he could get over three of them and by their old wooden and leaning gates he'd be close to one of the new borders to their land. Cross one more field awaiting development and push through its hedge - already growing too high and thin at its base to keep any stock secure – and Richard could enter his own little, neatly manicured back garden. And how sweet for once that would be. Normally, he loathed the manicured garden even more than the little two up two down house. Every fork tine stabbing into what had once been his ground felt like a wound. Now the cut grass and easy access was a goal. He could already see himself opening the door, phoning his father, then falling onto the softness of his bed to rest.

The ground was suddenly softer: a damp sponge now with an explosion of wild flowers. Their scent felt soporific as they enjoyed and shared this heady moment of freedom before the bulldozers arrived. Sleep in this field of poppies the breeze invited, and Richard paused. Then he saw the dryness of the milking tank waiting to be filled. And heard the bellowing of the distant herd, waiting. He crushed some orchid underfoot and moved with fresh force.

Thorns: blackthorn, or sloe: a bitter and astringent fruit which, as his aunt had taught him could, just after the first frost shrunk and wrinkled its skin, be seeped with gin to make a warming liqueur for Christmas: so sexily pink with a poisonous hint of almond. Then hawthorn: Aunt Flo made a jelly and wine from those little berries: "Good for the heart," she'd state tapping her own bird-like chest. Richard tugged himself free from the grip of thorns but not, as easily as normal, from the memories of Flo. The last barrier between him and his house was just the vicious net of briar: a web growing strand by strand, each re-rooting as it curved into fresh earth. He felt the thorned hooks tear and scratch through into his flesh but pushed on recalling briefly: bramble-tip, wine and hours of blackberrying. And one time in particular, when a long afternoon gathering a large crock full of berries, he'd carried them in for inspection, praise and reward. "The Devil's pissed on them," Aunt Flo spat: "throw them to the pigs." The first frost, he knew now, finished the fruit, forcing its sugars and acids back into the roots and soil and giving the Devil their souls in return for his gift.

Richard swathed through the final clutching fingers and saw a movement the other side of their patio door. Even in pain the adrenaline kicked in and let him make it at a rush and a crouch to the back of the garden shed. The panic that he was disturbing a burglary ebbed slowly as he let his face rest against the recently creosoted wood, ignoring the burning which felt cooling against what was igniting inside.

Selina was bending over their coffee table. The one *he'd* made for them out of a piece of elm after the disease took the last of those trees from their land. Her long, long-nailed fingers were clutching either side of its knurled and burred edge holding herself up: her head nodding up and down, reflecting, Richard knew, in its deeply polished surface, her long hair just flicking the pools of knots and growth rings that he had sanded until their swirling histories made him feel dizzy. Lew was standing naked behind her and driving it into her like, the words came back to him: his bull planting cabbages with it. Richard was held like some rabbit hypnotized by a weasel: knowing he must move to survive, but unable to resist the glamour of the spell.

Selina once told him, during an early row about her never wanting to have a child, that Lew's wife, Kirsty, had talked him into having the snip. "You will never get me to do that," Richard assured her. "No," Selina agreed: "you would not be man enough." And he had made himself choke with laughter at the notion of beanpole pen-pusher Lew being a man. "A wether more like," he'd chided, before adding one of Herbie's attempts at humour: "one quick snip and you are two stones lighter, ha ha."

Now he watched as those two, heavy-looking stones were slapping against his wife's firm arse. Selina was still wearing her very smart, charcoal and black suit. The short skirt rolled up like the belt Madeline had once called it. She was wearing white stockings and her breasts looked the same colour as they spilled out from her blouse shaking and registering every impact. Richard saw her turn her face toward him but knew that she could see nothing. Then he heard the noise.

Selina was groaning and moaning – a sad noise really, he thought. It made him think of Roly Cart that day in the barn, "The full bull," and that grotesque, but now he realized as she began to squeal, an accurate impersonation of her – though never with him. Once, just after they were married they stayed with some friends of Selina's. Laying in their guest room that night he listened to the husband and wife making love in the next room. When Richard realized Selina was still awake and listening also, he whispered, embarrassed by the noise and length of what was happening, "I guess it comes with practice." "Yeah," Selina had replied loudly: "just like playing the violin."

He saw Lew go rigid. A look of agony waved across his face as he emptied his barren seed into Selina. Richard saw her sag slightly as if disappointed then her whole body take a deep sigh for her. She stood up as Lew drew back and they both began rubbing with their feet at what must have spilled onto the new carpet. Selina grabbed Lew's hand and almost ran up the stairs dragging him with her. Richard noticed that the front room curtains were wide open and, though the house was detached, it could be overlooked by others and any passing residents. Richard also saw Lew's back as he followed her up the stairs. It appeared as if he had been mauled, so he realized, there must already have been more. And then another memory came thudding back: one that suddenly made terrible sense for the first time.

It was at another party. Everyone apart from Richard was well on the way to being drunk – Selina, first as normal. One of the men, a builder, started telling this dirty story. It was about another builder on a site they were both working. Richard was struggling to keep awake so listened. This man, who liked to 'play away from home', found out who the local tart was and claimed she was the 'village bicycle' and could not get enough riders. So he slipped off one lunch time to oblige her. When he got back into the site Porta-cabin, he'd shown his naked back to the rest of them. "Look what that filthy little bitch did to me," he said: "how on earth will I explain this to my wife now?"

The rest of the men decided that he should claim to have done it trying to get through one of the barbed-wire fences that surrounded the land they were developing. "So, to make it look real," the builder continued: "we took him out and got his shirt and pants – because the horny little cow had scarred his butt as well – tangled up in one of the fences. Then we left the dirty, lucky bastard hanging there."

Richard recalled now that the whole time the man was telling this tale, the other people not up dancing had started nudging him and giving him nods of disapproval. At the punch line of the story, the teller himself appeared to have realized something and his face went from its smiling to an expression of horror mirroring all those around him. Richard had been slipping quickly into sleep to really notice but made sure he gave them all a wide grin to let them know he was not so easily shocked. That was the same night he got another punch and gave them all another laugh at his expense.

"So," he said to himself, moving his cheek off the coarse whiskers of the shed: "so now the last to know, knows."

He could already hear the bed going and knew they were in no position to witness his departure. Richard forced himself to walk straight and firm back through the thorns. He was going to go back and milk the cows regardless of any pain. If Herbie turned up he would not even mention the bull and take any insults about how slow he was getting without reply. What really mattered was the plan growing in his head.

He knew how to quieten a filly down. And how the more wild they were the better they ended-up for the breaking. He was determined now, to have what he wanted from her. It was all going to be a matter of timing. The exact moment was vital. And for that all he needed was his usual charts. Plus a few other items: some old and magical; some new and clinical.

CHAPTER EIGHT

Selina suddenly backed out of the Kafeneon and rushed away, ignoring Yannis's welcoming, then startled look. He felt a wave of disappointment that she would not be brightening up his terrace and day. "Off again," he shouted after her, "always in a rush, always forgetting something." Yannis stared at the young family seated on the corner table. It almost seemed that they may have startled her – or even annoyed her by being in the place she usually sat. More likely, he thought, she'd been fighting with Perry again and wanted to put some distance between them. At it all night and day, according to his aunt's sister-in-law, who rented them the house and lived next door; at it one way or another non stop. "Ah," he sighed, and thinking of that perfect description of all of the young temptresses in his favourite book, Patouchas: "But what a 'demon'." Yannis looked over at his wife and sighed even deeper.

"Please," the Englishman called him from his regret and fantasy. "This wine, my wife, Lorna, says it is too bitter."

The prim, red-faced woman would not meet Yannis's eyes. "I make it myself." He told them: " it is good Cretan wine, straight from the barrel, no chemicals, just grapes and love."

"I like it," William assured him.

"Daddy likes all wine," the little girl, a mirror of the burnt, now angry-looking woman, giggled.

"I will get something else for you," Yannis told Lorna. He guessed they were renting his second cousin Erghina's restored 'long house' on the edge of the village. That meant they were probably here for two weeks. If the mousy little woman found his wine bitter and deemed not to speak to him, it would add up – it always did for some.

"Let me recommend the Afelia," Yannis watched Selina drive past, fast and alone. Another row for certain, he decided and marched off wondering how much to charge for this bottle and how long it would be before Perry arrived with more wounds to need soothing.

Selina had recognized Lorna first. And with it came the first clamouring memory of the day: her shock at the time when she learnt they were sisters-in-law. Of course to have found anything else out from any of them back then was impossible. The child sat with Lorna was obviously her daughter and, without needing to confirming it, the stooped figure with his back against her plane tree, William.

Selina's first feeling was that she'd been tracked down in some way and needed to escape. Then, as she'd sensed William's eyes discover her and the same feeling from all those years ago began to surge into her, to find some place to think, and try to understand again. She parked the jeep under the shade of a tamarisk and tossed her shirt onto the passenger seat, then did the same with her bikini top and stepped out onto the sands of Almiridha in just a red Brazilian thong with a book in her hand. Selina sensed some of the tourists staring at her. The locals also looked, but differently - with an interest that was considered polite and without greed or envy. She was used to being glared at but still it felt as if only one man had ever really seen, and he was now sat a short way off with his wife and daughter. Selina lay on one of the bed chairs knowing she would not be asked to pay or disturbed and glanced down at the novel. The words meant nothing. Maybe, she thought, a long swim might help. Then Selina knew she must go back.

"But why here ?" she asked herself, turning round and watching while two English-looking girls - probably with the encouragement from their men, since her arrival – removed their tops. Stretch marked, she noticed. And sagging paps, now drained, but once no doubt full. So good mothers to the toddlers basking under the brolly. Good mothers; good milkers. And she was back.

Back at Porlock Weir. Another little village, like this one that used its nets to catch tourists now rather than fish.

"They say the harbour is filled with treacle and once you have sailed in you are stuck for life." Selina recalled the landlord of the small hotel telling them as he opened a bottle of champagne. Even now that word with its touch of golden viscosity held her struggling like some insect in amber as she tried to fly from what had happened to her there and its aftermath.

Richard had not made love to her for months at this time. Selina needed sex. Always had. It filled a void, temporarily. So she took Lew. Then, as usual, he became a nuisance and needed to tell his wife and wanted her to leave Richard. He started phoning all the time and growing more pathetic by strides. Even declaring that he wanted to have the snip reversed for when they were together. Selina did not bother to explain that one of the reasons she was with him was down to her husband's desire in that direction. Are all men, she wondered at the time, obsessed with impregnating women ? Is it some ancient demand swimming inside their heads as well as their balls ? Or just another attempt to chain women down ? When she got to hear about William and

Lorna she'd despaired.

Then without any warning Richard announced that he'd booked himself a room in a hotel for three days and was going to take a break from the farm. He said that he understood it was short notice and that no doubt she already had made other plans. Selina stared at him. His thickening features and coarse hair appeared to tremble as he waited for her decision. "Did he know?" her mind screamed. "Was this some crude farmer's trap to leave her and her lover alone ?"

Selina had heard the famous story of how Silas's first wife turned out to be a 'gold-digger' just after his farm and already cheating on him. So one night with Herbie's contrivance and aid he came home, smeared in fake blood, claiming to have been in a crash on the back of Herbie's bike. They were both being taken to the hospital he told her. Later Herbie called pretending to be a doctor and saying that both men would be kept in overnight for observation. She heard again the tone of delight in her father-in-law's voice as he described the two of them bursting in with some private detective in tow and catching them in the 'dirty deed'. The photographs were still in the solicitor's safe, he told her once, with all the other deeds. Just in case. Selina imagined her and Lew lying together in the same solicitor's safe, bound with some purple ribbon bow in the act itself or just pulling apart in shock, that moment frozen forever.

So Selina said she would love to go.

"The honeymoon suite was it ?" the receptionist asked, smirking at them.

"Actually," Richard said, "it was a single room, but my wife decided to come after all. So if you have one with two single beds that would be ideal."

The first night Richard was charming and easy company.

Much as he'd been when they first started dating: giving her that sense of security with freedom which at that time felt so necessary. And like then, they drank too much without his tutting disapproval, though somehow, Richard – very unusually – appeared to handle it much better than her. In fact, Selina required his assistance to get up the stairs, as her head swirled, like one of the eddies in the wake of the boat they'd stood watching earlier, bubbling its way out of the treacle trap .

"Why don't you stay ?" Selina asked as he helped her into bed.

"I did not bring any with me," Richard replied.

He sounded more sad than angry she thought, "I bet they will sell them in the toilet," she offered: "get a fruit flavoured one and I'll give you a banana split for your breakfast." Selina heard his grunt of disgust and did not know why she had said such a thing. The one time she tried to push him down on her he'd struggled like a man about to be ducked. "I can't see the point in any of that," he said. "It's what the bull does to the cow to see if she's ready." When she tried to do it to him he went limp in her mouth and she got the message. She was still trying to work out where the suggestion came from when the bed began to spin faster, and his snoring joined the sea whispers all around them.

Selina's sleep was full of strange dreams that night: vivid and too weird, as if the poet that once walked this shore was leading her into his measureless caverns. In the morning she woke with the most awful hangover. Richard was sitting up in bed with a clipboard on his lap and nearly jumped out of his skin when she spoke. Selina guessed he was doing the farm accounts or something and was ashamed at being caught. Afterward, he was so kind and understanding, almost guilty, she imagined, that for the rest of the day Selina tried to find a way of discussing their lives. It felt the perfect chance to try and make him understand the differences between them and how they could not be changed. And how she felt an open marriage and freedom for both partners to live within it could be made to work. Each time she tried to get him to talk, Richard led her away with some fun or joke that made her feel like the one guilty of being stifling or restrictive. Only one thing slightly threatened to spoil what was such a light and blissful day: Selina tried to refuse the champagne that night. "But I've already ordered it," Richard said angrily. "To go with all the oysters."

"It gave me a terrible headache and the strangest dreams," Selina told him. "I saw Coleridge and all of his 'slimy things crawling upon a slimy sea'."

"So, you are going to spoil my holiday already," Richard snapped, downing his own glass quickly as Selina had never seen him do before. "And you are supposed to be the big drinker. I think you must be getting too old – or overdoing it behind my back."

That night Richard climbed into her bed. Selina was asleep but she felt his weight as she drifted in and out of another dream. This time the garish spectrum was replaced by a monochromatic seascape. She was walking along the edge of a leaded sea, each wave heavy and ponderous, balanced between breaking or falling back on itself. There was someone walking close to her - or even accompanying her: a man, though not Richard, a thin more aesthetic figure in a black cape who would not let her see his face. Then a bell rang. A dead knolling as if it was finding its way to them from a deep drowned church:

"Run," the man yelled turning and moving away too rapidly for her to keep up, with his coat flying behind him like smoke. "Run for your life you fool. It is the riptide."

Selina's legs were moving. Pumping faster than her heart

even as she felt the ground become liquefied and hold her wriggling as the sea began to swirl around her ankles. "Sound a bell," she remembered a local telling them just after they arrived, "when the riptide comes and a rider on a fast horse could not outrun it."

The water reached her crotch and a thick, icy-cold finger of it entered her and made her wake. Richard was on top of her thrusting mechanically back and forth. "Richard," she felt him jump and his rhythm falter: "you got some did you ?" she asked, her tongue heavy inside her mouth. He began again without answering as if the beat of some silent metronome were driving him on. Selina began to feel herself drifting away and gave one last effort to stop. She felt him pull roughly out of her,

"Feel," he said and brushed one of her long-nailed fingers over a ridge of something circling his penis. Selina felt its rubber tightness and sagged back onto the bed as he stabbed it roughly and quickly inside her. Almost immediately, she found herself returned to the black and white seascape. This time she was swimming in the water. Men were staring down from the harbour wall. Some were laughing at her attempts to keep going, others encouraging her: "Swim, swim baby," one of them yelled down. Then another: "kick open those legs good and wide. Like a good froggie. Like a good spawn."

Then she went under and was filled by the sticky liquid that surrounded her. She actually felt herself swell and bloat with the force of its pressure from within before being dragged legs first upward. Whatever had lassoed her ankles was wound around and around and pulled tighter so that her legs were bound together, before lowering her back and letting her hang above the jetty, her head and shoulders only just touching the smooth, sea worn stone. "Breathe slowly," her rescuer said. "Relax and breathe deeply, please." For the rest of the night it seemed that she was left strung up on the quayside for various men to pass and take a good slow look at her naked form. "Quite a catch," she heard someone say.

"She's caught alright," a voice said from whoever was slowly massaging her ankles back into life.

"Reeled her in nice and slow," I heard.

"The only way to do it. The only way to be sure."

In the morning her head felt worse than the time before and her ankles *were* covered in red marks and felt bruised and sore. It was late and Richard was not in the room. She found him sat out on the quay watching a boat getting ready to go fishing. Selina felt a wave of nausea turn her stomach at the thought of it returning and spreading out its catch.

"What the hell was going on last night ?" she demanded as Richard looked up and smiled.

"I should be asking you that !" he replied. "You were dreaming and babbling like a mad woman all night. At one point you got your legs all tangled up in the sheets and hung out of bed. It took me ages to unravel you. I cannot imagine what the people in the hotel thought was going on. Kicking and flaying. I did not get any sleep all night."

"You screwed me. I remember that much anyway. I felt your weight on me for ages."

"You insisted, loudly. I think it must be all this sea air and fresh fish. Maybe you ate some bad seafood. My one aunt.."

" Fuck all your aunts, I want to go home. I have never felt so ill in my life. It is as if I've been contaminated by some pollution or something."

Richard looked shocked, "Just one more night," he tried, struggling she could see to remain composed. "How many breaks do I ever get ? We'll leave the champagne and seafood alone. I hear they do a very nice rare steak and stout at the pub. We'll go there tonight, please, trust me. Or do you want to go back on your own for other reasons ?" Richard threw something into the water and Selina watched a flesh-coloured ring flutter and dart into the depths.

These oneiric memories - that Selina could recall now, with such clarity as a different sea inched toward her brown unshackled ankles - faded quickly at that time, and may have been lost forever if it had not been for a bird. One thing left alive for another part of the lie probably. But still, she hoped: flying free and untainted.

By the time that Selina began to have her continuing bout of morning sickness, Lew had, on the only occasion he managed to get anywhere near to her been beaten half senseless and had his arm broken. Richard arrived just as Lew pushed past her on the doorstep where she was struggling to get rid of him for good. He was actually trying to drag her up the stairs at the moment the tractor roared up their drive. Afterward, Richard did not give her a chance to try and explain anything,

"I knew it was coming," Richard said. "he's tried it on with loads of girls. Herbie caught him on the village green once, running around in the nude. Of course it was no good trying to tell you. I just bloody well hope he goes and calls the police."

Of course he did not. And Richard became more kind and attentive than she could stand or find a way of escaping from.

Then the jackdaw came down from the chimney to rescue her.

Selina was home from work with another morning of terrible sickness, a red burning glow to her face that happened every single time she managed to sneak a drink of any alcohol and a pounding deep threat of an advancing migraine. Her whole body felt as if it were in revolt over the terrible invader that had somehow found a way to grow inside. She wanted to deny all of the feelings; to dismiss the blue line that appeared on the testing kit each time she tried - as stark and bold and cruel as an open vein. She still refused to mention anything to Richard who seemed oblivious to her symptoms.

The jackdaws had nested in their chimney and Richard said he was going to shoot them. Selina insisted they stayed. "Next year," she told him, "you can block off the chimney and stop them doing it again. We never light real fires, so they will not hurt. Besides, they may already have babies coming. You must leave them alone." Strangely, Richard agreed and gave her a glowing look as if she had said the most wonderful thing in her life.

Selina sat on the sofa trying to concentrate on the comings and goings of the birds, their shadows passing like small clouds outside the window, and ignore the taste of acid bubbling its way back into her mouth, when a perfume and whisper of soot stirred by wings came into the room. The young jackdaw shot out of the hearth in a puff of dust as if conjured up by some magic performed for her distraction. It began flapping around the room, streaking the walls and windows black.

After two or three attempts, Selina caught it and held it gently in her one hand. The bird immediately went calm and turned its head to observe her. Selina was startled by the pure clarity of its eyes that appeared to look much farther than anything she could see: into the depths of a sky and dimension beyond her understanding. Then she saw a fleck of red touch the dark, greyish- blue lens and for a moment feared it might be blood and that the bird was injured. She turned and followed its gaze as the red package finished its fall and settled in the cold, unused cradle of the fire grate.

Selina opened the window and let the young jackdaw tumble softly onto the lawn. She waited as both parents landed on a telephone wire and began to craw angrily at their wayward offspring. It took off at a rush and both of them whirled after it trying to stay dignified and track its clumsy flight path. Selina watched it reach the fields and crash land like some primate into the arms of a hawthorn. Both adults joined it and she knew that it was safe.

She went to see what the bird had dislodged, sensing, no matter what noted thieves jackdaws, magpies, crows or rooks were - gold wedding rings and coins from some hidden hoard a speciality - it was a different type of criminal who'd stashed this treasure out of sight.

Selina unwrapped the red oilskin, its texture shaking off the soot like droplets of black rain falling onto the carpet as she read her own name. It was on one of the farm's breeding charts. The special type that Richard used as he attempted – in spite of Herbie's opinions and objections – to improve the herd, and produce in the future, an award-winning beast. She could remember sitting with her husband and feeling - though unable to share - his excitement as he told her of this dream. On the top of the chart, where the number of the cow should have been - no pet names for any of their animals except the bull – Richard had written, in fussy, florid, calligraphy her full name. It looked as if some patient monk had laboured for hours to produce it. "So," Selina thought, trying to find any way of shutting out what must have been going on in his mind as he worked on this: "you have some of your brother's artistic abilities, no matter how hard you struggle to deny it."

The rest of the page, and pages clipped to it, were a series of dates and a graph. Selina knew exactly what it was. One of the girls at work, struggling to fulfil her desire to have a child, brought in the more human version for them all to look at. "See," she'd explained to them during a coffee break: "this is the moment: our best chance. I should be going home for a light supper, flowers, a little wine, then a full night of passion; instead, he is going to see his stupid football team play. The clinic worked out this chart for us. They even told Rikki to save himself for this night. Mind you they also suggested he stopped wearing his 'little boy' Y-fronts and give his balls some air and room for production. So of course his mother bought him a dozen pairs of extra small ones." Selina could recall them all having a laugh at the man's expense and, as she did, her own private laugh when Richard recently bought himself three pairs of expensive, Italian boxer shorts and started wearing them to work. It had even briefly crossed her mind - with pleasure more than anything else - that he might be having a relationship of his own.

Selina carried on going through the pages, watching the circles and other symbols move like particles being drawn by some inevitable attraction until they all became united on one date. The number was surrounded by a many pointed star: a supernova exploding off the page and making her swallow the cold bile rising in her throat. She sat back and tried to concentrate: to keep as calm and calculated as the person who'd done this. There were other dates marked and highlighted in different ways but she guessed that he knew his chance would be very limited and this was his best shot.

The rest of the stuff made her feel sicker than what she now knew to have been forced inside her. The cold realization of how she'd been manipulated and violated; and just how cunning and desperate Richard truly was to have his own way and gain control over her. She thought of Madeline's babbling about Herbie's relentless pursuit of her and how nonsensical it used to sound. And yet the warning was there if only she'd listened. Behind each light niggling tale there brooded a more modern interpretation and she'd missed it. Selina recalled her father's explanations, as he read to her many times, what exactly lay hidden behind the apparent manners and respectability portrayed by their favourite writers. All wasted on her, she now realized.

"Oh," Selina heard Madeline again: "how he followed me around. Turning up outside my house always with roses though I had told him I did not want to see him again. Even when I *fled* to London he managed to *wangle* my friend's address out of my STUPID mother and just turned up on the doorstep. And I thought: 'Ah well I can't *escape*: I may as well accept the inevitable and *give in*'."

So Herbie was a stalker. That, Selina realized, could easily be the dirty realism, bottom line of *her* fairy stories. Now he sat back, she decided, and let her try to tell that version, watching as everyone dismissed it as the vanity of a vain old lady trying to find a way of capturing her fading beauty. Selina pictured herself, sat in the same farm, telling her sons' future wives a similar yarn,

"Why," she could say: "he even used roses. And of course these, my dears !" Selina placed the two leather straps on the sofa next to her. She could hardly bear to touch them. "How neat though," she thought, "the stitches were holding the layer of black velvet to their inside: how considerate of him not to have used glue and remember that her skin was allergic to it and broke out in a rash instantly at any point of contact; or more like, she quickly understood, that there was no point trying to hide the marks left by them if another set gave it away. Selina looked at the old, brown wrinkled and cracked leather. "What other creatures had been restrained or led around some show or slaughterhouse before it bound her flesh ?" she asked herself.

Selina used a pencil to lift and then drop the rubber ring. She had seen and experienced them before. A friend once brought the real thing back from India: a delicate object carved from ivory with precision and wisdom to hold back the male orgasm and stimulate the clitoris at the same stroke. "You wait," Selina's friend told her "until the premature little sods get this beauty on." Selina could recall being jealous of it and making her friend promise to find the same antique bazaar next time she returned to Goa and get her one. This one she knew had been used to fool her into believing it was a condom, and maximize not pleasure, but his chances of success.

Richard must have bought two, Selina realized, seeing again the object vanish into the depths of Porlock. She picked up a container of pills: different sizes and shapes, rattling dully inside the small yellow bottle. Next, she opened some cuttings. The first from a glossy, women's magazine on how the female orgasm played its role in conception, with a series of photographs showing the contraction dip something hungry and beak-like into a tidal wave of semen if the timing was exact.

The second was a newspaper article on a famous rock guitarist that recently came to live in a nearby village. He was already associated, the paper said, with black magic rituals. Now he had driven his young 'child bride' half-crazy. She needed to sell her story as part of the 'catharsis' she claimed. 'He became obsessed with his orgasm', she told the readers. 'He would not allow himself to ejaculate. Day after day, week after week he would keep bringing himself to the point with his hand or in different parts of me. Always stopping. During these times he would sleep on the cellar floor wrapped in sackcloth so as to prevent wet dreams. In the end his testicles would be so big and swollen he could hardly bear to stand or walk. Then he liked to climb on top of me and let the dam burst. I could almost feel myself explode there was so much. Then I had to lie with my legs up above my head while he watched. I would get whipped if any spilled out. He even once tied my legs together after he read that the old aristocrats used to do it to their wives when they were desperate to produce an heir. Not that he wanted a child. Not unless it was Satan's of course." The third article was on a rape drug being slipped in girls' drinks at clubs and pubs. She could hardly read the descriptions of their suffering as *their* memories returned.

The final thing was written in a different hand on a piece of old parchment: a delicate, spider-like scrawl of strange names and instructions: a spell, in fact. Selina recalled another of Madeline's tales. How another of the great aunts married a gentleman farmer. A tall-in-the-saddle, dashing, ex-cavalry officer. She'd even showed Selina a sepia print of them in their finery, seated on a horse and trap. They were unable to have children but 'so delighted' in each other they learned to live with the sorrow and forget about it. Then on one visit to Aunt Flo she'd got told there was a 'wandering look' in her husband's eye.

Aunt Flo gave her one of her potions. Three months later, at the age of forty two, the woman went to the doctors and told him that she had a growth in her stomach. "Growth, be damned woman," he was said to have cried: "you have a child in there !". Two months after their son was born she conceived again, even though she'd taken no more of the potion. Selina thought of the exotic meals he'd cooked for her a couple of times as a 'special treat' - and how she'd tried to encourage him to do some more.

Selina put everything carefully back in place. She pictured how many times before the trip to Porlock she'd found Richard locked in the toilet claiming to have an upset stomach. She saw him again shuffling around saying that he'd hurt his back and that he needed to sleep on the floor for a time. She felt herself swell again that night as he had let his 'dam burst'.

The final thing Selina placed back in the oilskin was a little notebook. It was the only thing that made her smile slightly with its list of expenses, including receipts from an Ann Summers' shop for love rings, boxer shorts from London mail order, hotel and petrol. Also, a largish cash amount recorded as going to someone named 'Spiker' - Selina guessed for the drugs he must have given her. She even saw the cost of the bloody magazine and newspaper.

Then any flicker of a smile went as she read the last entry: the date when her period should have started and exactly how many tampax there were in the bathroom. It was followed by: 'First day due: same amount. End of first week: same amount. A month overdue: ditto.' To end the record, he'd written in the same florid letters: <u>THE DEED IS DONE</u>.

She carried the package and lay it in the bottom of her suitcase as she began packing. Only, if there was any attempt to fight the divorce after she sorted out her abortion would this go to whoever was necessary. If the agreement was amicable then he could have it back and keep it for a reminder of what sort of person he really was; and exactly what he was capable of doing.

The memories of that tainted her again. Selina got to her feet and sprinted out into the sea. She swam until a cleanness engulfed her and she turned on her back to let the sun burn off anything that remained. In the distance she could see the peaks of the Lefka Oris. A sad feeling came to her that by the time the White Mountains became white again, then burst into their spring spectacular of wild flowers: the white would not be so pure this time, the wild lupins and narcissi not so vivid. As the sadness grew something light brushed against the back of her thigh in its passing. Selina imagined it could be the smallest tip of some giant creature or the largest part of a minute life form: either oblivious to her or her needs. Life moving on regardless. Suddenly she felt desperate to get back to the shore and then to see William before it was too late.

~

William was already struggling to find something to say when the Jeep arrived back. He did not need to turn around and see who was getting out and making the short, plump man smile with pride. He'd seen Selina the moment she ran up the steps of the side entrance and saw him. His reaction – though less than hers was also noticed by Lorna who now looked puzzled again, this time at what was stirring in both men.

"So," William thought, smiling to himself at this seeming coincidence – and the fact as usual that rumours were often more accurate than radar - "this is where Selina's 'rich catch' brought her – or she led, more like." He'd heard something about it at work from one of the secretaries who was a mutual friend to Lorna and Selina. Everyone, it seemed knew about the schism between William and his family and fished around with interest for anything connected. William ignored all the gossip about the messy divorce, and those that followed after it was over. He struggled to hide his delight at the main news: knowing inside that it had nothing to do with any bad feelings toward his brother and everything to do with the girl now arriving.

William ran into Miles shortly after his brother's remarriage to Annie. The card and two slices of cake arriving as mysteriously as any fungus on his front lawn: and the photograph of the marriage at the registry office as far removed from any fairy ring as his own had been, "Of course," Lorna assured him: "she is probably pregnant. Even if she doesn't show as obviously as I did." Miles appeared two days later – out of breath and comical on a drop-handled racing bike with a baseball cap on his head and his corduroys tucked into his socks. The breaks shrieked to a halt some way past where William was taking one of his ever increasing walks; as if the decision to stop was an afterthought.

"I'll tell you something for nothing," Miles wheezed: "whoever decided that exercise was good for you must pray to that same god that believes in the virtues of hard work and abstinence."

The two men walked for a time, trying it felt to William, to find a way of avoiding all the possible questions and their answers that could trip them both over.

"She's found a right one this time, *our* girl," Miles announced: "went to a top public school, learnt bugger all of any use to anyone, and ended-up with only the church willing to avail themselves of his *qualifications*. So he promptly sticks ten holy crosses on a pools coupon and wins over £100,000. Selina met him in Italy."

William had felt the jar, from that possible coincidence, hit him harder than any of the other news.

"She'd gone there after...well you probably know what. Went there to 'find herself' again: and found Peregrine. Brought him home: charm itself – they certainly teach them manners at those places. Drank nearly a keg of my strongest homebrew and did not have an original thought to share, even though to his credit, he could still totter a straight line."

They walked to the crossroads which would take them in their different directions,

"William," Miles said hesitantly, "I would like to say something to you which is not perhaps the correct thing, but I must. There are men and women in this world who one feels should be together, but through fate or circumstance, or whatever you will: miss and miss again. They might be termed, unlucky. But I believe, blessed by the grace of love - even if it does not physically come around. There are others for whom it does not happen that way and they force the issue hoping that it can grow. But the worst are those who know it is all wrong and then after they have tricked or stolen what should not be theirs, seek to corrupt or force that person into what was not there naturally. Do you understand?"

Without speaking, William had embraced Miles and quickly walked away feeling too choked to speak. But there was something that he needed to say and he turned to do so even though Miles was peddling furiously away,

"Miles, one day we'll..." William had carried on shouting and imagined, or did, see a nod of understanding and happiness.

"Selina?" Lorna said in astonishment. "Selina, *is it* you?"

"Hello Lorna," Selina said, trying to recall when or if they'd ever actually met. She glanced quickly at William and then at Perry who was seated with them. That was no surprise: he would have made a beeline for them the moment he heard their language. He looked stunned that they could be known to her, and she could see the usual questions forming and storing in his head.

"Hello William," Selina said trying to sound casual. "and this must be...Florence."

"Hi Selina," William replied pleased that she knew as much probably about him as he did about her. "I was truly sorry to hear about your father. He was a fine fine man."

Selina sat down and William watched Perry move over to her and place a podgy hand on hers.

"Fancy you meeting friends," he said.

"Acquaintances," she said quickly. "just from around the same area."

William backed her up trying to ignore Lorna's flaring nostrils.

"I was just telling your friends," Perry continued. "about 'Under the Volcano'."

Selina noticed the copy of 'Freedom and Death' by Nikos Kazantzakis close to William's glass of wine. Perry would have latched onto that as a way of telling his only literary story again. Of how he had read Lowry's masterpiece exclusively for the last decade, two, three, four, even five times a year: but had never read the last pages. He never wanted to know how it ended and believed this was a true understanding of the work. Perry claimed to go deaf if anyone tried to tell him and on two occasions since being with Selina actually ran from a room when someone insisted on trying.

"A couple of more glasses of this stuff and I will show him how it ends," William joked.

Perry had made his way into the Kafeneon to get Selina a drink as Yannis managed, as per usual, to ignore his affected finger snapping.

"Wait for me to catch up," Selina said: "and we'll do the last chapter." And their eyes met and held for too long.

Lorna shuffled her chair angrily, "I obviously must read it," she said.

"And how is Florence enjoying the wonderful Kreta ?" Selina asked.

"Actually," Florence replied haughtily, picking up on her

mother's disapproval and apparent dislike of this beautiful lady, "we are in 'Crete'. And this is the first time that *any* of us have been abroad properly; though daddy once went off somewhere for a quick visit. Mommy and I don't like the food: though *he* ate snails last night."

Selina did not question herself as to why William had kept part of his life secret – that was something she understood too easily – but was slightly disappointed as she felt him tense as if he suspected that *she* might betray him.

"Well," she said, beginning to enjoy herself, "if this is your first time we must all make sure you have a great time."

William saw his wife's eyes cloud darkly as she lifted the glass of wine for the first time to her thin lips. Perry banged a carafe of the house Retsina down,

"You must all come and have dinner with us," he said, obviously having listened to every word. "And I do mean egg and chips," he added to Florence, then stared hard at William.

William had drifted away and was glaring off at the massing of Lefka Oris. He suddenly found himself wishing that he could be up there, walking maybe through one of the magnificent gorges, or groves of citrus and olives. He saw himself returning in the spring when the wild flowers burst through the dry earth: perhaps even with a pad and some paints. The shock of that notion coming from nowhere after so long brought him back with a slap. He stared in surprise and with a feeling of guilt around the table under the old plane tree: everyone seemed to be smiling and chatting: unaware of his experience. Though William believed that one person had been with him. Hand in hand in the ancient light of Greece. Under this bestowing sun. Hotter than any volcano.

CHAPTER NINE

Madeline was struggling to recognize her son. When she took him in her arms - earlier in the day for the first time in fifteen or sixteen years - he'd felt exactly right. But then the look and smell was all wrong. He was bloated and soft. His beautiful cerulean eyes - that used to melt her as they pierced and then drifted away into the skies and seas beyond, were dark and stagnant like waterholes on the farm, with reflections of red stubble-burning dancing around their margins. And a smell clung to him: a prison smell, she imagined: one of strong disinfectant, stale alcohol and tobacco, sickness and odour. Her precious artistic son – who'd always found the stench of the farmyard so repulsive; the landscape so inhibiting - was back: transformed and trapped by everything he once loathed. "What have they, we, all done to you?" she wanted to cry out.

William was seated on the deep window-sill of their barn conversion. Herbie was telling him how he found the cherry wood for their construction, cut it himself, then made sure the builders set it so the grain caught the light correctly. Next it would be the fireplace. She knew her husband was nervous, and that this was much more than his usual bragging. He was working himself up into showing William the other barn. The one supposedly constructed for holiday lets - but which no stranger had ever entered, or would if Herbie had anything to do with it. Madeline recalled at the time of its work that Herbie insisted the huge area upstairs was left open-plan and all the openings glazed. "A great studio," he'd even said. "And what would you know," her bitter reply at the time.

Most of last night, and the rest of this day, she tried a similar but silent mental attack on his artistic attempts. Ever since hearing from Richard about William's arrest, and their instant and mutual decision to have him home, Herbie kept on working - freshening the barn and hanging William's early paintings around the place. His idea of how a 'studio' should appear. Madeline guessed how far off the mark he would turn out to be, and refused to help or comment. She hoped it was the main reason for his anxiety now. Especially, after witnessing him hang that one painting from all those years ago in the most prominent place as if he was now so proud of what he'd hid away.

Herbie was now laying the stones of the fireplace again, and boasting about how the builder wanted to take a photo and claim the design for himself. Struggling, she thought, for some claim on William's artistic character; though anyone with eyes to see, knew it must come for her. Madeline watched William's small sensitive fingers moving back and forth over the polished cherry wood as if it were still living and needed comforting; or that he could divine, without needing to ask and open any wounds, some truths about their lives from its patina. They'd agreed not to ask any questions about his: to let the last decade and a half remain a blank if that is what their son chose.

"So," Herbie asked, puffing himself up: "what do you think of our retirement home ?"

William glanced at his parents again, and again, hardly able to bear the pain of what he saw. They'd grown old. He could hardly believe they were so changed. How much of their lives he'd missed. Their vulnerability glared out to him through the thinnest carapace of pretence. Any remaining feelings over Lorna and Florence seemed incidental by the side of the loss and guilt he was now experiencing. The worst thing though, was the sense of failure he was getting from them. Their disappointment over what they'd not managed to achieve or experience felt almost tangible; and no matter how hard he tried, he knew he could not take the blame for most of it. "It's great," he heard himself saying. A minute ago a pick-up truck roared by outside. William saw by the expression on both of his parents' faces that it was Richard doing some work on the farm. He watched them look and read his thoughts: would his brother stop on the way back and call in ? William could read the answer in their eyes – though he'd already known it.

"Have you anything to drink ?" William asked as the vehicle returned, then deliberately, he felt, made a big deal of accelerating away as it got close.

"Sherry," Herbie said. "A very nice cream sherry that I found."

"Nice to know some things never change," William wanted to say, but the lie behind that statement would have choked him more than any sickly syrup.

"He comes shopping these days," Madeline added, as he scurried off to get it. "Can you imagine what a help he is !"

William poured himself a second glass as Herbie concentrated on the cakes. He stared out of the barn window as something flashed past in the quickly, fading light. "I'm sure I just saw a barn owl," he called out. And Madeline saw his face transformed back into the William she remembered so well. "A barn owl."

"What did you think, we'd evicted them all to make room for

us !" Herbie said, his mouth full of caraway cake. And Madeline heard them laugh and relax together - which was something she could not recall clearly from any time. And it came to her, as pure and white as any creature in the darkest night; both of them wanted this chance.

"Your father," Madeline said, enjoying the sound of that title again, "put up nesting boxes all around for them so that they would stay and others return."

William saw in his mind a picture of those ghost-like shapes returning easily and content; while he was struggling to find his way back to anything here. He could not see any way of bridging the gap that must lay between them now. Any hope of comfort and warmth felt as if it had a thin layer of ice floating over it, waiting for the first confident step, before springing its trap, then closing again - thicker and harder than before. But then, at that moment, it suddenly seemed worth the risk. He decided at that precise moment to stay for a time; to try and do the work Herbie once claimed his birthright and duty. The decision came just as he was about to refuse the offer of the other barn and say that he intended to leave for Greece or France,

"Well," he heard Herbie ask again, sounding a little doubtful this time, "are you ready to come and see it ?"

"Before I do see it," William said stalling for a time to gather his thoughts, "I would like you to tell me something about your lives. I don't care if I've heard it before or never: just a tale before we go out."

Madeline heard sorrow and regret in his voice; along with something that sounded more positive for the first time. She moved closer to Herbie on the sofa,

" A bit old for bedtime stories aren't you boy," Herbie said as his hand closed on hers.

"Catching up on lost time." William managed to say.

"Roller skating," Herbie said. And Madeline found herself remembering it for the first time in decades. "All of us used to go on a weekend. Up and down the seafront, gangs of us skating for all we were worth."

"And couples," Madeline added: "holding hands, or arm in arm."

"I was always the fastest and most daring," Herbie said.

"The maddest more like."

"Skating," William said, seeing in his mind a painting by Degas of Parisian couples in the moonlight on a frozen lake, "you used to skate arm in arm along the esplanade with the tide lapping below ? You two ?"

"Sometimes it was crashing over the wall," Herbie said.

"Or," Madeline recalled, "miles out. Lost behind the horizon with the mud banks glistening silver."

"It's what we did most weekends if the weather was fine," Herbie was remembering the first time that he managed to get close to Madeline though he was 'sort of' engaged to her best friend. He'd taken her arm and sped her feather-light body a long way from the rest of the gang and his fiancée. The long row of oblong drain lids, with their multi diamond-holed eyes into the hollow concavity of the sea wall had sped by, and seemed to glitter like jewels, denying their cast iron rust and salt crystal age.

"And then," he heard his now young again wife say, "all of the men would sit around and smoke their pipes."

William saw his father smirk at that recollection. He was famous for his strong opinions on smoking. What, he'd always stated, could be more ridiculous than someone puffing away their lives and money ? William waited for him to deny it. "We thought we were so fashionable," he said, "dragging on our pipes and even wearing cowboy hats from America."

William pictured the seafront the last time he saw it, when Florence was young and they still went for picnics. No skaters, gently weaving; but couples with too many children being harassed and chimed out of their money by rows of cheap arcades and fast food outlets. Gangs alright - though not puffing on pipes or wearing funny hats; but leaving syringes and shattered glass to bespeckle the tide-line, and half-deflated bags smeared with glue to roll like spume balls across the sands. A vague idea of a painting flickered across his inner vision, then began to take a familiar hold so that he found it hard to remain seated as Madeline started another tale.

"I always see Richard coming home just as he was learning to ride his first bike," she said sensing the silence was lasting too long. " 'I've found a dead man,' he yelled. 'A real dead 'un !' Even Aunt Flo nearly managed to come and take a look. He dragged me and your father up to the spot and there was Nevin Paddle lying by the side of the road."

"Dead alright," Herbie recalled: "dead drunk."

"That was when the cottage at the crossroads used to be a cider house," Madeline continued, "and all of the men would stand around drinking out of their own mugs and helping themselves from the different barrels as the old lady watched them. Sat in a rocking chair with a better beard than any of them."

"You had to put the coins in a tin the moment you filled your glass and she could tell by the sound of the spilling coins if you were cheating. At least," Herbie added, "that was what Sorley reckoned."

Once, just after William had started painting again, he drove out this way and saw that cottage: a cross between some fairy tale image and a hacienda. He recalled his disappointment at so many things he saw just that short while ago and how nothing inspired him. Now he tried to visualize it as it might have been: glowing yellow and garish across the levels as the late night drinking carried on and one of the mists came creeping in.

"Of course," Madeline said, "Nevin, and a lot of the others, would never have gotten home without their horses. That was a common sight around here once: the old horse plodding back at night – or sometimes first thing in the morning – with its master flat out in the cart, or asleep in the saddle. The horse knew exactly where they lived and always got them home for their poor wives or children to carry them in."

"I never even knew it was a pub," William said. "and it is hard to imagine horse and carts moving along these roads now."

"Once," Herbie told him, "everything was done around here that way and for a long time after cars and tractors arrived. Once, we even had our milk delivered that way. A couple of old spinster sisters used to come along with their beautifully hand-painted cart with all the churns and brass measuring jugs sparkling. The horse's main and tail all plaited and curled, its coat gleaming and hoofs varnished. And the milk still warm as they ladled it into your mother's jug."

"Jersey cows," Madeline added: "all milked by hand and kept as pretty as their horse."

As his parents talked, William thought, that in a way now that they were not tied so much to the farm and its endless demands, there was, if not real love, a closer bond between them; he tried to picture how they may have been before it took over their lives. Also, that it *would* be important while he was here, if he tried to catch some of these images before they faded forever - if only to give them something back for what had been taken.

"Of course," Herbie said, "Nevin Paddle was one of the first to die when the typhoid came."

"Typhoid !" William said, shocked out of his own reverie.

"Spread, some folk said, from the new bacon factory and the way it slaughtered the pigs and then handled the meat. Others said that it was the rhines becoming contaminated. Whatever, it killed plenty. They laid old Bertie on a table in the pub and the men carried on drinking as if he'd just taken a drop too much, as normal."

"And," Madeline carried on, "Dolly took her life when the proper milk round got going." Madeline stopped for a second and stared out past William as if she could still see something on the Levels. "Drowned herself in a dew-pond. She must have waited for the time when there was enough water gathered in it. All of the ditches must have seemed too filthy for so clean a woman. I can remember it so well. Her sister stopping me and just saying, 'Oh Mrs. Halliday, Dolly has made an end to herself.' That was the only thing she said, and then pointed across the field to that sump in the ground full of crystal clear water, just as the local policeman fished her body out and covered it with a tarpaulin. Even at the distance I was, I could see how swollen that mound was. I was carrying Richard at the time and it made me shudder and go funny all day."

Herbie began to yawn and suddenly William felt very tired himself. "Well," he said getting up. "Can I go and see my new home and studio." Even as the words came out there was still the urge to take them back and flee; but Herbie sprang up instantly as if it was exactly what he was waiting to hear. Madeline was going to ask William to stay this first night in one of their spare rooms as she did not want this special night spoiled by her son's probable reaction to what she knew lay a few hundred yards away. Now as her husband blustered out it was too late.

The second barn was bigger than the one Herbie and Madeline lived in. It was also much older and had been more difficult to restore and convert. Richard used to complain non-stop during the work about the expense and design. "How many paying guests would it take to ever see this money back ?" and "Why was the place being made so open ? Why such high ceilings and so many windows ?" She could never get anymore satisfactory answers than her son to similar questions and tried to dismiss any nagging doubts about Herbie's motivations and schemes. He often saw things differently, she convinced herself, and was by nature stubborn once he'd made his mind up. Madeline stood at the door with them as the outside lights flicked on and saw something in his face that changed that opinion.

This was Herbie's moment. An event that he always knew would come no matter how long it took. He fingered the key – the original old iron one that was dug up during the building work after some fifty years in the ground. His fingers were trembling and he was glad nobody was going to see him try and fit it into the lock. "This is yours," he said handing it to William.

William smiled, not understanding exactly what Herbie meant or wanted him to do.

"I mean," Herbie said, "this place is yours. It is *our* gift to you. The deeds are with the solicitor and will be made over to you as soon as your troubles are over. This is your home and studio now, and forever."

Herbie could see that Madeline was too surprised to react, yet. He reached quickly past William and flicked the lights on before she got the chance to recover and speak.

Then, as he turned the key and was about to refuse the gift, William was too shocked to do anything but stare. His early paintings were everywhere. Images he'd forgotten but now remembered so easily. He was stunned to see his own face staring down at him. William compared it to the two he'd just completed. So many changes. And yet a similarity; a link to what he'd been recently searching for. A real key to the secret world he feared lost in Italy and the barren years following. All the anger and frustration, since he'd started to try again began to fade as the honest, childlike freedom of his early work, showed him a way back clearer than any drink or rage had managed. He felt an urgency to bring his recent work here and begin to mend it; then go forward.

Herbie was explaining as he led William around - ignoring, or oblivious to the dreamlike state he was in – about how he made the builders leave part of an old tree in one of the walls, and how some of the beams were so old they were harder than iron and could not be cut. The main double bed was actually part of the original building. A cider press with grey smooth sides which now held instead of grain a king sized mattress. William looked down at the bed which seemed to be almost growing out of the floor. He let his hand press its firmness and smiled. Madeline saw the same wicked grin cross Herbie's face and then pass between the two men. That nonsense, she realized, was obviously something these two did have in common; while Richard she was certain, for once took after her.

Madeline could not keep her eyes off the row of nudes leading up the polished stairway. Many of them, she knew, were paintings and drawings of her. More than that: of how she was really inside. Madeline wished Herbie would stop yapping and look at them. Then, as they reached the top, and stepped into the huge open area Madeline saw the three large paintings. The last ones William had completed before leaving. More nudes. And not of her. Madeline saw clearly again who they were. As she tried to look away and saw on the other side of the wall a self-portrait of William looking straight through her and into the flesh of that girl she despised. Madeline thought of Richard and all he'd suffered from contact with her. A chillness entered her, whispering of troubles yet to come.

Finally, in front of the one end, which was virtually a wall of glass, Herbie and William stood together looking at the early painting. Madeline stayed back, trying to flick through one of William's old sketch pads. She still feared if there was going to be a reaction to any of this it would come now. Instead, just silence. She joined the two men and stared properly into the painting for the first time since Herbie had carried it away.

A beam of light shone through her old kitchen window and fragmented into rays that illuminated each person gathered around the table. The brilliance and intensity of its glow seemed to have made transparent all the outer garments and even skin. The people were dissolving into shadows and then being remade from deep inside. Madeline recalled the shock she'd received the first time she briefly saw the work. Still it disturbed her and made her question what her son saw every time he opened his eyes.

Herbie had looked at the painting many times since that day. And saw the dandy gentleman, spectral and hiding inside the heavy crude body his son had caught so well; he'd loathed and denied the greedy expression masking his face and staring out at his wife and children. Many times he'd longed for a chance to be able to explain to William a different truth. Now, he felt, let him look at it again, with this proof of generosity surrounding it - see it in this light - this reality.

William was looking at the shape he'd given to his brother. The brooding sullen man he imagined he was destined to become. And then at his own shape, empty of everything except the particles of sunlight. Gold dust swirling into colours then becoming drained motes of dust, desquamating into the flagstones. He could not help thinking there was still much to like about the work. The colours were not bad, the idea strong. The vision of his parents though was completely wrong. He'd been too easily fooled by them. Too naïve and arrogant to see and understand.

William put his arm around his father's shoulders and felt a slight quiver pass through their solid strength. "I am going to redo that painting," he said "and I am going to get it right this time."

Herbie nodded as if he expected no less.

That night, long after Madeline and Herbie were gone, William was still awake in the stone bed even though he felt exhausted by all the things he'd been through since his arrest. His head was full of skaters and gaily painted carts, men in a smokey shebeen with their heads bowed and lips moist with cider as a bearded lady heard the fall of coins and a man lay dead on the table. Then the dawn of horses leading some of them home as pure creamy milk swirled out of bright copper. And very strongly he saw a new version of the sun touching his parents as they were. It felt important and vital that he stayed and worked on what he was starting to see again. Willam had claimed enough in the last eighteen months – mostly to himself - during the rows and battles since he gave up his job and struggled to return to painting - that it was an artist's task to chronicle and record as much as to create. This was the perfect chance to prove it. And he was going to take it.

As sleep came, he realized that he felt more determined than since he first left this place to really paint. He would work with a fury until everything was caught by his eye and brush. Nothing would get in the way or have any other claim on him again. The last scene that floated into his mind, was of a mist licking its way back from the cottages and farms into the depths of the Levels, leaving a pond revealed in the cold dawn light: a dew-pond glistening like silver with something heavy moving and blemishing its sheen, before growing still and sinking.

That would be his first painting, he decided, 'The Dew-pond', and whispered its title softly like a barn owl falling from the darkness onto its prey below.

CHAPTER TEN

Richard had still not spoken to his brother – and did not intend to start. Apart from, of course, that night when William called from the police cells and, not only spoke to Annie - as far as Richard knew for the first time in her life - but then gave him his first word in half of their lifetimes: 'help', naturally enough. It was true, that he lay awake following it, remembering and getting sentimental; even making plans for a way of coming together - before stupidly ringing his parents to inform them. "Never send a letter that you've written at night until you've read it again in the cold morning light," Flo once told him. And when, finally, *he* got to hear what his parents did following that call, he wished he'd heeded that bit of advice.

"The best piece of property on the whole farm and a couple of thousand square yards of land thrown in," Richard had raved at them both, "he's only been back a few months," a look passed between them. "Oh I don't suppose he had to wait even that long for another gift did he ?"

"You have the farmhouse, the rest of the land will all be yours one day and our house," Herbie said, as Madeline held her latest grandchild and would not meet Richard's glare. Annie insisted when Richard told her the news that he took the child: "Show them who they are robbing," she screamed, shocking him with the depth of her vehemency.

"I've worked every single day to keep this place going, to build it up." Richard said, feeling as betrayed by them as he'd once been by Flo. "Hard, back breaking work day in day out."

"Work never did anyone any harm, boy," Herbie, still content to do a longer day than Richard, threw at him.

"Your brother works hard, Richard," Madeline added. "Every single day. And you think what that terrible woman put him through. All those lies in the local paper. He's lost his home and child."

"He is still painting in that studio at gone midnight and up before you," Herbie said.

"I have to struggle to get him to come and eat a single meal with us," Madeline told Richard as he'd got up ready to leave them in disgust, "and you begrudge him a chance to have somewhere to live and work. I cannot understand why if *we* are willing to forget, you are so set against your brother. Are you sure this has not got something else behind it ?"

Then, as he snatched away his child he found he could not, for the first time in his life look her straight in the eye; Maddy's standard test for honesty - and he failed.

Richard was trying to forget that meeting and the anger that still existed inside him about all of it. He came in from milking to find their 'paying' guests were already up and being served breakfast by Annie. They were fishing on the full, peat-black drains for pike. Now that autumn was underway the giant predators would be in prime condition and hungry to kill and prepare for the coming winter. Twice they'd asked Richard to come and join them. "Too busy, too busy," his usual mantra. Though in truth it was a quiet time and in-between milkings he could have joined them. Richard loved fishing like some men love women, others wine.

And what was more: it had always been *his* own thing. Herbie was a: 'Worm on one end a fool on the other' quoter. The rest of his relatives, Annie, and all of the other 'young farmers' or farm workers: part of the 'can you eat it brigade ?' Richard was longing for his son to be old enough and to have the excuse – he somehow felt he now needed – to go again. Maybe, even two 'excuses' he imagined, as Annie was pregnant again and another boy to go with the two girls would only be fair. Richard carried on levering his boots off trying to block out the pain that still came with any thoughts of pregnancy or *his* children.

"Slouching around like Van Gogh in that movie with Kirk Douglas in it," he heard one of the pike anglers say.

"What was that film called then ?" another of them asked.

"Wasn't it the moon and something or the other ?" the third of them joined in.

"I only know him as a cowboy, or a Viking," Annie said as Richard stepped in.

"The Moon and Sixpence was based on Gaugin not Van Gogh," Richard told them all - seeing by the surprised looks on their faces that he'd overheard another gossipy conversation about his brother: "the film you are talking about is, 'Lust for Life'." He sat at the roll-top desk sensing they were all waiting for some other reaction from him; or searching for another subject that might divert it. He'd seen his brother many times already, stalking the Levels and lanes and farm, a small wooden easel strapped to his back and two bags flapping like crow wings at his sides. Sometimes he even saw his distant silhouette, set-up and making sketches or small paintings of what Richard guessed he must work on later in the barn. Richard spied him at that one night too. He'd just stepped out from helping Herbie with a difficult litter of piglets and stood for a few cooling seconds in the star-clustered darkness. He saw William working away through the large window: oblivious it felt to everything: from the sidereal birth light of galaxies to the acrid heat-lamp wrigglings of the new-born pigs. Richard did not think he'd ever witnessed anyone so concentrated on what he was doing in his life and could not look away himself. It had actually seemed at one moment that he could see the colours radiating around, forming and then flowing from his brother onto the large white area in front of him. It made Richard shiver and hurry away to his home and comfort.

" 'The Horse's Mouth' was another," Richard said as they all remained silent: "that was about Stanley Spencer with a touch of Augustus John's desire to paint large murals thrown in. Then there was the 'Agony and Ecstasy, which was Michelangelo Buonarroti and the Sistine Chapel." Richard saw that their looks of surprise were turning to shock, especially on the face of his wife. For a moment he felt proud of his knowledge; then ashamed how his interest in such films would be interpreted. "Always in agony or ecstasy these 'artists': it must be the *pain* of lifting those brushes or pens: then the *joy* cashing all those cheques."

The men all began to add their opinions and he saw Annie put some extra rashers of bacon in the frying pan for his breakfast. There was a look of smug satisfaction on her face reflecting from the stainless steel covers on the new royal blue range they'd just fitted. For some reason both things made him feel angry and frustrated - especially as he suspected she'd instigated all the talk about his brother in front of these townies and strangers,

"I think I might slip down a bit later and spend a few hours showing you amateurs how to catch a big pike," Richard announced.

He kept all of his tackle in pristine condition and knew a quick phone call would make certain all the necessary licences were in order. The idea went quickly from being no more than a reaction to something that felt vital. "How long," he asked himself, "since I've done anything just for the pleasure of it ?"

"I shall go and get my hair done then," Annie said quickly. "and properly. I am just sick of sitting in my own kitchen having it cut. Your parents can have the children while I go – that is something else that is overdue, anyway." She banged his breakfast plate down on the table. Since William's return, they'd both kept the children away in the hope of inflicting some hurt on Herbie and Maddy. Now Richard did not care, he sat at the table gulping down his breakfast as usual, trying to ignore everything except the vision of a red-tipped float dipping slowly under the surface and shattering the calm as a giant pike tail-walked across the water in a bid for freedom. Vaguely, he felt the men looking at him and this disturbance in the normal smooth currents of this place, and heard, from a long way off, Annie shouting down the phone and making her hair appointment.

~

The drains were the main arteries that allowed the blood of this land to be fed into the sea: held back behind its wall: brooding and whispering on the prevailing winds of its plans to return: sometimes raging in its chains: and once even breaching the defences and coating acres of pasture and gardens in silt and seaweed. The pumping stations were the huge mechanical hearts that pulsed the water acclivitous to the clyst gates, which then allowed the fresh to follow the receding tides and mingle with the saline before its diluted return found the gate opened one way only. Sometimes a high tide formed a bore and found entrance into one of the steep-banked estuarial rivers just to show what it could do: its brown unfurling anger rushing landward: mocked by children on safe, high iron bridges, or ridden by surfers in rubber suits on brightly painted boards: its only potency, the stench of raw sewage filling the noses of its captors and tormentors.

Richard knew the manager of the main pumping station well. He was an eccentric character, noted for driving off any angler who strayed too close to his station with one of the massive spanners, used to maintain the pumps, raised above his head. Also, to the few he favoured, for a supply of freshwater eels, illegally speared salmon, and a still that made a rough brandy out of cider. Today, he was waiting for Richard with a bucket containing three rudd that swam, red and brass scaled in circles around the filthy plastic constraints of their shrunken world. Richard handed him over a couple of pound coins,

"Mind out for them mink, young Halliday," Royston said to him, as if it was just days since their last meeting; and not years. "Wild mink: they've escaped – or been set free by those 'liberation' wankers – and are killing all the fish and birds now. Last week it was a fisherman's turn. Came after his Cornish pasty and he took a swipe at it with a bank stick. It jumped out of the way easily – fast as greased lightening they are – sprang onto his back and very nearly bit his ear off. Vicious bastards. Come here and have a look."

Richard was desperate to go and get tackled-up and start fishing, but knew better than to upset the keeper in any way. He followed Royston into a cathedral of a building: this edifice, Richard always thought, maintained beyond any necessity and to the point of real worship or obsession. Every single bit of the Victorian pumps was as freshly painted as the day steam drove their pistons, all of the valves and pipes glistened like gold, and the glass dial dazzled him as he tried to read them. "Looking great, Royston," he intoned, as expected. Richard stood on the clearly demarked floor space, knowing it was sacrilege to walk where only the anointed were allowed. His toe nuzzled the white line between the two areas, impatient and waiting to be summoned. He felt the hollow floor vibrate, gently; not shaking like a earth tremor, as when the pumps kicked in and the torrent was sucked below.

"Come," Royston called.

Hidden behind one of the pumps was a bank of mesh cages. Inside them there was a mass of wildly moving creatures: black-furred and going, or gone, insane at their recapture,

"I'm just waiting for the bounty to go up and then I will lower them into the water and drown the little cunts. If you were to push someone's fingers in there, they would bite them clean off and eat them before you could say, ouch !" Royston waved his own fingers close to the cage and a terrible thought came into Richard's mind as he felt the violence and smelled a strange, almost sinister, melange of musk and urine.

Richard hurried away and joined the men further along the drain. They'd been fishing since first light with only a small pike – a jack it was called – between them. "We've seen a much larger one," they all told him excitedly; "much larger, scattering shoals of fry and rolling near the baits."

Richard guessed from their voices that Royston must have sold them some of his 'poison brew' and made a mental note not to let them near the landing net when the time came. He knew they were fishing dead baits: a half mackerel hard on the bottom with a stream of oil seeping to the surface and flattening out the wind ripples, or sprats, suspended mid-water and glinting as if alive. He set up his own rod and line. On the end he attached a vicious double set of treble hooks on a heavy wire trace: a jardine snap tackle. Richard saw the men watching and read the words on their lips: 'out of date and barbaric'. Next, he took one of the live rudd and twisted one barbed hook through its upper lip and then from the second treble another through the root of its dorsal fin. The fish made a gasping noise and squirmed. Richard saw the other anglers do the same. 'Live-baiting' was officially banned now. Another notion, in Richard's estimation: dreamed up by some do-gooder sat in Whitehall who knew nothing about the countryside with its own self-regulating laws administered judiciously by the true custodians.

He tossed the bait softly toward a likely spot – more instinct and feeling than anything he could explain – and sat back as the heavy float: bright red top and disguised dark green bottom: carved delicate patterns on the surface as the impaled fish attempted to escape. "Swim for one last time," Richard whispered. When it ran out of steam, he would have to draw it in and put on another. It was, Richard knew, the struggling of an injured dying fish that sang a siren song to old Esox lucius, the pike. Or at least, to the one he wanted to catch.

Annie still tried to relax in her seat. She'd decided on having a new modern style, with some strong highlights. Twenty minutes of listening to a lecture from Madeline on: how beautiful *her* hair remained after having two children. Followed by a long description of how it was once bobbed and she wore a little French berry, while Herbie grinned and smirked in pride was as hard as usual to stand. But the final, "Of course yours is so long and natural and not really suitable for too many styles," was too much. Especially as her father-in-law seemed determined to drive the two toddlers crazy, and make sure they woke up the baby so she could hear it bawling before she drove off. Annie was about to show them, for the first time, that she was not the timorous little thing they were too willing and happy to accept. And then he walked in.

Now, Annie's earlier plan about getting home and changed into something pretty and, along with the new hair style, showing Richard what he was willing to start neglecting for some smelly old fish, seemed a waste of time. She had not exactly expected to drive him wild with lust – that was not, she knew, and was glad of the fact, in his nature. But there were other passions that he could be driven to. It would take just one: "We've all met Uncle William; and he is nice", from Tim or Maddy to awaken them instantly. Richard was - and rightly so, Annie believed after the way he'd been treated - obsessed with loyalty. So how to beat the children into subtly and gently breaking the news was one problem she was considering. But that was no longer the main issue; or the one that was making, even the catching up on the usual gossip feel shallow and unsatisfying; or the reason Annie only half-heard,

"Of course, even though she is back, *she* was still much too high and mighty to come in here – even with what we all know about her !"

And then, only just hear the scissors stutter in their rhythm, before pausing as something passed between the two stylists that must have concerned her and should have been pursued. Annie was far too busy trying to find some way of understanding the complexities of what up until now she had considered so simple.

It was so easy to see his return as nothing more than a slight blip in their lives. To believe what she heard, then read, about him. To share and feel anger for herself, husband and children at the fact they were being robbed by some drunken, and, according to what was reported about the case: perverted, failed artist. But ten minutes in his company had changed all of that, and, she realized, would not allow it to return or be easily hidden or ignored.

Annie could just remember seeing William before – though never close up - as he came into the kitchen to collect some sandwiches. No one heard him enter, though she saw him first. The silence was instant: Madeline halted her chattering; Herbie held Timmy frozen in mid-bounce; and even Maddy stopped doing impersonations of her namesake and granny. Madeline broke the spell,

"Well at least you've kept your promise, this time," she stated trying to sound firm. Then to Annie – as if she were concerned: "I've made him sandwiches every day for weeks and he's left them each time for the chicken. Last night we made him promise. Don't you think he looks too thin ? Half-starved even ? Annie, this is your brother-in-law, William. William, meet Annie and your nieces and nephew: Tim, Maddy, and fast asleep, Beth."

Annie nearly jumped-up, grabbed her children and marched out. But his smile and something else filling the room with him made it impossible. She could see a hint of her husband in his features – but no more than that. Nor any real close resemblance to Herbie or Madeline. And his eyes were unlike any she'd seen before in her life. They were blue and piercing and could not be held for more than a few seconds before she needed to look away. In those moments though, she felt they were as young as her children's with the same sense of wonder; then that they were too bright and unnatural for any normal sight. Annie sensed he was not concerned with anything they understood as necessary: their values and assessments did not apply to him. How many people, she wondered, would have spotted that as clearly as she did ? How many ever had, and what would they have done with the knowledge ? She knew that if her first words to him were: "Could I have the barn back for my unborn child ?" that the deeds would have been in her bag and probably his sandwiches in her mouth before she got to the hairdressers. The knowledge made her cringe and feel greedy and exposed. No wonder, she thought, he'd found it easy to 'squander' his share of the farm. It meant nothing to him and never could.

"I must catch this light," he said, his shyness, another surprise she felt.

Annie also noticed that he made no attempt to coo over the children, or ruffle one of their heads, or say who they took after. In fact, she understood, that he did not particularly care for them – or even notice they were there.

"He does look as if a good meal would do him no harm," she replied dutifully.

"You try getting him to sit down long enough to eat one," Madeline said, handing him over the greaseproof packet with a look that Annie had never seen before. Nothing close to it, not with Richard, Herbie or the grandchildren. The slight wave of anger it made her feel passed as she also saw how desperate Madeline was for the look to be returned, and how far away her son was already staring. Then, briefly, he was back with them, and Annie sensed them all being scrutinized. The feeling of discomfort was intense, almost brutal. Then he smiled and it was over. William moved to the door,

"Uncle William," Maddy called: "Daddy's gone fishing today."

Annie saw Herbie nearly leap out of his seat. William stopped, "He took me once," he told his niece: "but I was no good."

Annie heard sadness and regret in his voice.

She could still hear it now above the hot breath of the hairdryer. And felt that somehow it was her role to try and bring the two brothers back together. She'd heard that cadence of sadness too many times before from Richard not to recognize it and want to do something about it. And that was muddying everything else. She wanted to shut her mind to it and return to the earlier, simpler equation, but knew she could not.

"Now girls," she said, leaving the disturbing tide of seashell whisperings and wanting to indulge herself for a little: "Who is back ?"

~

The float paused. To the other anglers, who were now much more attentive of Richard's efforts than their own – spotting quickly that he was in a different league to them – it seemed that the third live-bait must just have joined the others, and expired. Richard tensed. He knew that the stop was far too sudden. It was through fright this time and not death. The float lifted a fraction, and, against all the normal rules of waiting for the run to develop, of allowing the pike time to turn the prey in its jaws, or even swallow it and end-up deep or gut-hooked, Richard struck instantly. The rod slammed over. And it was the moment. The one where the peace and meditative state Richard only ever found when fishing was deepened and shattered in the same instant.

All the illusory calm that fooled so many people about fishing became transformed into what it really was. A battle waiting. It exploded now as the heavy fish sent its energy back along the almost invisible line and through the buckling, curved rod into Richard's nerves. The link with something unknown from another dimension was now forged: and would remain for as long as his skill allowed it, until they met: or be gone forever if the fish's strength and cunning was greater and it escaped. The pike left its aqueous domain with an airborne dive. It shook its head wildly trying to throw the hooks and curved its body for more flight. The group of fishermen gasped at the size of the fish. And Richard knew that he'd never come close to a specimen like this before.

The pike came down in a shower of silver droplets and spray. It used its uncoiling to go deep and fast toward a distant bed of waterlilies. If it managed to weave the line around their stems the fight was over. Richard eased the pressure slightly instead of increasing it, allowing a gentle side-strain to encourage the fish to enter them. Its suspicion or belligerence caused it to turn and make a long run straight up the middle of the drain. The line sizzled and sliced through the water in its wake: a cheese wire cutting the liquid and whining its tension back into their ears.

Once, many years ago, Richard read in a fishing magazine that his great hero – and the man he liked to think he was named after – Richard Walker who caught the record carp, 'Clarissa', could charm a fish into the net. They said he was so skilled, that often a giant carp or rainbow trout did not even know it had been hooked. Tugging matches were for macho men without any skill or art. Now Richard began to take control. He sensed the weight of the fish as it began to sulk and ponder heavily.

All of the other men's lines were cleared out of the water and they stood watching – Richard only vaguely aware of their existence now, along with the presence of Royston. Twenty more minutes passed in what felt to him like an eternity; or seconds. The fight was now contained to a small square that bubbled and swirled like a cauldron near their feet.

Richard could tell though that it was far from beaten, even as the eldest of the anglers picked up his large landing net. The reel screamed its agreement as the fish took off on another run, this time in the direction of the pumping station. He just managed to stop it in the pool before the gridded entrance to the inflow.

Above it the windows of the station caught the scene and held it like a stained glass record as the fish began to judder and submit. Richard drew it slowly, slowly back.

Richard could not help looking at the picture of them all reflecting in the dark glass. It made him think of a different scene. When he was young and made a mistake of telling his family and the workers, gathered at the dinner table, as the haymaking stole his chance of another opening week of the fishing season, that he did not really want to be a farmer. Nobody but William appeared to be paying any attention, so he went on: "I really want to be a professional angler," he said, needing to share his greatest secret with them. "Like Richard Walker. I want to teach people to fish properly. Show them how to respect what they catch and the places they fish."

"No such thing, boy," Herbie told him.

"Worm on one end..." Silas added.

"Only got to respect what you eat," Roly said through a mouthful of crud and bungo.

"I think Richard is the best angler in the world," William had suddenly said. "all of the fishermen say so too."

Richard could still hear their laughter and then see his brother's tears for him. He returned fully to the fight.

The man next to him put the net in the water ready. Richard looked at his eyes to see if they were bleary from the drink. Netting a fish was itself a skill. Take a stab at a beaten fish and it could easily be panicked into a new desperation to escape, lift the net too soon and the fish could flip back out and snap the line or tangle it around the net. The man blinked too many times then licked his lips,

"I'll take the net," Richard stated and reached for its handle with his left hand. He held the rod high with the other and placed a finger on the spool of the reel to stop the pike taking anymore line. The veins and muscles in his arm bulged with the effort as he inched the massive fish closer the softness of the net.

"Hey, I've got a gaff," Royston said staring at the size of the fish. "Or a fucking eel spear. Both of them hanging on the wall. I could run and get them."

"Or your gun," the man who was now sulking about being deprived of the net said: "I know someone who shot one once."

Richard silenced the two of them with a warning look. The pike came in sideways, gently until it filled the length of the net and its tail still hung over the edge and flapped freely. It was in truth much too big for the net and he was sure it would escape as he tried to lift. But guns or gaffs were not for this beautiful creature. Then, with a positive heave, it was his.

Flecks of green, yellow, pink, amethyst, sparkled off its minute, silver chain-mail scales and its small eyes stared wickedly into the dryness of this world for the first time. Richard knelt by it and opening the enormous jaws unhooked it easily. The plates of curved teeth gently brushed the back of his and the only blood he saw was his own.

"It's a record for this county, for certain," one man said.

"Probably, the biggest caught in the country for years," another added.

"Unfucking believable," Royston said. "Now I know what has been eating all my poor ducks."

"You should kill it and have it mounted," the eldest angler said. "I have a friend that could do it cheaply for you."

"Imagine that monster in a bow-fronted glass case in your front room. Sat with a whiskey and watching the flames of your fire dancing off its scales and remembering this day forever."

"Or in the pub," Royston said. "You would never need to buy

another drink in your lifetime. Not with your name and the weight and the year it was caught wrote in gold for everyone to read."

Richard saw its gill case open and close: the red rawness exposed for a second. He opened its mouth again. "How many times," he wondered, "has this predator closed them after some lightening fast lunge and killed without a moment's hesitation or sympathy ?" There was only one law. The hunter and the hunted. Now it was over. And he was the victor. Richard had killed many fish: trout, salmon, eels – all for the pot. Also, fish being used for live-bait. But never a specimen. And this was his best by far. Also, something else that came to him during the fight and now. Possibly his last. He already doubted that his children would want to learn or that he had any real desire to teach them if they did. Ideas were changing too fast for this to have a place soon. Too many people already were doing damage. And time: even this bit of stolen time would have to be paid for in more ways than one. So why not a record ? A solid object brought out of this dream-time before it was over.

One of the anglers handed him a brick. A heavy stone lifted from the margins: its base pitted by history and crawling with life; its top: dry, bleached and smooth.

"A good hard blow on the head."

"Let it suffocate. You don't want to risk damaging its shape."

"It will loose some weight and colour if you do. Tap it on the bonce.

"Whack its fucking brains out."

Richard grasped the fish under its jaw and lifted it with one hand. He dropped the stone and hooked his arm under its middle to cradle it. His hands were wet from the net as he did not want to burn its epidermal layer with his dryness. "I don't suppose any of you tossers carries a set of weighing scales ?" he asked, watching them nod their heads as if to say: 'What for ?' He judged it and knew he was fairly accurate : high thirties, maybe forty pounds. Richard stretched it full length. "Nor a camera ?" Praying this time one of them would say yes. "Ah well," he sighed and turned to the water.

Then he saw his brother. Sat like some wretched scarecrow among a row of pollarded willows: a sketch pad waving some flag of surrender as he carried on working like fury – oblivious, it seemed to this little drama. Richard looked away. Even his presence was not going to spoil this. He lowered the pike's tail into the water. Then, grasping its jaws with both hands, began to let the fish melt slowly back into the drain. Finally, as his hands entered its world for a instant he held on as it began to revive. As he let go the water erupted in a shower of crystal back over him. And the fish was gone.

Richard glanced up and saw his brother now standing and staring. "Missed that one," he thought.

"I'll be late for milking," he said. "Enough of this time wasting."

He was already struggling to see the fish clearly as the water calmed and he began to break his tackle down. But the memory was there. "That was enough," he told himself over and over, wishing there could have been more.

CHAPTER ELEVEN

Selina listened out for the noise again. It had come into a dream, as she was sitting quietly with a glass of ice-cold beer in her favourite corner of Chania harbour. The rigging on one of the yachts twanged like a bow string, slapping wet against the bone-hollow alloy of the mast. The sound made her jump and spill the glass down her front. Then as her hand wiped the liquid from between her breasts, Selina knew that it was too warm for any drink and if she had placed a finger in her mouth it would have been as salty as any of those droplets just fired into her dream. She let her hand wipe the sheets, confirming that the bed was empty before trying to drift back to sleep.

Next, it was the change, as the steady creaking of the sword fishermen's boats suddenly crashed violently together: a dull crescendo of wet wooden cymbals that seemed to carry on reverberating through the house, even though she knew that she was awake again. In this new dream, she'd left the main harbour and was taking an early private volta, enjoying the looks of the men mending lines and nets as their colourful boats rocked the slow rhythm of the afternoon in Crete. This time the noise woke her properly. Outside, something screeched: telling her clearly that she was not lying awake in a mountain village listening to Scops owls debating with their ghostly, monotonous 'poo poo' call, but back in Somerset. And that the sound still moving slowly below could be worse than any nightmare.

Selina climbed into the chill and found her father's beloved dressing gown: "A touch of the Noel Coward's," she heard him say, as she pulled it on and hurried to check on her mother. Selina opened the door gently and held her breath. The shape appeared peaceful – if far too small, as if shrinking by hours now – and showed no signs of having been writhing in agony, or falling again from bed, before struggling back exhausted. Her mother's breathing seemed, as far as it was possible to tell from its light shallowness, at least regular. Selina stood in the doorway trying to normalize her own. As she watched her mother a stupid, almost selfish, question came to her: "When did the roles change and the parent become the child ?" If there ever was such a thing as a clear demarcation in lives, this one was drawn while she was away - without the chance to prepare.

"I think that you should know that your mother, my dearest sister, has had a terrible fall. Of course, this is not the first, but this one has hurt her badly and it is a sign, I have to tell you of far deeper problems. Something that out of concern for you she has insisted on keeping a secret."

Selina had just got back from a hospital herself and been given the message from Yannis. "You must call your Aunt Ruth in England – it is urgent." She refused his offer of going into the taverna and using the phone. There was going to be enough looks, opinions and questions when she did put in her next appearance. "An ambulance again!" "You must be driving the poor man to it!" "But why when he loves you so ?" Without them watching her, as whatever tragedy inspired her aunt to call was revealed on her face.

Selina fed the pay card into the phone – its bright hologram of a dove alighting on a rainbow became one of the lammergeier vultures carrying her own body easily in its talons as the words flew across space. She listened without arguing or even trying any defence as her aunt delighted in making her suffer; and for much more than her mother's condition. In the distance she saw her friend Lefterios switching lightly the flank of a large, dusty, near-black donkey, as it carried him through to foothills to his vines. The donkey arrogant; the man kingly.

"A Cretan four-wheel drive," he joked the first time they met. It was tied up to a strange, cup handled ring of stone that jutted, puzzlingly, out of the walls of many of the older village houses. Both the joke, and the sudden understanding of their purpose made her smile. He invited Selina and Perry to join him at his table in the shade. Yannis brought over two small glasses without being asked and Lefterios poured all of them a full measure. "Yamos," he said touching both of their glasses and throwing the drink down his throat, all in one smooth motion. Selina did the same and saw his eyes widen in appreciation. Perry took a slow sip and made a face,

"A bit like schnapps, I'd say. Not the best German stuff of course, but the home brewed type they do so well."

She saw a look of anger and pain touch the old man's face. "I will tell you something the Germans do well, young man. They die. Once we fought them over those hills. They dropped from the sky like olives and we shot them as they fell. The only problem we had was not killing them but counting the bodies. Our women gathered up the parachutes and made dresses out of the silk. And the brave Germans said they would hang any woman they caught wearing one. But the women were so clever with their stitching, they could not tell. So they put red streaks in them so they would see. And the women made underwear out of them so they did not; every night the washing lines dried the garments in the dark so the colour was lost to the moon's cold eye. A scarlet red: exactly the same red as the ones your beautiful lady is now wearing. So drink your *raki*, then you pour the next round as I am no waiter."

Perry had filled all of their glasses, then, without being asked so did Selina: she could see the rage and jealousy in Perry's face. This time over a close to eighty year old with a white beard – though to this day she could not explain how he'd known what she was wearing under her dress.

But it was not that memory that made her keep watching him as she seethed and boiled to respond down the phone. And then, afterwards to give her mother a tongue lashing for not telling her straight away. It was an important lesson she had learnt from him one day in the same taverna – though without Perry, who refused to enter the place if the 'bigoted old peasant', or his friend who claimed to have been in 'Zorba the Greek' were holding court. This day one of Lefterios's cousins – which included just about every young person in the village – was being a pain in the arse over some trivial matter, connected as usual with money or land. After he finally left, Selina asked Lefterios in Greek: "Do you like Giorgos ?" The old man looked totally baffled by the question: as if his perfect English had failed or Selina was attempting to destroy another Greek verb.

"He is my cousin," the puzzled reply. "He's family."

And Selina understood something of what she had witnessed day after day. Family was everything. From the smallest child to the most aged patriarch: all were included and cherished. It was more a part of the magic this place breathed into her soul than anything to do with landscape or food and warmth. Selina had felt her own loneliness and isolation strongly ever since. Now she was made to feel selfishness and blame that others attached to her.

"I am very sorry, Aunt Ruth," she said. "I will call mom

straight away and contact you as soon as I get home."

Perry came back from hospital later that day. Selina was already packing, or at least making a secret start as she did not want him to find out until she could try to explain why. She could not imagine his reaction if he walked in and caught her. Especially, as the reason for his latest trip to the hospital was inspired again by her *telling* him she was leaving.

And this time he'd tried pills. Luckily, perhaps, Paracetamol were banned on Crete or he might have actually done some harm. Instead, she thought, he just looked a little sicker than usual: more sorry for himself and in need of comforting. That was what he claimed yesterday when she told him she was going. "I need some sympathy," he said.

"Yes," Selina replied. "And sympathy is close to syphilis in the dictionary and they both do you about as much good." One of Miles's. And within an hour Eva was hurrying in the Kafeneon to tell her that "Perry has taken his life again."

Selina could easily recall the first attempt. That one was still a slight shock. She got home, late, after a beautiful day visiting the 'Virgin of the Golden Step', then swimming in the Libyan sea, picking shellfish off the rocks - doing anything other than going back to his earlier nagging. The blood was everywhere: all over the cool marble floor and being absorbed into the white walls and turning them shades of pink. Perry was spread out on the ground, ashen and trembling. Selina held him all the way to the hospital - trying to recall the icon in the church and then imagining that one of the steps had turned golden for her and she *was* pure in spirit. By the time they returned home with Perry's cuts not even deep enough to require stitches, she knew that she'd fallen for a different type of trick.

But it was too late. Perry sat in their avli with his pathetic bandages on display for all the locals and tourists to walk past and witness; while she walked through the square like some contemptuous widow without her weeds.

Then it was the gun. One of the antiques hanging on the wall. This time it followed a more direct row. Now that, finally, the ones about how she never said that she loved him, were worn out - even if he still refused absolutely to believe the truth, and was convinced, that through some desperate act or attrition, he could make her.

"When the money goes," Perry had said: "I suppose that will be it for me." He was looking at a bank statement and doing his usual: scribbling down sets of figures to work out how long they would last.

Selina was getting ready to go to one of her jobs. She was teaching some mature students English. And had started acting as an agent for a real estate broker: showing viewers around old houses and plots of land. Selina was also working on a book with two Cretan women. Helping to capture the supposedly, 'lost' cuisine of the island and put into words what was mostly an oral, almost instinctual set of recipes. And though she enjoyed helping students and improving her own Greek at the same time and did get a buzz when someone fell in love with a property, it was the book which gave her the greatest pleasure. She could not believe how much satisfaction it gave her. Every new page was felt as if it was something cut in stone. She had plans to finish it, get someone to do some art work, and then find a publisher. Perry hated it. Criticising any meal she tried out on him and her own weak prose style and sloppy grammar.

He was working on his autobiography. Or so he claimed. So far Selina had not seen a single page of it. "Too secret for you," he liked to say each time she got close to the thick book he carried around. "Not for your greedy little eyes yet." She tried to imagine what, if anything, it could possibly say: "Went to top boys' school. Learnt everything about nothing. Won a packet. Bought a tart. Came to an island to lose both."

This day his lethargy and wining got to her. They'd been living equally on her earnings for some time now, even though he still insisted on paying the rent. In return Selina did all of the cooking, shopping and cleaning. And she still let him fuck her. Though it rarely satisfied her, even physically these days, and often seemed to make him more miserable than content. Selina still had some money left over from the house sale agreement with Richard, there was a small legacy from her father and an allowance her mother kept on paying into another account. Last time she looked there was over ten thousand in that one alone though she swore she would never touch it. So Selina knew that she could leave Perry easily now and survive. And was struggling to explain, to herself, why she did not.

There remained a bond between them. Some friendship, occasionally, and he could still make her laugh when he chose. But the main reason was a thing that she hated to face: fear. In truth, he did something no other man had got close to doing: he scared her. Not in a violent way. That had been tried by others and failed. In fact, it held a strange allure for Selina that she was puzzled by and wanted one day, with the right person, to explore. It was in a haunting way. Almost, at times lately, it felt as if the child she terminated was determined to find a way into her life through another means. To make her pay for thinking she could escape. What had started out as such a leap into freedom was reverting into the opposite. She'd even began to believe that perhaps this was just payment for her sins. Though she recalled Miles's contempt about all that nonsense. And his warning when she left that was probably closer to the truth: "You cannot run to contentment; it is something that you carry inside you."

Or, and this was what really frightened her, that Perry was much more intelligent than she supposed and was playing a more sinister game with her than the obvious one.

"Perry," she said before going: "*who* exactly are you trying to kid ? I will leave you one day but it will have nothing to do with your money. Contrary to your opinion: I am not, or ever was, for sale."

Some way into the English lesson a gun went off. Guns often went off in the nearby mountain villages. The Cretans loved guns. Often, when Perry and Selina still enjoyed exploring the island together, they would come upon road signs so full of heavy, dull unfurled silver holes that the words were impossible to decipher. Selina always found it more amusing than threatening. A few minutes after the shot, one of the builders Selina recognized from working on the restoration of a village house, came charging through the archway and into her class,

"Perry has shot himself," he announced.

Stupidly, Selina translated it into English for her startled pupils before running back with the man. Just as they reached the taverna Selina saw that he was laughing and the men inside the courtyard sipping drinks were also joining in. Selina slowed down, already furious at whatever joke Perry must have put them up to. Then, coming from their gateway, she saw Lefterios and the local doctor. So it was true. "Malakas," she yelled at the men and heard them laugh all the more.

"I have called an ambulance," the doctor told her, and unbelievably she saw him pass a smirk to Lefterios. Inside, a strange blue haze diffused the room and a smell of fireworks tingled in her nose. Eva was sitting on a chair placed next to their sofa. She was holding Perry's hand – like a lot of women, their landlady was somehow desperate to mother the so 'well mannered' young gentleman. He turned and grinned at Selina as Eva glowered and she felt her own laughter begin to swell inside. His teeth were black and most of his hair burnt off along with his eyebrows. The rest of his face was scorched in black and red, his clothes hanging in tatters.

Selina turned and left the room without a word. She saw the gun laying on the floor, its barrels opened like some giant metallic flower blooming for the first time in the centuries since its birth. She went straight into the taverna, guessing the men would probably be both amused and hostile toward her, but feeling lost and suddenly lonely with nowhere else to go. Instead, Yannis brought her a beer without being asked and Lefterios and his builders beckoned her over to their table,

"I think the fool," Lefterios told her, "must have got some modern cartridges and emptied all of their powder into the gun. Much, much, too much. Then put the barrel in his mouth and used his toe to pull the trigger."

"A sort of Hemmingway," Selina said, "half-trying to see something noble in his action."

"Ah yes," Lefterios said: "only this young bullfighter did not bother about putting in any bullet. In fact, he must have also blocked the muzzle with something which is why it blew up like that. Cretan guns do not explode in your face. Anyway, it managed to catch him on fire for his troubles."

And the laughter began again as the raki glasses chinked.

Some time after the ambulance left and Selina judged Perry was probably having the rest of his clothes cut off and gauze put on his face, she was tearing the clothes off the young builder and letting something hot and soothing cover his face. She also made certain for Eva that the shutters were left open, and after a very long time - forcing her too keen lover to go slowly and wait for her – she came with a lot of noise.

The pills - especially with the news from England still poisoning her slowly – were impossible to find any such easy consolation from. Selina looked at Perry, trying to ignore the green tinge to his skin and the hospital smell clinging to him. It disgusted her to think of wearing these self-inflicted wounds to try and restrain her; while her mother hid real ones to give her freedom. Selina also felt a different type of disgust at herself for feeling elated that there was an even better excuse for leaving now,

"Perry," she said: "I am sorry for what you believe I've made you do, but I am still leaving. I have to. My mother is seriously ill. She has bone cancer and I must get home to help nurse her. My aunt called while you were in hospital to tell me. I've spoken to my mother and I can tell she is very afraid even though she will not admit it. I need to be with her. Do you understand ?" Selina could see in his eyes that he was dismissing this as an invention: even as the terrible, unspeakable name of the disease reached him he was just drifting into his own devices. Getting ready, she felt to make an appropriate move: a subtle one this time. She felt afraid of him as he smiled reassuringly.

"Do you remember that deserted village we once walked to ?" Perry asked her, staring out to the white mountains.

Selina nodded. Perry had been obsessed by the place and its remoteness. He struggled to find a way of buying up one of the old village houses and taking her there to live. It turned out to be impossible, with each property belonging to many different relatives who could not agree. She thought with almost horror now of what life might have been like if Perry's persuasions had succeeded.

"I was talking to the doctor and telling him about how happy we used to be - and what we tried to do."

Selina pictured Perry bleating away to some psychiatrist: making certain this suicide attempt was all put down to her.

"I said that I thought if we had bought a house in that village and been able to live there, we would have grown together instead of apart. He, naturally, agreed, but then told me something terrible. Some of these mountain villages are deserted because of vendettas. Like those in Sicily. Long running ones that some say will never be resolved. Those places are damned now – even cursed by what has happened and still waits to happen if anyone dares to return."

"And he was trying to help you !" Selina attempted to joke. Perry was making her flesh crawl. She was desperate to get packing and away from him. He ignored her gibe though and carried on peering into the Lefka Ori.

"Imagine being able to love and hate so well that nothing could ever be forgiven or forgot. And the passion is so strong that it can be passed into the blood of your children and they will carry on until there is no one left. Only then can it be over."

"Imagine," Selina replied, trying not to make eye contact with him as he flicked her a glance then returned, she imagined to that ghost town in the mountains.

Perry spent the rest of the day sitting in the same chair, accepting a meal and watching as she carried on packing without saying a word. That night he climbed into one of the small single beds in the old sleeping galleries claiming he did not want to keep her awake with all the arrangements she had to make the next day. Also adding, that he was going to have to get used to sleeping alone anyway. Selina hardly slept at all expecting any moment the door to burst open, or something worse to happen if she did. It was the same pattern for the remaining days until her flight. He talked about nothing, sat staring out of the window, and climbed early into his own bed. Selina waited, at least, for the inevitable questions to be asked: "How long do you expect to be gone for ?" or: "You do intend to come back don't you ?"

She felt foolish, and slightly vain, when the day of her leaving came and the cases stood by the door and she ordered the taxi and without a question or word about anything that was happening. Perry took himself for his first trip out and left her waiting for the seconds to pass alone. Then he hurried back in,

"Lefterios and Zorba are in the kafeneon and are desperate to wish you goodbye," he announced. "They were so shocked to hear that you were leaving and that they might not have got to wish you well. So I said I would come and make you go to see them. So hurry. You still have plenty of time."

She knew how much Perry disliked the two old men and would normally have gone straight past and to another place rather than sit in their proximity.

"You better go alone though," he said, "I'm feeling a bit drained now."

Selina went, wanting to take her cases and the passport and tickets from the fireplace, but unable to find an unobvious way of doing either. She pictured herself coming back as the taxi arrived in the square and finding everything slashed to ribbons with Perry lying in the debris grinning at how easily she was fooled. It made her unable to concentrate on her friends as they wished her so many things with tears in their eyes. Then as Lefterios held her hand and wanted to tell her something he thought important. It was something to do with a house he was restoring,

"A dream home, to think and find peace in. When I have

finished it," he whispered, "you can come and stay in it for as long as you like."

Selina gave his hand a squeeze. She tried to imagine herself ever coming back and being able to live alone in such a place – it made her forget for a moment what she suspected was taking place a short way off.

"There is an old bread oven that I will have mended. It cracked when my father died. That often happens when the owner's spirit departs. You can try out some of those cooking book ideas and feed the man you will bring back," Lefterios teased.

"No more men for me," she told him. "I've done with them forever."

"I see you in that house with a fine man," Lefterios assured her. "I read it in the bones one day after you finished eating. You did not know that I could do that. Or what I saw. Now you do."

Selina knew Lefterios was full of strange superstitions and beliefs. He would never eat or drink off or out of anything made of plastic. A special silver knife and fork, and an antique plate were always carried out if he deemed to stay for food. And she'd often noticed many of the villages calling him over and showing them their plates after a meal and listening attentively to what he said. She always imagined it was to do with the quality of olives, fish or meat. Now she looked deeply into the faces of both men and could see that they believed absolutely what was being revealed,

"Well," she said: "was he handsome ?" And Perry arrived.

Selina's reaction made both the old warriors start. He was carrying her suitcases and had her handbag stuffed under his arm. "I've decided I will drive you to the airport," Perry announced. "I am feeling much better. Don't worry about the taxi,

I've already cancelled it." He stood by the table waiting for her to move.

Selina could not keep the trapped wild look off her face as she stood up.

"What a fine and nice idea," Lefterios said, letting go of her hand – letting go of her, she felt. "And we will come too. A splendid sight it will be: two old men weeping at the Nikos Kazantzakis airport over a young and beautiful girl: even he would have hoped for no more."

Lefterios was up and carrying one of her suitcases before Perry could respond. Levendis (not really Zorba, except for the tourists) grabbed the other one and followed.

After Selina got home and saw just how ill and wasted her mother was, she closed her mind to any doubts and concern over Perry. She was determined to concentrate all of her will and spirit on helping to win this battle. Ignoring also, the realization that nothing had changed for her here; including the all pervading feeling of resentment and jealousy she tried so hard to flee from. It had waited intact for her return: glaring and whispering at each outing to the shops or surgery. Selina tried to imagine what might happen, if one evening she took herself – as in Crete – so casually into the local bar for a cold beer. The thought of the likely results very nearly drove her to do it, and she promised herself the moment there was any improvement in her mother's health that she would.

Selina did expect, nearly every time the phone rang that she would hear Perry bleating on the other end. But there was nothing, and as the weeks passed she began to convince herself that he was probably as relieved as her to be apart - he even went up a notch in her estimation over it. Her mother only mentioned him once.

"I knew that he was not the right man for you," she said when Selina attempted to explain. "So did your father. 'My girl will have him for breakfast', he said after the first meeting. I don't think he could hardly believe you were together just before he died."

Selina tried not to imagine him going to his grave and never knowing that he was right. Two days later they were sat together for another evening in front of the fire going through the family photo albums. She was pleased to see that the few photos of her and Richard were missing; their blank spaces unfilled and appropriate to how that time now felt. Selina saw the ones of her and Perry sent over from Crete: she put them aside and saw her mother smile, "You never did have any sentimentality, did you ?" she asked. A car pulled up outside and there was a loud knocking at the door. She heard the car drive off as she reached the door handle,

"Thought you could get rid of me that easily did you ?" Perry said, shoving past her and leaving a large canvas bag at her feet. Selina smelled a strange, yet somehow familiar smell mingling with stale whiskey and hurried after him. "And how is the invalid ?" she heard him almost shout and saw her mother struggling to hide her alarm and cover herself up. It was one of her bad days already without this. Selina kept things calm and easy until she managed to get her to bed.

"What are you playing at ?" she demanded the moment she got back down.

"Do you know what those silly old men told me a couple of days ago ?" Perry asked, standing and blocking the fire with his hands clasped behind his back, and rocking gently on his feet like some Edwardian caricature of the enraged squire. "They said that you would not be coming back to me and that I should start accepting the fact and forget you. 'Become a man', they told me with their moustaches dragging on the floor; 'maybe even consider leaving Crete'. I answered them, 'I thought you were the men that never forgave or forgot !' That shut the pair of old goats right up."

"Perry, I have come home to be with my mother. She is very very ill. I want to spend some quality time with her – just the two of us. I need some time alone as well.

"We have all the time in the world," Perry sang in his best Louis Armstrong impersonation.

"Perry you cannot stay here," Selina said trying to keep her anger and fear under control.

"Your mother, my friend Nancy, just said that I could. I heard her with my own fucking ears."

"She was just being polite, Perry." Selina wanted him out of her parents' house more than anything she'd ever desired. She felt he was contaminating it beyond any chance of repair.

"We will all have to talk about it in the morning," Perry stated: "I am much too tired after all of my travelling to get to you. All I need now is our bed."

"You can stay tonight - just tonight," Selina decided. "And on the sofa." She went to get some blankets and a pillow. Perry began rubbing his hand between her legs as she bent to make up his bed,

"Shall I sneak up later ?" he whispered. "Or will you come down to me like the last time I stayed."

The memory of that - when her father was alive and, she knew, must have heard her creeping down the stairs, and what followed - sickened her more than his fingering, and stinking breath: it filled her with the spirit Miles had always encouraged.

She slapped his hand away: "You will never touch me again. Tomorrow you are going to get out of this house and my life for good. I never want to see or hear from you, ever."

"Did I tell you ? When I left Crete I gave the keys to the jeep to Lefterios. 'Have a proper four-wheel drive for a change', I told him. I don't think he got the joke though and just said: 'I will look after this for Selina's return'. 'Our return', I said. Though of course I gave up our house and we will have to find somewhere else. I am still thinking of that deserted village. It pains me to think of all that killing and revenge. And that perhaps a little love could bring the place back to life again."

Selina had lain awake for hours listening out for his footsteps on the stairs. She knew that she would not be able to fight him off without her mother hearing and running in to help – and what that might do to her. Selina saw herself keeping still and being raped in silence rather than adding to the damage his arrival must have already caused. Then the noise came that awoke her and finally made her run to her mother's aid.

Now, as she carried on watching her breath peacefully, the memories gave way to the here and now. The man behind the noises *was* downstairs, probably awake and waiting for her to go down, or getting ready to come up. The sound must have been him tapping on the ceiling or something worse. She began to see him searching through all of their personal things. Or even piling stuff up and setting fire to the place to drive her out and back with him. She closed the bedroom door gently and began to tiptoe down the stairs. It was better anyway, she thought, to go and face him down there than just keep dreading the inevitable. At least she could get it over without disturbing her mother's sleep.

Selina crept into the front room and approached the sofa as quietly as possible, just in case by some miracle he was asleep. It was empty and she span round expecting his attack. A shimmer in the darkness made her turn again, and she caught the faintest whiff of that bittersweet smell again, oddly this time, reminiscent of her best perfume though she hadn't worn any of it since leaving Crete.

The lounge was empty, as was the dining room, Miles's study and library. Selina stood in front of her father's desk and saw Perry's signed first edition of Under The Volcano open on it. He must have sat here reading, she realized, and swept the book onto the floor in disgust; only vaguely aware that it was opened on the final page. Selina stood at the bottom of the stairs and strained to hear anything. She knew that when she went back up, Perry was going to be lying in her bed waiting. And that while she was standing in her mother's room: ruminating on their sordid past, he was crawling along the corridor in his own attempt to keep it going. She cursed herself for not moving quickly when she was first disturbed. Then a similar creaking noise to the one in her dream called to her from the kitchen.

Selina pushed open the heavy door and was almost flattened by the shock. The air inside her froze and her heart felt as if it could stop as she staggered against the wall and fought to keep standing. Slowly, the initial impact calmed and began to shape into a deeper horror.

Perry was pretending to have hung himself. He was very cleverly swinging from the meat hook in their old kitchen ceiling, attached by what looked like a public school necktie. To make the joke even worse he was naked, apart from Selina's red, designer label, swimsuit. She could recall packing it now, but not, she suddenly realized finding it on her return. So he must have stolen it the day she was saying goodbye to her friends. "For what ?" she wondered: "A keep sake ? This latest attempt ?" The thong stretched over his crutch and arse: and for some reason there was a fine chain wound around his ankles with a small golden lock securing it, so that there was no way Selina could pull it down if she'd wanted. The top was cutting into his fleshy, hairy chest and he had managed to handcuff himself behind. "Probably swallowed the keys," she thought, "just to make things even harder."

Selina tired of his game and wanted to shout at him to get down. She looked at the stool tipped sideways on the floor. It was one that Miles bought at a craft fair. Selina could remember the man cutting it out of a tree trunk with a whirling-bladed chainsaw in a shower of sweet-smelling sawdust. She could not recall if it took six cuts or seven. Never very stable though: so it could have toppled by mistake. 'Kinky sex games go wrong'. Better, perhaps than: 'Lover takes life after being abandoned'.

"Very good Perry," she gasped. "A great idea for revenge. But you can get down now because I am not buying it. You've played it too many times for it to work now. No more attempts at blackmail."

Perry turned very slowly to face her and answer. Selina noticed that he had bitten clean through his tongue and the only thing coming out of his mouth was blood. And that it was washing over the flagstones and her feet were already getting sticky, and cold in it.

CHAPTER TWELVE

William studied himself in a triptych, covering three different times and guises, but held together by stronger forces than any hinges and hiding nothing. The first one painted a short time before he left for Marche. William did not need to try and recall the moment or its inspiration. It was just after – and the reason why he'd placed it along with the other two from the pile – he first met, and then from memory began the paintings of Selina. He could feel those other paintings of her looking down at him from where his father hung them. William smiled sadly at his thin staring face: saw exactly what he'd felt at that time and what it meant then; and still did in an unexplainable, yet always present way.

He did not want to look closely at the second of them and began trying to concentrate on what he was supposed to be doing. His first solo exhibition in England was coming up in a few months. A gallery in Bristol with important connections in London and New York were mounting a show. William was both excited and nervous and could not help recalling his only other one. But that was not why these self-portraits were lined-up just as dawn, silent without any piper or chorus, began to reveal a bluish mist outside his studio window.

He knew the exhibition would be a success by its own standard. The gallery had already hung and sold several of his paintings. The London branch wanted some. Four more landscapes were sold after being selected for hanging in the highly competitive and prestigious summer and autumn shows at The Royal West of England Academy. Those sales led to William being given a part-time lecturing post at two colleges. Also, there were three early commissions accepted and nearly completed. Those followed Oscar Whitting's purchase of a large oil of an old tithe barn, which now hung in the cold corridors of Bristol Crown Court.

At the time of its purchase, William accused Herbie of bribing him to do so. Nobody, except his 'uncle' Silas had bought a painting before. And that one, William believed, out of something approaching guilt following Roly Cart's lonely, wretched death. William came upon him one day as he was laying a hedge. Roly was about half way round an ancient paddock, owned by a couple of old spinsters that still milked their few Jersey cattle by hand. In front of him the hedge was tall and leggy: hawthorn and blackthorn battling to become trees and neglecting their responsibility to restrain domestic beasts and giving fruit and homes to what was wild instead. Behind him they had been bowed: cut and bent, then weaved as if by some creature of infinite skill and purpose.

William made his sketches in silence that day, letting the hedge stretch in its two forms either side of the stooping man. Expressing, he hoped, without any comment or condescension, the craft and toil, and its effect on nature.

"I heard you was back," Roly said, stopping for a few mouthfuls of cider. "Everyone comes back in the end. You always was a good boy. Not like that bastard brother of yours. Never given me a day's work since he took over; nor let me help Silas since they bought him out. What did I ever do to he ?"

William carried on sketching without comment. When some

months later Herbie asked him to come to the funeral and even read something out, as Richard had refused, William agreed. He stood in front of the small group of mourners in the church with the plump parson breathing sweet sherry and mint over his shoulder and read from Ted Hughes's 'The Day He Died', ending with:

> 'From now on the land
> Will have to manage without him.
> But it hesitates, in this slow realization of light,
> Childlike, too naked, in a frail sun,
> With roots cut
> And a great blank in its memory.'

Later that day, William made some sketches as he saw how clearly those old faces in the frail sun of the cemetery understood those words. He caught something else that day: Herbie and Madeline were working overtime in trying to make their son fit back, and become accepted in this place.

William stared now at the second painting. He saw the bloated, bleary-eyed face; with a pale glimmer of something just beginning to illuminate the mask he was still wearing. William guessed the paint on this self-portrait – the first since his return to art – could hardly have been dry before his wife and child were gone and he was locked up in a cell. It would be though, by the time he received a letter from Florence. Months after the court case, in which, even with a dramatic performance by both Lorna and his daughter - and some terrible stuff in the local papers - he was found not guilty of all charges. And still more time after the divorce in which despite some long nights of loneliness, the overwhelming sense of freedom kept him from ever attempting to make contact.

'Daddy I love you,' it read. 'Mommy is a stressed-out bitch. She has a NEW FRIEND. He is a bore. He made her throw all of your paintings away.'

William remembered all the fuss Lorna made about keeping pieces of work he'd completed in the period after quitting his job. He felt a little pain at this part of Florence's letter. The first bit did not even register.

"I had to stay in my bedroom and watch as the dustmen came and undid the string holding them all together, then they took a good look at each one, before throwing them in with the rest of the rubbish anyway. I felt so sorry for you. I want to come and stay for the weekends. I also want to meet my grandma and grandpa for the very first time ever."

William spent the rest of that day unable to concentrate on anything except the pleas and sadness of his child. Many times he nearly went over to his parents to tell them he would like to have his daughter to come and stay and to get to know them. Each time something held him; a slight dread of what she may become a bridge to; a mistrust of her motives. He went back over the letter and felt that it *was* deliberate and contrived. That it smacked of Lorna's scheming for something. A voice inside told him that he was his father's son. That like him he was detached and cold to anything but his own needs. A selfish, spoilt man who needed to change if he was ever to experience true human emotions; another more calculated one told him to wait.

A week later he got another letter: "You are a bastard. Mommy was right. I hate hate hate you. And one day I will make you pay and understand exactly how much you have hurt us." William balled it up and then, having definitely one side of Herbie's character that he'd been grateful to, placed it carefully in an envelope and kept it for safe keeping.

William tried to see in his portrait what he was guilty of through that whole period. He was ashamed, momentarily, of the shallowness and cruelty he imagined he *could* see in his face. Then delighted with what he *did* see. Not a person gloating, or enjoying the suffering or frailty of others; but one hurting for what he could not give or receive. He went quickly from it to the third of the images.

His only self-portrait since coming to the barn: and still unfinished. Not so long between the last two really. And yet they could have been different sitters. William saw that it was the first, and this one that had everything in common: sitting either side of whoever he'd become in-between, it seemed almost as if the young man had stepped into the middle one, remained hidden and then emerged again.

And all because he had seen her again.

Selina gave the light to the first and was now illuminating this one. A part of William had always believed he was not capable of loving anyone. Art was his love; detachment the price he paid for it. Now he questioned was it possible he loved too much ? He'd heard Madeline say many times that Herbie was obsessed with her. But obsession was not what he felt - he knew all about that emotion. And this was nothing so easy to explain.

William made some feeble effort when the news story broke like an incendiary over the village, to go along with the horror and revulsion his parents and seemingly everyone else felt. Madeline hated her with passion,

"The little whore is killing her poor mother with all this scandal. When I think what she put *your* poor brother through. How she could even dare to come back. Now this. Perversion and pornography. I truly believe she is a curse."

"Or cursed," William whispered.

"Did you see those photographs of her. I cannot even imagine what it must have done to Richard and Annie to see such filth."

William had seen them. The ones always rumoured to have existed - dredged up, he imagined, by some enterprising hack with his eyes on bigger things than the local press. Selina posing for a planned LP cover of another doomed local band. Naked, with a tattoo of a rainbow-shimmering snake slithering down her spine, its forked tongue vanishing into a censored ball of blackness. He also saw another: her standing by her parent's door, pleading, William guessed – the same as on the local TV news – for them to go away and allow her ill mother some peace.

He took the photos and held the posed one next to the paintings he did after their first encounter and, trying to ignore the fact and reasons behind the blurred facial features, was pleased to see how accurate his young eye was in visualizing her form. William began some sketches for a full length nude from the photo – minus the snake tattoo which he could see was false. And a portrait from the other picture. It was also the beginning of his own latest self-portrait. Even the sketches and painting began to make all the other stuff wait and seem, at first, slightly less important.

Then William saw her in the flesh. And nothing on the canvases in front of him could answer all the questions.

Selina must have slipped out for an early morning walk and taken to the fields behind her house rather than risk being spotted by anyone. It made him touch her sadness and shame as he saw her walking along the old railway cutting, head bowed, so that her long, raven-black hair veiled her face. William was making some plans for a dawn view of an old steel bridge. He hid as he saw Selina - not wanting to intrude into her desire for solitude - scared even more, to actually meet her again; and desperate to do so. In the following weeks he began to spy on her every day, before coming back and attempting to work on commissions, preparing stuff for the exhibition, students notes, any of the half-finished paintings. None of it now – except for the self-portrait or sketches of her – felt important or challenging. And what was worse, with each passing day, he realized it never truly would. There was no *real* light in this place for him. No illumination except for what she gave him here all those years back. It was beginning to feel that he was paying off a debt he'd not really incurred or already already cleared.

When William started painting again and was transformed by the relief of it, he tried to work on a painting of Selina from their meeting in Crete. One screaming, acrimonious day, Lorna grabbed the canvas: "Don't think I'm stupid. Or blind. I know who this is no matter how hard you try to disguise her. Why don't you paint me ? Or your beautiful daughter ? If you are determined to destroy us you might as well have a record !" And William tried to catch them as they would have wanted. He was pleased that those were the paintings Lorna chose to keep. And even more so that they were now floating in some cavern of methane and rotting waste.

At this precise moment he wished that nearly everything else since then was with them. That little voice again - which up until now, was content to whisper its nagging doubt - was now delighted to roar its contempt. William took one last look at his portrait and made up his mind. He grabbed a coat and rushed out of his studio. He was going to meet her this time: nothing must stop it. He knew exactly what the consequences might be. But there was no other way. If anything did happen - and he knew or sensed on every previous meeting that they both felt something strong – it would be the end of so much; but also the beginning of so much more. Time to risk everything or gain nothing, he decided.

The old railway cutting sounded hollow, as if instead of having once carried silver rails, it was a river that smoothed the stones and compressed the earth into this form, before sinking into a deeper blacker world. Selina could almost hear it below: a Stygian meander under her boots, waiting. The nurse had been carrying a bowl of something dark and foul from her mother's room this morning as they passed on the landing. "A mule's hoof full of Styx water to poison Alexander the Great," she thought. The association made her stop and heave a deep sob. Her mother *was* dying. Slipping in and out of phases of pain and drugged muttering into moments of lucidity and ease - or some semblance of it. At times she could still recognize pictures in the album and talk for whole minutes at a stretch about Miles and their happiness.

On other occasions – and worse for Selina in some ways that even the groaning or heaving – she struggled for sentences only to be able to make sense and order out of her daughter's life. To find an explanation for it; or a way of carrying blame on her frail shoulders before it was too late.

"I did not know," she said yesterday evening, "that you had a tattoo of a serpent. Your father would have hated that. You know what he always said: 'There are enough ways of being tagged and recognized in this bloody country already, without having some unmovable badge stuck to your hide'."

Selina searched under her mother's pillow and pulled the pile of newspaper cuttings out. She thought she'd destroyed every one that their *kind* neighbours posted anonymously through the door. Selina suspected one of the nurses: the local one that could still not force herself to speak to her.

"Mom," Selina held her hand: "it was a body painting, just done for the photographs. It was for an LP cover. You remember I went out with Larry, the keyboard player. You liked Larry. You and dad came and heard his band a few times."

Larry was Selina's first real boyfriend. She lost her virginity to him. On the beach in the back of the group van. Too proud and haughty to let him know that it was her first time and ending up on top and then bent over one of the front seats as if she had been doing it for years, then pretending that the blood was just left over from her period. Selina wished for some stupid reason she could go back now and tell him.

"Brrr," her mother brought her back: "I've always hated snakes."

"What about Herbie's one ?" Selina tried. "He claims to have seen a giant one in his house once when he was still a schoolboy."

A different look of anguish and pain filled her mother's face as that name opened up another can of worms to crawl and slither over her daughter's image,

"When I am gone," she said, brushing aside Selina's attempt to silence her and deny this: "you must sell this house and leave. There will be enough money, including what we have in the bank for you to get far away and live sensibly for a long time."

"Mom *I* am not ashamed of anything I have done. And I will never run away again from anywhere. I am staying here with you for a long time yet."

She heard her mother breathe a sigh and thought, in panic, of that stunning, terrible line in R.S. Thomas's poem as his wife died: 'for the shedding of one sigh no heavier than a feather.'

"Mother," she cried, rocking her until her eyes opened again and their dull, glazed vision gave some recognition, and more, as Selina watched: a flicker of hope for them to still hold together.

Now she was stomping passionately along, daring the ground itself to open and defy her will. "I *will* stay here," she told the mist shapes spying on her from the hedgerow. I'll defy them and their knowing looks. It is my parents' home and I am going to keep their memory with me. Alone, forever. 'The scarlet woman.' 'The snake lady.' Whatever they want to believe. I shall wear drab clothes and no make-up. Find the most mundane job and see what can go wrong then. Oh, and just when everyone takes me for granted, I shall start smoking again at seventy years of age. And find some way of causing another scandal before I go. And no one will ever have known or know the real me..."

"Hello," William said. "I've been waiting for you."

CHAPTER THIRTEEN

Richard was carrying a gun. It was his late grandfather's and to date was unbloodied by his hands. Tonight he was going to change that and something wild was going to die. Herbie never allowed any shooting on his land. Richard could recall many bottles of whisky being handed over by hopeful hunters for the chance of, "Just a few duck, Mr. Halliday, as your rhines and ponds are so full of them." "And that's because I keep them clean and never let any bugger shoot on them," the usual reply before the bottle went down to the cellar to join all of the rest.

Great Aunt Flo told Richard as his young arms struggled once to hold the heavy damascus-barreled gun steady, "Your granddaddy, my brother, was a fine shot – some say the best in the county. He always won the prize shoot at the fete. And a great huntsman too - bolt upright in the saddle and the first to any kill." And behind her was his portrait: giving truth then, as now, to her words and outliving all the reality behind the big-drinking, heavy-smoking waster. It often seemed to Richard that one brief moment of illusion was enough to give most people their heroes, or villains. They wanted the lie to give truth and justification to themselves. Now apparently, he'd been caught; and knew exactly in which guise he would be seen.

He clutched the gun tighter as Selina came unexpectedly - and rarely these days - into his mind, created as a display of lights flashed and dimmed luminously in a towering hawthorn. "Jack-o-lantern ?" he whispered. "Wills-o-the-wisp ?" Then answered himself: "No boy, some ugly little wingless beetle looking to get fucked; or a moth flashing out its final duty before death." That's what Annie called Selina when she burst into all of their lives again. "I already knew that little bedroom moth was fluttering around again. I heard it in the hairdresser's first. Then saw the butcher nearly chop his fat finger off when Mrs. Lillycrap thought it necessary to tell me in his shop full of people. Maybe, he thought even his swollen charms were still enough to attract *her* attentions."

The lights blinked out in perfect synchronization as Richard forced her from his mind and concentrated on the recent event and its unfairness. Some dumb, drunken stud dangles himself from a ceiling dressed in a tart's drawers - a man, who according to the reports had never done a day's work in his life - and everyone goes into a state of hysteria over him. Local headlines on TV and all over the newspapers. Nobody able to stop talking about it. The waste. The tragedy. How sordid. How fascinating. While six farmers, that went to the same agricultural college as Richard, had already taken their lives, and only got a slight mention when someone decided that the ever-increasing suicides amongst farmers might be down to ingesting too much sheep-dip.

Never mind, Richard thought, leaning now against the wave-rippled sides of a rusting Dutch barn, that the banks were foreclosing quicker than ever, there was falling prices, mad cow disease, and even madder rules and competition flooding in from Europe. It just had to be down to some extraneous influence. Why else would a good old boring sod-buster want to cast off the joys of their rich and wonderful lives ? Of course there could be nothing dramatic or poetic about a man in overalls and wellies spilling his blood and brains back into the soil he spent his life working and had just lost. Or drinking in mouthfuls of carbon monoxide from his own tractor while another cow tottered in its death waltz in the corner of his clouding vision. No great moment worth recording.

And now, Richard was supposed to be delighted that he was. His brother had painted him and he must go to see himself on public display and make peace with the artist. Richard broke the gun and let the brass ends of the cartridges catch some starlight.

"I think you are jealous," Annie had shouted at him a few hours ago as she ran from the room. "You are just jealous of his talent." Even though, as he'd tried to remain calm and tell her, "you've not even seen any of his recent work, - including this *masterpiece* of me."

Earlier, his parents were equally bias. "What is your problem, boy ?" Herbie demanded to know.

Richard shrugged, unable to find words to express exactly what he felt – even to himself. They never really got on too well when they were young. Then the way he was welcomed back and given so much. The way he was always given so much. Now the real 'prodigal's return. It was all part of it – but not all. Sometimes, he felt it was a balance he'd invented a long time ago. His way of tipping the scales back a little, as his efforts went unnoticed and were taken for granted, while his brother's talent blazed like those damn blue eyes of his that pinned you down and made you squirm. Jealousy, then, if that is what it must be called.

"And he's done this most beautiful painting of you," Madeline added, breaking the news. "Especially for his big show. And it will be one of the most expensive in the show. Herbie found that out. Even though we're not allowed to see it."

"What !" Richard shouted. "He's got no right to use me. And

how the hell do you know it's beautiful if you haven't even seen it? I am not going to allow it."

"Don't be stupid boy," Herbie said. "Artists and writers always use people they know as models and characters. Why he's even redoing that painting of us around the kitchen table for the show. Says he's got your mother and me just right this time."

"All of his paintings are beautiful," Madeleine added: "you should see what he did with poor Roly Cart."

Richard had been amazed that anyone would want to paint the man, and then ashamed, briefly, for the way he'd treated him. "He's not using me. I refuse to give my permission." He heard the impotence and childishness in his voice as he stamped out of his parents' home.

Now he was feeling it again as the night proper closed its fist around him and the distant shape of the barn brooded against the shrinking horizon. Its lights burning into his eyes telling him that his brother was still awake and most probably working.

Painted me, Richard thought, turning and walking away. Caught in some pose or action that would, or could, outlast all he might do and achieve with his real life. Richard imagined with what ease and pleasure his brother would have done it. He also knew what a lie it would be. "This is not me," he could state without bothering to look. And then state it over and over without anyone caring enough to listen.

Earlier on, he'd tried to convince himself it did not matter. If some idiot wanted to buy a disparaging, mocking version of his life, dreamed-up by his malcontent brother, more fool them. It gave him some comfort until Annie started. The children were going on about William again. Richard tried to ignore it. Listening to them telling him how 'funny' and 'kind' he was every time they went round to his parents now. "Why," Richard asked

Annie when the last of them was finally persuaded to bed, "is *he* always around our children ?"

"Maybe he likes them and misses his own one," she replied.

"Should have thought of that before he chucked in his job, started boozing again and making threats," Richard snapped, trying not to see his brother playing with the children, making them all laugh as he was working.

"I thought the court said that he was not guilty and that Lorna was making it all up because the marriage was failing and she wanted out of it."

Richard stared at his wife. Up until now they'd never had a serious disagreement over anything. Nothing. No recriminations about the breaking of their earlier 'understanding'. No questions about her own brief first marriage. They worked together solidly and in unison on decorating and altering the farmhouse after Madeline and Herbie left. Agreed on children. Well not quite: Richard wanted to stop at four, Annie wanted six. She had stood, pregnant herself, helping him to deliver his first pedigree calf. No conflict or disharmony before now. Until his brother came back. Or rather, until she met him.

"You don't want to take any notice of that," Richard assured her. "Old Oscar Whitting could persuade the Pope he was Jewish if he was paid to. Why do you think he is so fond of Herbie ? I'll tell you: Herbie is the only bugger he has never been able to fool. And he wants to keep trying."

"A bit like with those snakes, you mean ?" Annie said, making the motion Herbie used when telling his tale - wanting to charm Richard into a sweeter mood before she told him of her decision.

He could not help smiling at the thought of Oscar being grasped like some glove puppet in a wig and gown by his father. Annie wiped it off his face though with the next statement, "I want to go to the exhibition next month. Herbie and Madeline are going and said that *we* can travel with them."

"Never in a million years. Do you really think I want to see any of my world and life through his eyes ?" Richard got to his feet.

"It's not just about the paintings or giving the appearance that you have forgiven your brother is it ? Or resentment over the way your parents are treating him ?" She probed desperately for some reaction. Annie was already hearing all the talk. It was impossible to do anything in a small village like this, however clandestine you were, without someone, then eventually everyone, knowing. Annie knew if there was ever to be a chance of any sort of reconciliation it must be soon; and before the next storm broke over them all. It felt more important now than ever; and more threatening, but she had to go on. She saw him blink twice, too quickly for his normal cool control.

"Well I am going." She said. "And I want to tell you something before you argue. The thing I like most about that strange mismatched relationship of your parents is its real openness. Herbie can puff up his chest and shout and bluster all he likes. Madeline never flinches. She can say what she wants and he listens knowing at least he is hearing all of it. Last week, Madeline thought it might be fun to slip over to William's studio and take a sneak preview of some of the paintings he is getting ready for the show. I said I did not want to, because I was *afraid* of what you would have to say if I did. And of the fact I might have to keep it secret from you. Madeline read it in my face and said that I was right, we should wait and all go to the proper show together. Do you want that feeling to grow into something more ? You stop me from going and I know it will. And it is well past time that you faced whatever it is that you are *afraid* of."

Richard could hardly take in what she was saying. That he was a coward and bully,

"I never said that you could not go. I just said that I am not. And I look in a mirror if I want to see my face, okay. And now I will tell you something you might like to know. While my parents and wife were discussing art at the 'William Appreciation Society', I was with the vet discussing TB in cattle and the fact that two of *my* cows have contracted it and will have to be slaughtered."

Richard saw the look of shock and pain in her face. He knew that Annie loved the animals and always tried to be present at the birth of a new calf. He had wanted to try and find some gentle way of breaking the news but now it felt perfect, cruel and just.

"I'll keep you all informed about its progress, that is of course if you are not too busy staring at the latest works of real importance." He began searching through the drawers for some cartridges. Then grabbed the gun. Annie looked as if she was about to cry and he paused for her tears,

"That," she said, getting to her feet, "was a despicable thing to do. To use such a thing for your own ends is well below what I would have expected. You cannot go on blaming your brother for all the problems in the world. I just think you are jealous. Jealous of his talent. And how people admire him; even love him - especially one person."

Richard heard that again, and puzzled over exactly what she'd meant as he got close to the badger set. Badgers carried TB and spread it to cattle regardless of what any clever ministry bod said, or do-gooders believed. They'd even given it to one of his fellow students from college, a once wild man and good friend, cursed now to live with brucellosis. The thought of them snuffling warm and poisonous in his ground kept his feet moving when already all he really wanted was to return home to his wife and make peace. Now he slowed and let the night breeze carry his scent away. His thumb cocked the two hammers on the shotgun: slowly, letting his body heat flow into the scrolled steel and figured walnut as his grandfather must have done many times. But he, the gentleman taking a high bird or bolting hare for the sport of it. The first hammer clicked silently into place, then the second as he moved forward. This set, he recalled, was claimed to be over a thousand years old. Brock was digging here, some said, when the Knights of the Round Table were chasing around searching for dragons to slay and maidens to be rescued; or the Holy Thorn at nearby Glastonbury was a sapling.

A cold, old moonlight made a stage out of the incline before the main entrance. Flowing to one side was a spoil heap, littered with stark white bones. Below these remains, the killers were playing.

Richard watched as two young badgers growled and practised their fighting skills. An older, much larger animal kept its back to him – the hoary of its bristles giving away its age. Then another adult came from the entrance, sniffed the air and then, almost joyously, moved over to the older one. Immediately, three very young badgers followed her and snuggled close. He let the gun come up slowly. Richard knew that if he fired both barrels at the same time he could kill or at least maim every one of them.

He fingers found the two triggers. His eye the bead. A silver speck as gentle as a pearl wanting to find some warm body to rest upon. Richard let his fingers whisper off the triggers and backed away silently so as not to even frighten the badgers. A short way off he released both hammers as carefully and safely as his trembling hand would allow it. 'Farmer shoots himself' he imagined Annie reading if he had an accident now. He could no more contemplate the real action than killing those animals a few seconds ago. If the disease was traced to them and it was necessary to have them gassed then that would be a different matter. But killing things out of anger or through some stupid notion of revenge was not inside him. So why had he come ? Richard knew the answer to his own question and began to stride toward his brother's studio.

If he was still up and working, Richard told himself, and just happened to glance down as he strolled, casually across the yard, gun broken over his arm as if it was a normal event, then that was fate. Richard was pretty certain that this was one of the few times at night when his father was not likely to be awake and spotting the fall of every leaf. He tried to make himself appear calm and at ease. But how, he suddenly thought, does one fool an artist's eye? It would be a bit like someone showing him a sick or weakly calf and expecting him to carry it back from the market. It almost stopped him. Let him see, Richard made up his mind, and carried on to the first gate that let his feet move off the sponged silence of moist pasture onto the cobbles.

If his brother did happen to notice him then he would stop and wait. Making the gesture. If William came down to the door and opened it, then, Richard decided, he would go in. And welcome him home at least. After that...

Her naked body filled the largest window almost completely as she stretched and swayed. Richard dropped low into a crouch and scuttled across to the old milking parlour and squeezed himself into the shadows of its opening. She brought her long arms together and held them clasped above her head and stared out across the fields in the direction of the badger set. Selina, with the person he had always known and dreaded from that first meeting she most desired. Richard felt a numbness holding him physically and mentally as he stared.

He could not help noticing that she was still beautiful. Her graceful neck and body just as shapely. The surprising, almost masculine broad shoulders and heavy breasts looked as firm and proud as the first time he saw her naked. And, he recalled with a shudder: the last time and how crazy she had driven him by then and his desperate attempt to keep her. Richard could not stop his gaze fixing on the always so neat, and trimmed oblong of jet black pubic hair – the colour and texture almost tangible to him at this distance. Selina's long thin legs appeared to be just as well muscled and unblemished. He saw her spin round angrily as his brother must have commanded her return. The same haughty gesture of defiance, he remembered. And the same round firm buttocks. "Not yet succumbing to gravity," he whispered, thinking of Annie's recent description of herself. And then, as she came back into his thoughts, the words from the row and their meaning made perfect sense. "So," he whispered, "once again I'm the last to know. Fooled every time, boy."

Then, as she turned back to the window, Richard saw one of the studio spotlights shine its ray through the gap at the top of her legs. A gap that remained even with her legs squeezed tightly together – or strapped. It made another memory fill his head. The words of some men at another party as she bent in a mini skirt to pour another drink: "Plenty of gripage and gapage there my friend !" "Made for it. The arched entrance to the temple of Venus. Never closed: Never filled." And never would, or had been, by him, or any of those that liked to gossip and fantasize.

Richard watched as she tossed her head arrogantly again at whatever her persistent lover was demanding: that dismissive flick that could cut deeper than a cartman's whip. It gave him the slightest frisson of pleasure to believe that his brother would learn to suffer those lashes and be no more than another victim.

But, as he thought it, she smiled, then laughed with a look of compliance and willingness that he'd never seen before; clearly she was delighted to do whatever was being requested. She stretched her arms back above her head again and clasped her fingers like some cage that could hold a heart still beating and warm forever; or shatter it into shards of ice and watch in pleasure the pretty crystals glitter as they fell and faded to dust. Selina began to dance, slowly and sinuously as if caught and controlled by some ancient Eastern rhythm. Richard heard the strange music filling the Somerset night. The noise and her dancing, knowing what he was watching now belonged to his brother; and that he was waiting for her, made Richard go rigid and cold. He closed the gun noisily. Flicked both hammers back. Three beats out of time.

Once there had been a clay pigeon shoot as part of the village celebrations. Herbie, who as far as Richard knew never shot a thing in his life, broke twenty-five out of twenty-five clays and carried off the prize. The rest of the competitors - many of whom shot all year round with fancy modern guns – were stunned. Richard could remember carrying the gun home with so much pride that day. And his father's advice following the event: "Never think: just snap the gun to your shoulder and fire. All this swinging and counting is rubbish. Trust your eye and instinct. Look. Snap. Fire. And you will never miss. Shut your mind to all other thoughts. Look. Snap. Fire."

Richard looked. But he thought. He pictured the implosion of glass tearing with the shot into her white porcelain body. Heard the scream, maybe filling his waking parents' ears after the dying echo of the shot. Then his naked brother lifting her in his arms. Or worse, staring down as Selina fell and her blood became a dark shadow running across the cobbles to meet his own. The only way she would ever, in reality, have happily done so. He saw Annie and his children; the farm in ruins and shame; and his brother still painting her: catching her beauty and freedom. Then he imagined that painting sitting alongside the one he knew had already been made of him, while he sat in some cell, and she in her grave. And everyone kept looking and judging.

Selina stopped moving and stared out as if suddenly aware she was being observed. She looked toward Richard and he felt his fingers tighten around the gun as her eyes peered into the shadows. Then she gazed back into the studio. Richard made his move. A darting run across the yard and out along the drive that led to the road. There were better ways to settle this and leave a clarity behind that no one would ever be able to gloat over. Richard was now in a hurry to get home and tell Annie that he would go to the exhibition. That was the exact, and perfect place for all this to end.

CHAPTER FOURTEEN

Selina wanted to move, "I'm getting stiff," she said quietly.

"Then take a break," William replied, carrying on painting as his model slowly rose from the high-backed chair. He still found it hard to believe that she was physically with him. After so many times of creating her from his imagination or a photo: projecting her to similar poses as the one she had just left: he actually felt the need to reach out and touch her just to confirm the reality of her body. But that, he reminded himself, was strictly banned.

Selina move easily and without apparent concern for her nakedness to the huge glass window. She remembered William telling her that it was once the opening for loading the harvested cereal and grain. Men would have stood below and winched up heavy, bulging sacks of the stuff: their food for the year; and seed for the next. As their Pharaoh watched, from horseback probably: too rich to need work with so much cheap muscle available. Nearly all of the population employed in agriculture then: slavery and drudgery. Wheat for bread: barley for beer. Before the machines and Frankenstein crops arrived. Selina pictured their ghosts stood below and looking up now. Seeing what it had all come to. Seeing her.

Selina felt William looking and watching each pulse in her body move, she sensed that he could spot every stain that was ever washed away, every bruise and scratch that had faded, then add them to her image or remove them as he saw fit. Selina was anxious and longing to see the finished painting. So far William had refused her even a glimpse. She loved the earlier ones and was amazed by the power of her spirit and youth. "When did you do these ?" Selina asked him. "Oh, after the first time I saw you, then after I could not stop thinking about you." She'd held the recent sketches he was working on from the newspaper and saw herself again for the first time as she actually felt.

But what, she wondered again, clasping her hands together above her head and doing some stretching exercises, was he seeing now. Now that his dream girl was real. And had given words to taint his vision; and others to stop anything else.

Just over two weeks ago as they first walked together between the narrow hedgerow. Side by side until the railway cutting opened suddenly into what must once have been a station or yard. It was littered with strangely-shaped metal objects, rusting into a red ochre dust of iron oxide or a desquamation of burnt sienna. The ground was dry and black with clinker and lumps of vitrified coke as if it had been scorched in some catastrophe. The atmosphere of the place seemed to change their light chatting into something deeper too quickly, moving it inevitably to where she knew they must not go. Selina saw their reflections in the soot-blackened window of an old tar-painted hut: its dimness not able to dull what was happening. Selina felt a growing panic and became desperate to stop it.

"I do not think I will ever find anyone to love," she told him. "Every time I have a relationship the person ends up trying to change me or destroy themselves. All of the trust has gone for me." Selina watched the look of hurt cross his face. "All I want," she continued, "is to be free. To take some time to learn about myself and heal a few wounds." Selina did not feel able to tell anyone truly about her pain and hurt; how deep it went. "It is a promise I have made and intend to keep."

"All I want," William said, "is to paint you. To be allowed to do a full length portrait of you for my forthcoming exhibition."

"I would have thought that everyone had seen more than enough of my body recently," Selina saw another look of distress – this time worse than the first. "I just meant," she said puzzled by him now. William did not let her explain.

"Will you come to my studio and pose for me in the nude. I'll give you an absolute promise that I will not touch you, or attempt to hit on you, or anything else. Just paint you. I want the picture for the show. Something new and vital for me. To change back and alter the things I've been doing. I also believe that it might help you to see yourself differently. To change a lot of the past. I really think we should do this one thing together. Trust art if not me. Art shows us how and why we live: it does not seek to destroy anything except lies."

"And what will your dear parents have to say when their terrible ex daughter-in-law and the scandal of their precious village puts in another appearance?" Selina was feeling the darkness of the place filling her thoughts, the ashes and dust in her mouth as she struggled to drive William away. Everything had felt simplified until this meeting. Her closing down to survive. Now already she could feel herself being opened again and was afraid.

"I don't care what anybody else thinks. I thought you would have at least given *me* credit for that. I always believed you and I were kindred spirits. But if you have been beaten down and are too scared to take a chance I will just do it from photographs. But I am still going to paint you. And your picture will be at the exhibition."

"Okay," Selina decided. She crunched her heel down onto some melded, shining and solid looking mass and watched it sparkle into fragments. "But I will only come at night."

"I would love to see the sunlight – even this excuse for it – on your skin. I've told you I don't care what anyone thinks."

"Nor do I," Selina told him truthfully. "But my mother is very ill and has a nurse with her all night now. I like to spend my days with her."

William agreed that it would be nights only. Now he called her back from the window,

"Selina, can we do some more work, please."

She span round, "I'm thinking," she snapped at him. "Don't be such a slave driver." Selina turned back to the window and grinned as she heard his long sigh of resignation. She was trying to catch the memory again of their first night. After the nervous talking and her viewing some of his early work, wondering why he did not want her to see any of the recent stuff, they'd both gone silent. Selina knew why instantly. She had worn a full-length black coat with a large hood and a pair of high black boots. Slipping by the nurse and out through the slumbering village, passing the farmhouses and other barns like a wraith. Now he wanted her uncloaked. Maybe, just the coat to start with. Then a coffee or glass of wine to help her relax. She had already made her mind up about it before leaving home. This was going to be done professionally. It was why, she stated to herself, that she was here.

Selina had jumped up, unzipped the boots and kicked them off, then unbuttoned the coat and stepped out of it in one quick shedding. She stood feet away from William, her naked body close enough for his breath to touch her skin. It felt easy and natural after viewing the early paintings of herself. "Spoil it," she said to herself, by ogling or leering, changing your breathing or body language: any of the actions I've seen so many times before and I will weep before leaving."

Instead, he dressed her. That is exactly what Selina sensed as his piercing blue eyes washed over every inch of her looking way beyond what any man had ever been allowed or felt capable of seeing. Now this fortnight felt like the purest time in her life. Selina knew that it was coming to an end and dreaded anything taking away what it had already given her before it was over.

William watched Selina stretching in front of the window. The painting was nearly finished. He could complete it as far as she was needed by tomorrow night and knew that he would not make any pretence to bring her back while he finished it. Selina would be gone with all the things he wanted to say, unsaid. And no way of saying any of them now without making a mockery of what they had achieved together. William understood that one word could be the sabre, slicing through the fibres of the canvas in front of him: denying its value as anything other than a piece of trickery. And nothing felt worth that to him. Not even love.

"Stay there," William said as her hands entwined. "I want to make a sketch of you from behind."

"No way," she giggled. "Just the *one* painting you said. No more."

"Don't argue," he commanded, trying to hide the slap of disappointment she'd delivered so easily and catch one more impression of her. He pressed the button of the cassette player and let the music she loved, and liked to hear as he worked, fill the studio. The strange hypnotic, almost oriental-sounding Cretan music with Psarantonis playing the lyra held her swaying in its endless repetitions: washing in ecstatic waves of nine and seven eight rhythm from an ancient civilization who worshipped sensuality and light, Selina had explained, while cursing those they stole it from for being feminine and decadent. Ever the artist's curse, William had replied.

"Concentrate," William ordered himself now, trying to ignore the equally hypnotic movement of Selina's body. He tried to fill his head with the words from Ray Carver's poem 'What You Need for Painting' as he hurried to finish,

'Indifference to everything except your canvas.

The ability to work like a locomotive.

An Iron Will.'

His will held. The moment was recorded.

"Selina," he asked, the harshness of his language stark against the singing of Nikio Xylouris, "are you going to come to the exhibition ?" William had asked her every day since the start of the painting.

Selina stopped dancing as if something outside had caught her eye, "I don't think so," she said, sounding almost afraid and nervous suddenly.

"Please," William said, louder to call her back. "I need you there to see what you think of the painting. Really it will be the perfect place to see it. I will have varnished it and the gallery will have it framed."

"Are you trying to blackmail me ?" she said, staring down into the yard suddenly, all the sensuality leaving her, cowering almost it seemed to William.

"Sort of," William said. "Selina what's wrong ?"

Selina turned as if released quickly from some constraint. She gave him a dazzling wild smile as the music became frenetic and danced back to her chair. "You win," she said, "if I can leave my mother I will come. I'll arrive and surprise you." She tried not to imagine the surprise it would give Herbie and especially Madeline if she did. "But I want to see the painting before."

"You might. Or I might make you wait and surprise you on the night."

For the briefest moment Selina felt another movement outside. As if the darkness all around them had suddenly drawn in a breath and was waiting for their next move. Their slip or mistake. She tried to wipe any look of doubt that may have caused it off her face before William's brush held it for others to interpret forever.

CHAPTER FIFTEEN

William was collecting: catching her movements, expressions and poses: pinning them safely and perfect in the deepest vault of his mind. To be only opened at the right time and painted quickly, before, like any exhumed treasure, time could corrupt. Now she was pulling on her boots: sat naked, one black and pointed, stabbing into the heart of the green oak floor, the other, just closing the almost pelt-silver fabric, coarse against the ivory whiteness of her skin.

It made him think of Bonnard's 'Nude in Black Stockings' and how blessed he had been to have his love and muse with him all of his days. William gave a title to his: 'Woman Leaving', and saw himself painting it at fifty years of age. "Woman Leaving," he whispered, and imagined the sadness that would be there waiting along with this image. "Maybe sixty," William decided: " the heart seared enough surely by then to set this one free."

"Are you going to show it to me or not then ?" Selina demanded to know, standing in front of him as she had the first time: letting him take a long, final look. She pulled her coat on. "Well ?"

"You said that you would try to come to the exhibition. Can't you wait just two weeks ? There is a lot of detail still to add, and there is the varnishing. The light will show it better when it is hung properly." William was desperate to at least have some chance of seeing her after this.

"William, I don't know if I will come. My mother is getting worse by the day now. And besides: I'm not sure it is a good idea. Your parents will be there. Madeline will not walk in a shop if she sees me there. She crosses the street if she sees me coming. Herbie still waves and smiles, but never in the presence of her."

"They'll see you on the wall," William said, knowing that what Selina was saying about his mother was less than the truth. Once she made her mind up to hate and become bitter, nothing could penetrate or touch it. William suspected it had more to do with her own discontentment and misery, but it made no difference to the result.

"Yes, I know that. But being there, perhaps having to speak out of politeness. Knowing what she was thinking and how she was looking at me and the painting. I don't know if I want it. I have a lot of things to deal with at the moment that are painful and unpleasant. I don't want to risk adding something else."

"Oh they would probably just ignore you," William tried to assure her, feeling her slipping away from him. "Herbie is the master of stony silences when it is politically expedient."

"Um, maybe," Selina hesitated and nearly told William something. That in fact she'd recently spoken with his father.

Selina had been walking in the small market town when she heard the droning voice of the auctioneer from behind the walled enclosure. Then smelled and sensed the brooding fear of the penned beasts. The murmuring complaints of the farmers came next when the crack of the gavel always fell too soon. She cursed finding herself in town on the day of the sale and would normally have avoided it by miles. But this morning, her mother, seemed to brighten and, after sitting up in bed and having her hair brushed, said, "Do you know what I really fancy, Selina ?"

Selina waited.

"Some dandelion and burdock. I am so sick of everything tasting of tin and smelling of medicine and sulphur. I know its strong taste would still be there. It always reminded me of spring. Miles loved it too."

Selina tried the small supermarket in the village and may as well have been asking for powdered rhino horn, for both the look and response she got for her effort. Then she remembered the old fashioned tobacconist in the town. 'Pouncy's' by the market. She could not have numbered how many times she'd stood in that place, bewitched by the endless jars of sweets that never seemed to empty no matter how many mixes were bagged and sold. Or counted how many packets of cigarettes were handed over without a word about age or health ever being exchanged by Mr. Pouncy, who did once comment to them that a packet of Player's Weights was more healthy than a bag of cough candy.

Selina guessed that it was probably long gone, but the thought of her mother actually wanting something drove her on. Even the reality of Market Day and the gathering of the farmers could not stop her. "Let them stare and whisper," she told herself. "See if any of them are so brave to come close enough to be contaminated."

The shop, unbelievably, was still there, the window dirtier but with what looked like the same array of pipes, smoking mixtures and snuff. A bell tinkled and stepping inside Selina could easily have been nine or ten again. Old man Pouncy looked at her from behind his counter as if she still was, "You wouldn't have a bottle of dandelion and burdock ?" she asked in what sounded like a child's voice - almost overcome by the sense of dislocation.

"Wouldn't I though," he replied: his stock answer, Selina recalled to every request. She heard her best friend Janice asking once: "You wouldn't have a packet of Du Maurier cigarettes would you darling ?" And for a moment she was not dead: not killed in a car crash in Nassau with the guitarist from Larry's band she'd tried to escape with: but standing here again, showing the rest of them how to be sophisticated. Her memory reminded Selina of how easy they both thought it would be to escape this place. She rushed out of the shop, clutching the bottle of near-black liquid, afraid of every genie waiting to materialize from the dusty jars and welcome her home. The bell sounded again and she ran straight into the arms of Herbie.

Selina was so sensitised she recalled in an instance the last time she'd been in his arms: outside the church the day he rescued her. She felt the same solid chest and scented the same sweet aftershave. Smaller, she noticed, stepping back, but still vain - dying his hair and eyebrows now.

"Selina," he said, clearly surprised and looking caught and awkward but only momentarily. "How are you ? How is your mother ?"

There were many times during her short marriage to his son when she struggled to try and get to the bottom of this man: and knew she never got close. He appeared to be at once shallow and materialistic, then complicated and generous. Everyone said how honest and willing to help he was and yet she always suspected him of cunning and self-importance.

She saw a glimpse of that cunning pass over his face as she said her mother had suddenly rallied and even wanted this, holding up the bottle.

Herbie responded quickly before she had any time to wonder what it was for, "Ha, dandelion and burdock," he said. Wanting to hide from this unlucky girl, the fact that in most of the mounting number of deaths he was becoming ever more conscious of, the person usually pulled themselves together just before the end: gathering their strength for dying rather than living. "That's the stuff. Dandelion and burdock wine. Aunt Flo used to make it by the gallon and my father would pinch it before going down the pub. 'She'll only leave it to turn into vinegar,' he used to tell me, taking a few good sups and then topping the jar back up with water so that she wouldn't know. Or at least that is what he thought. 'Only virgin left in the village,' he said to her again, one day after a session down the local. 'Yes,' she'd replied, 'but even this old virgin knows the difference between water and wine !' Stopped him in his tracks that did."

Selina began to suspect something. The Herbie she recalled, certainly did not stand around gossiping for nothing.

"Did you know that my boy was back home ?" he asked. "Back in the arms of his family. And doing what *I* always hoped he would. What *I* always knew and told him he should. Painting his own landscape. Doing very well at it too."

Selina listened without responding. 'Never play poker with Herbie,' her father had once warned her. 'He is the most stone-faced artful bugger on two legs.'

"Who wants to look at a load of foreign skies and sun when they can have a good English landscape. It never did Constable any harm to stay put, did it ? And as for all those gloomy self-portraits, who would want one of those staring down at them ? I won't even mention those nudes he used to churn out." Herbie held her eyes with his own.

Selina guessed he knew. She sensed some desperation coming from him. What did he want ? she wondered. Was he just a control freak as Madeline always used to claim. Or was he genuinely concerned and wanted to understand and help. She was as puzzled by him as ever,

"I think there is a crowd of men waiting for you," Selina said calmly, gesturing to the steel gates where Richard and about twelve other farmers were stood staring across at them. Their mouths open and eyes unblinking.

Now, as Selina pushed for William to let her see the painting, she decided not to mention that meeting. She imagined Herbie's face and expression at the exhibition when he got to see her. Unshocked, she judged, as he stared and smiled. Maybe, giving her likeness a quick wink, just to let her know.

"Okay," William said. "You better come and take a look."

Selina got home later that night than usual. It was nearly light by the time she laid in bed trying to picture her real self again. She had thought the moment her eyes saw the painting, and felt the light and warmth of its truth and her awakening that it could never fade. Selina wanted to bask now in its afterglow: to see again and again how her spirit still radiated and was unbound. But already it was becoming obscured: the dullness and gloom of this place misting her vision and senses; with the smell of medication an acrid, bitter reminder of guilt and responsibility over illness and death, emphasized by the loud, brittle, deliberate noise of her mother's nurse, saying 'I heard your comings and goings'; and the dawn tractors raging and rejoicing, as they began to turn the sky darker with their emissions, and rut the earth red with their steely claws. And William *had* tried to kiss her.

She did not mind his arm going around her as they stood together in front of the canvas. It felt natural, almost parental and supportive as if he sensed clearly her feeling of starting to be reborn as its power drew her in. Then, just as she wanted to stay inside it for as long as time would allow, he turned her away and tried to kiss her. Selina felt she had been torn back prematurely into a rebirth she did not want; and with the cruellest insensitivity. Worse still, that the person who created such a thing was willing to destroy it so easily. A betrayal, it seemed at that moment, more dreadful than any against her before, and by the very person she'd trusted most.

She stormed down the studio steps ignoring William's pleas for her forgiveness. Then his calling her back. Asking her still to come to the exhibition at least. Selina walked straight past the other barn conversion not caring for once if Herbie did see her. And William was suddenly by her side, still bare footed as he liked to paint. "I love you," he said. "I always have and will"

"No," Selina said, desperate to hurt him as much as he'd done to her. "You love the girl in the paintings: the one from your imagination. But it is not me. You got it all wrong: from the first one to the last one." She'd left him standing there. His feet white and frozen on the cobbles and knew that no slap across the face could ever have stunned any suitor in the history of that place more.

Now she wished she could take the lies back. And longed for it to be the start again and not the end. Selina remembered taking her clothes off for him that first time and the feeling that something weighty and soiled had been removed. Now it was back. She let her finger slide inside herself. She was bone dry. All night, every night of the painting she'd been so wet it was a struggle not to let William see her juices as they escaped and glistened each time she moved. Selina still began to stroke herself gently needing to try and find some comfort however brief or shallow. There was a tap on the bedroom door and she hurried from bed and pulled on a large T- shirt.

"Selina," Nurse Titmarsh said coldly, "I am sorry to disturb *your* sleep but I think you better go in and see your mother. I do not think she has got a lot longer."

Selina shoved past her quickly and felt the chill that had waited all this time: never really warmed by anything as trivial as art.

"I shall call the doctor," Selina heard the nurse say.

"Mother," she called gently and pushed the door open.

There was no great farewell speech. No death bed revelations or last words of advice. Just the delicate shuck of her mother finally crumbling. And, for a few brief, glorious seconds a holding together long enough for a smile and touch. One last unspoken message of what could outlast even death.

Dr. Canin came and told Selina what she already knew. "I delivered you," he said letting her fill his arms and rest her head on his shoulder. "You were a beauty then and if you don't mind an old man who has seen his share of both entrances and exits saying it: you are a beauty now. I know both your mother and father were rightly very proud of you."

Selina was touched by his kindness but saw behind his back the nurse look down. "I will take care of my mother now," she said as Nurse Titmarsh began to strut over to her mother's body. She did not want her to go near her now. Dr. Canin understood and waved the old lady away before she could argue. "And I will stay and help," he announced, daring her to look back.

Later, Selina came to realize, just how alone her mother had been since Miles's death. She read through the careful and organized instructions for the funeral arrangements. A quiet cremation. No mourners except her sister Ruth and another sister that Selina had not seen for over thirty years. And an old friend who had stayed in touch since her mother's schooldays by letter. No one else. A simple note in the local newspaper saying no flowers and inviting donations to cancer research.

It told Selina everything about how her mother had felt about this place and these people. Just about every single family in the village had arrived at Miles's cremation. "They turn out," he'd told her once, "for everyone just the same. It's a perfunctory as planting or ploughing. Another duty to be done. No more." Miles's death had been sudden and too shocking for any instructions to stop them. Clearly her mother wanted the message to be heard this time.

Then she wanted her ashes poured into the same river as she had poured her husband's. Their favourite place. A short way off but as far removed from the sluggish drains of the Levels as possible. A clear, rock-strewn trout and salmon river that was famous in the county for one act of treachery when it built up a reservoir of its own contriving, then let it burst and tear the cosy, slumbering town at its mouth to bits. Miles loved to fish it. And walk its banks with his girlfriend, then wife. "You were conceived on that bank," he'd once teased Selina. "And right in the middle of the May fly hatch. That would tell any real fisherman just how passionate we were for each other."

Selina prayed she could find the exact spot when the time came. And then she knew that it did not matter as she thought of a beautiful story she'd read after her father's death and wished more than anything at that time she could have let him read it. Or better still have read it to him. 'A River Runs Through It' by Norman Maclean. Miles would have loved that book. Selina recalled some of the beautiful poetry of its final paragraph. 'Eventually, all things merge into one, and a river runs through it.' Then, for the first time since she'd sat on his lap and wept, she let her own tears mingle with that endless current.

CHAPTER SIXTEEN

Richard swirled the acid. It felt too heavy inside its constraint: as if within the small blue bottle a weight appropriate to its power existed that was testing and searching for any weakness. "You be very careful," his friend warned him, "and only give it a minute before you wash it off, or your ancient farm implement will become ancient history. If you get any on your skin and don't get it off immediately, it'll find a way in and keep on going until it eats the marrow out of your bones. Get the fume in your lungs and they'll be vapour by the time you are dead of Pneumonia. So remember: gloves, goggles and mask and plenty of water at hand."

Richard placed it back on the shelf in the old farm refrigerator. He could imagine its blue glow still filling the space as its light winked out. The chill of the place inconsequential to the heat of its purpose. Tomorrow, he would have to take it home and up to their bedroom, then find a way of hiding its ribbed form inside his too tight suit jacket or trousers. Richard got himself ready to go milking; ignoring the sense of incongruity of leaving the acid amongst all the balms and medications used to treat and heal his animals. And then the much harder one of it travelling in the car with his excited parents and wife. He closed his mind to the feelings and let others take their place. Ones that would carry him through. Ones that might help explain afterwards.

Herbie was still sulking. It was an art he'd mastered in the days of his indulgent aunt and father. Now it was about a painting. Not the photograph in a frame that he'd once been *made* to pose for,

"Stop it Herbie," Madeline said. "William knows best what paintings he wants to show. It is not up to you. That must be a terrible blow to your vanity I'm sure, but one you best accept before tomorrow. Because nobody is going to want your opinions at the gallery either." Actually Madeline was sad that *their* painting would not be on show. Just themselves in the flesh with no mystery to stare and wonder at.

"I just said that it was a painting that he should exhibit," Herbie repeated for the nth. time: "one that showed his potential from the start."

"Shows you - more to the point," Madeline interrupted.

"I just said," Herbie ignored her: "that as a piece of early work it was worth letting others see."

"And he told you that he got it wrong and that the new version is not yet ready," Madeline heard the door close and watched the back of her husband hunched as he carried on with his game. It was still far too easy, even for her, to dash over and offer him some bribe to straighten and cheer up. She was glad that William had already left for the gallery and would not be back until all the hanging and arranging was done. Because one thing she knew for certain, was that Herbie was more than capable of pestering William silly all day to get his own way. There was no sign of any diminishing in that department, she sighed: still the centre of his own universe.

Herbie peered up at the studio window. He let his imaginary eye drift slowly along the row of paintings, not wanting to reach the last one and follow that beam of sunlight into his own body.

Not wanting to confirm what he knew: that it was still there. "Damn stubborn boy," he whispered to the black protuberance of oak. Ten years ago, he decided, he would have taken the spare key, opened this door and removed the painting himself. Then knocked a bloody nail in the wall and hung it in front of them all and accepted his son's gratitude afterwards when it turned out to be the hit of the show. He fumbled in his pocket as if searching for the key. His hand found two small coins and he saw two others spinning from his fingers that time so long ago. Herbie wondered where they were now and whose eyes they may one day cover. He trudged off to mend a gate he'd spotted hanging loose a day before. His other son seemed to be missing too many obvious things lately as well. "How could a man rest easy," he asked himself, "when everyone around him was half-blind?" Herbie puffed his chest out and rose up, knowing now he was out of his wife's vision. "Still the 'Hawkeye' to the end," he said loudly to a sty of piglets, noticing that their bedding had not been changed.

William had just finished throwing a major sulk himself. The three paintings he most wanted to hang did not fit in with Giles's and Caradoc's idea of an exhibition. In fact, did not fit at all. The two pretty girl assistants and the equally pretty boy, could not help but agree with their bosses' pertinent guidance and experience. William attempted again to explain that they were a different side to his work and very important, "Think of them as signposts," he tried.

"Yes I am." Giles replied: "Ones that will lead your buyers out of my gallery. We've sold everything you have let us have so far. And it is my opinion that we will sell just about everything on sale tonight – except those."

"What Giles means," his sweeter partner, Caradoc, added, "is that it is a question of not confusing the viewers. There are some very good buyers coming tonight and an important agent who has expressed an interest in you. He is talking about limited edition prints and has clients in multi-nationals and food chains and so on."

"Piped art you mean," William said, looking at the paintings running along both sides of the gallery walls, seeing them repeated endlessly - knowing now and wanting to tell: they are not what I meant to do; they will never be done again; they are for an escape not an internment.

"No, art shared," Giles sensed he better calm the situation down. "The therapeutic quality of landscapes like these on the stressed and harried lives they will touch is nothing to be ashamed of."

"I need those three canvases included," William snapped. "They are a little important for my stress level."

"I know," Caradoc said, placing his long translucent fingers on William's shoulder: "all of the landscapes for sale and on loan stay in the main gallery. We'll hang those *new* three in the small annex at the far end. A sort of private show within a show."

William was left with the pretty boy to sort it out while he heard Giles and Caradoc having a ferocious row over whether it ought to be Sancerre or Chardonnay, Australian red or Bulgarian. He could not help himself from hoping he was the real cause behind their disharmony.

Later that day, after he got home and managed to avoid another of Madeline's cooked dinners and a further debate about art with his father, William sat alone in the studio. He knew that, Nancy, Selina's mother had died. And that it happened a short time after her fleeing from here. There was no way he could find to approach her now. "Why," he asked himself over and over, "did I try to kiss her ?" With each sop of an answer William saw that ugly scene replayed. The look in her eyes as they changed from delight at her painting to disgust as his face approached hers. He reheard Selina's footsteps running down the stairs again, the blackness of her coat seeming to drift back each time and fall like some cloud over his senses. It blocked out everything including his vision and will.

William tried to sketch now and saw nothing but dark heavy lines running away and unable to converge. A stupid whisper came, a memory of Madeline's often told story about how his father had pursued her relentlessly. He saw himself firing up the old Buffs Superior and roaring off after Selina. It almost made him smile but not move. He could picture too clearly the response he'd receive if he tried to get Selina - instead of some easily flattered, ageing maiden - on the back of his saddle and roar away to some life of captivity and duty. Then an even more ridiculous notion came into his head: maybe she would come to the exhibition after all. He'd given the dates and directions enough times. "Or," the black cloud fell heavily again: "had she left already?"

"Just a question of time," Madeline said, the moment the news of Nancy's death reached her, "before the 'For Sale' boards go up and madam is off again."

"No," William said, and nearly let slip that she'd actually told him many times. "I think she is here to stay."

And strangely, William watched a look of satisfaction and delight fill his mother's face at this news. "Both the wanderers back for good," Herbie had added contentedly, as if it confirmed and assured everything he knew about the world beyond his own.

William threw the pad down. He stood at the window where recently Selina danced and posed. He saw his own dreadful reflection glaring back and knew it was what he needed to paint.

How he was now. And would be, it felt, forever.

Selina awoke and listened again for her mother. She'd done the same thing every day since the funeral and, though she promised herself not to, hurried each time in to the empty cold room to check. This morning she forced herself to remain in bed.

Last night, for the first occasion since being alone in the house, Selina became frightened. The house shifted minutely on its bed of peat and clay, or made some other adjustment she did not want to consider, and the noise creaked into her room just as Selina was drifting off. It made her think of Perry. At first with the usual anger and loathing at what he had done, then with an unstoppable apprehension about what was in the house with her now. Selina struggled to go into her mother's room, then to every room and window in the place, before, finally daring to push open the kitchen door.

Afterwards, Selina sat in Miles's study where she was starting to sort through all of the clutter of her parents' lives. She was finding some comfort in the familiar, or the sudden mnemonic kick from another hoarded item, but craved someone to talk to. A friend who she could joke and cry with; a friend who would demand nothing in return. There was no one. Selina had very deliberately cut everyone out of her life a long time ago. Still unsettled and reluctant to go back to bed, she began to go through another drawer in the curiously black-streaked desk Miles always claimed was made of stink-wood and had belonged to a judge. And made a discovery.

Her father was a poet. Selina read the first one in what she thought was another of the small journals he'd kept religiously every year since his youth. As Selina read it and realized exactly what it was, she heard him telling her again,

"Never trust any person who reads too much: they always

have secret longings."

"So, now we'll see what yours were," she whispered and began reading. By the time Selina had read through a small number of the poems, her fears – like those that her father touched, struggled to find words to express and then reach beyond – faded and she carried the book back to her bed.

After a while Selina got up and, unable to resist, went into her parent's room again. The bed was made with clean sheets and plumped-up pillows. Virginal and untouched, as if all its memories of love, dreams and deaths had been washed and smoothed from its embrace. She sat down on her mother's side and began to read some of the poems to her. The ones she believed Miles would never have revealed to her. Then she saw them looking down at her. Both smiling at her easy, comfortable presumptions and naivety over their lives.

Selina closed the book and then the bedroom door. Her mind was made up. Later today, she would go to the exhibition. A slightly late arrival, she decided. Quiet entrance or a spectacular one ? She pondered that only briefly, knowing that she was truly her father's daughter: full of passion and secrets that would never fade or stay hidden. Whatever the cost.

Annie waited for Richard to return from dropping the children off at her mother's. One journey a day, especially a longer one than usual, was more than enough. All of her pregnancies had made her travel sick and have an allergic reaction to alcohol. She tried not to think about the long drive in Herbie's big, leather-smelling, new car. His still - even with Madeline now attempting to slow him down - wild aggressive driving. Then the gallery with, no doubt glasses of wine or champagne, and her face and arms going a blotchy red, as she waddled around in her maternity dress. And to top it all off,

Richard insisted on wearing his peppermint green, double-breasted suit.

The couple of times Annie had seen it before in his wardrobe she vaguely tried to picture the man that once bought and wore it. Whoever he was, she did not know or want to. Last night she'd watched as he struggled to find a way back into this shroud from an early existence. It disturbed her to see the result and she sensed Richard's self-consciousness over her reaction,

"Maybe I'll get Maddy to move a few buttons," he said.

"No, you look fine," she'd lied.

Annie was still much too excited about Richard's agreeing to go to the exhibition to risk anything. Though she believed that he was doing it mostly to please her; she also recognized something else stirring inside her husband each time it was mentioned. Annie hoped it was a sign that Richard was pleased to be going and wanted this chance.

She looked at the suit again stretched flat on the bed waiting for him, also the narrow, flashy, almost snake-skin textured necktie. Annie pictured him wrapping it around his thick neck once as Selina was getting ready to lead him off to another party. She imagined what the gorgeous Selina might have been wearing or pulling on. And how Richard's eyes would have been on her. "But not hers on you my love," she said, hearing the sound of Richard returning. She let her hand rest on their unborn child and felt proud and defiant.

CHAPTER SEVENTEEN

Madeline looked wonderful. Annie was still amazed by how easily her mother-in-law could transform herself from dowdy to vibrant. One seemingly simple step from farmer's wife to an elegant, sophisticated woman. She watched Herbie swirling around her: hardly able to keep his hands from touching and grasping what had appeared. And how easily Madeline controlled him; and enjoyed rebuffing him; more than even the illusion she'd created.

Herbie was immaculately dressed: but then neither she, nor anyone else, had ever seen him off the farm any other way. Always the well-cut jacket to emphasize the size of his shoulders and chest, the shoes shone so brightly to reflect the many smiles, nods and gestures of respect his passing *usually* gathered and, Annie had no doubt, that he was expecting tonight. As Richard helped her out of the car, then moved next to his parents, she could not help noticing how much more strained and awkward he appeared than either of his parents. Almost, as if they'd deliberately given him only one side of their characters - either through nature of nurturing - with some cruel pragmatic decision that it was all *he* would need. Annie dismissed the thought and decided it was probably just nervousness over what was coming. They were both aware that Maddy and Herbie had promised not to let William know that his brother was going to attend and Richard must be anxious over the possible reaction.

In fact, Richard was feeling very positive and determined. His mind was made up and his plan set in place. He joined his father and walked by his side, their steps even and measured, while behind came his wife's flat-foot slap thickening and masking his mother's graceful high heel step. Something about that sound touched him and added to his purpose. Herbie knew exactly where to park and then to lead them. Richard could picture him sat with his brother making his map – bursting to tell William that *he'd* managed to talk Richard into coming and dreading not to be some major part of the surprise. Herbie pushed open the gallery door and stepped aside to allow the ladies to enter first. Richard waited, trying to suck in one final untainted breath, "Turn your lungs to vapour," he heard again and stepped inside.

Richard estimated with his quick, cattle-counting eye that there were about forty people in the gallery. He deliberately hung back and watched as his family moved into the crowd. Madeline took a glass of champagne off a very pretty girl and Herbie said something to her that made her smile then blush as he took his – charmed as easily as ever. He saw his wife refuse and guessed that she was now telling her all about her hormones. He turned away and saw the first of the paintings.

A wall. And Richard recalled it and its history in a trice. Once it was part of a cottage. A shepherd's isolated home without any electricity or mains water. The shepherd's wife had been killed: her neck broken when a bale of moisture-heavy spring scented hay toppled from the top of a rick and hit her. "Carrying home our morning milk," the old man used to tell anyone who'd listen, including Herbie and Richard every time they gave him some small task to carry out. "And do you know she never spilled a single drop."

The wall was stone built with a crude fireplace in its centre. The rest of the house had been demolished shortly after the shepherd and his son were evicted. Richard could remember Herbie's fury at the time when he got to hear that the wealthy landowner no longer needed a shepherd and they were being forced out and the place pulled down. Richard had gone and stood with his father after the task was carried out and this wall left standing only because it joined and formed the back of something more important than a person's home – a disused piggery.

"Do you know," his father told him: "five generations of that man's family lived and worked here. Think of all those fires: smoking peat or crackling green withy, burning and scorching the stones as those people lived out their lives. All gone."

But now, as Richard tried to smile at another gorgeous girl offering him some blood-red wine in a silver goblet, they were back alive. Amongst all these wealthy, pretty people, he could see their shadows in the penumbra of that long cold fire again. It was impossible for him not to see and feel their strength and dignity. And finally – as he saw a highly-polished copper pot standing on a green musty bale with a drip of pure white milk frozen in its fall – not to touch their tragedy. Richard read the price. "More," he told himself, "than I could earn in a year."

"Of course," he heard a posh-sounding voice telling two people stood in front of another painting of what looked like a corpse laid out on a pub table, with a mist, hazy outside its walls and a man asleep on one horse, while another pulled a brightly painted cart laden with golden milk churns: "as Ruskin said, 'Art is the only true biography'. And that is precisely what you are seeing here. Not another example of the collective madness masquerading as art: but the real thing from a genuine talent."

Richard moved away from the sales-pitch trying to ignore the words and shut off what he was beginning to see. It was becoming hard to concentrate as he found himself surrounded by so many places and people he'd forgotten. So much caught.

There was Roly Cart laying the hedge again. A hedge they'd grubbed out last week and was cut now into logs or still smouldering in ash. The hedge seemed now to have its place back, along with the man that knew nothing of the modern needs of agriculture. His billhook like a claw trying to cling to something precious rushing away. Roly portrayed as some Arcadian hero. "So who was going to be the villain in all this?" he asked himself, sensing the answer, and visualizing his own role in driving all these folk from their soot-stained, thorn-walled paradise.

Richard shook his head to clear it. He had never felt so full of colour and impressions and with them, questions and doubts. Then he saw his brother. Ten yards away in the arched entrance to a small side room. It was the first time in so many years he was this close to William. Richard could not help recording how thin and tired he looked. Also, that behind the plastic, coat hanger smile of acceptance and gratitude for the compliments and praise, there was sadness and pain.

In the corner of his vision Richard noticed a large painting of a frozen tractor: duck-egg blue and rusting in a blanket of snow. He'd learnt to drive on that old Massey and once he recalled, gave William a ride on it, letting him sit on his lap and take the wheel. He almost felt it cough into life: sucking in a mouthful of Easy Start: denying it was asleep or dead now. Richard looked away and saw Annie, Madeline and Herbie all standing just inside the entrance of that other room: staring past William to whatever waited inside. Their expressions were of shock as they moved in. And Richard knew at what.

He let his hand go into his pocket and confirm the bottle's

presence again. Richard moved quickly toward them. He could see himself already being exposed and betrayed. All of the dignity and grace his brother was granting to so much else, taken back from him in spades. "Crucified," he said aloud, shoving a couple of people easily out of his way.

Richard appeared under the arched entrance and saw his family. Both standing in front of him and on the wall. That early childhood painting his father once rushed out of sight. Only different. Richard saw them all sat at the table again with the same explosion of sunlight seeming to burn away what covered them. But now it appeared to expose just shadows and not alternative people. His mother and father appeared joined by a common, mutual need: not two people hiding their real selves, but using them for their own space and freedom. Richard felt he would have liked a chance to see all of the other changes. To try and understand some of the complexities that made up his parents through a different pair of eyes for once. He would also have liked to see what his brother made of the two of them now, but there was not time. Richard ignored the fact that his parents were standing below the painting and, actually, for the first time he could recall in his life, holding hands as they studied it. He turned slowly. And saw Selina.

Only it was not the Selina he'd ever seen. Instead, the one he once longed and burnt for. Her spirit and beauty caught. No, he understood, not caught. That was what he had tried. Given. She was giving what was there. Even his brother could not have stolen this image.

Richard saw his wife and brother move slightly back from where they were standing shoulder to shoulder before the final painting in the room. He stepped in between them, his eyes half-closed, hardly daring to open them, his fingers beginning to turn the lid of the bottle. Richard felt a charge rush through his body as he saw himself. Not ugly and grasping as he'd pictured and dreaded so many times. Not the petty, jealous, unforgiving person he expected his brother to have seen easily and delighted in exposing out of revenge. Not transformed into something that would haunt the rest of his life - even after its planned destruction allowed it to fade for everyone else. But glorified. That was the only word he could find to get close to how this gift was making him feel.

The pike lived. Every minute scale seemed to ripple and gleam with energy. The ribs in its tail and fins fanned translucent in the breeze. And it was the exact fish Richard had caught that day with every single detail perfect. The painting showed the moment when he returned the pike. Only in this it was as if he was some great magician drawing it from a peat black void. Goblets of silver dripped from its body and showered back into the opening of the water below. In the windows of the pumping station there were other pictures: each pane of glass holding a different image. Some of the actual fight with the rod bending and pulling into the next scene. And one that made him feel cold: two boys fishing together once so long ago.

He let his hand come slowly out of his pocket and placed it gently on his brother's shoulder. Thin, he could not help noticing, like the skeleton of a bird or fish. Then Richard saw the clump of flowers in the bottom corner of the painting. They were those strange flowers he'd found once in the snow and not seen since. It made him glimpse, as his brother's arm linked them together, what a terrible frightening memory William must possess and what it might mean to live with such a gift or curse. He could not speak. Richard felt Herbie and Madeline standing behind them. Felt them all looking at him. Felt enriched and alive.

Selina came in. She was dressed in a very short, silver dress that caught and reflected the light as she moved. A pretty boy sprang upon her with a glass of champagne. "You are in the painting," he blurted out. "It's in the other part of the gallery." He pointed as Selina felt people turning to look. She brushed him off easily as he started to follow her and offered to be her guide. Selina wanted, if possible, to pick her moment and not be spotted by William until she was ready.

Selina glimpsed the paintings either side of her. She knew from William's comments and actions that they meant little to him now they were finished. Nothing more in fact, than part of a journey he'd once failed to record. She also understood that he was leaving them behind both physically and mentally. William's record of his time here for others to see and remember. Selina had wondered - and feared in a way as she'd read her father's poems - that the portrait of her was for the same purpose. And in her fury, and arrogance over his attempt to kiss her, she'd failed to grasp a bigger truth. Now, she'd come to the gallery to confirm it or deny it for reasons she did not want to face or admit to.

As Selina hurried to meet the painting, she tried to shut out those thoughts, wanting just to see herself open and naked again; longing to see and get close to the image it had created without any of the doubts or questions she'd attached. Instead, what she saw stopped her cold. The whole family gathered together with their backs turned to her painting. Her ex. husband with his arm around William. William embracing his brother. Herbie and Madeline actually holding hands behind them. And Annie glowing with pride. While she glared at them from the wall and the doorway. Selina could feel their joy at this moment and knew exactly what her arrival would do to it. She turned, silently: a diamond-back shimmer of something slithering away that registered as nothing more than motes of sparkle in the periphery of their eyes.

Richard wanted that painting more than any possession he'd ever desired - but understood that he would never own it. And not because of the price tag which could have bought three of his pedigree Holsteins, or the fact that like the three paintings in this part of the gallery there was already a reserved sticker on it. But because of his brother. It was more than enough that after so long it had granted him this chance. To risk it by trying to *buy* something so special was not possible. To place his farmer's market value between them now an insult. Then as he looked, Richard felt something else between them. A lump of cold glass containing its fire. He thought of all the hate that conceived and then bred his plan of throwing it over this painting. Of standing in front of these people and dissolving what his own bitterness had visualized being here. Richard shook his head and pulled away,

"I've got to step outside for a moment," he said.

"I'll come with you," William said, as if the two of them should stay together.

Annie held William back as her husband hurried out. She knew her husband was overcome with emotion and guessed he wanted some time alone to compose himself.

Richard marched back through the gallery. He noticed the couple from earlier and tried to give them a smile of assurance as they panicked to get clear of him this time. A few steps past them and he stopped. At the door he could see Selina wrestling her arm away from some dainty-looking youth. She escaped him and rushed out of the door. Richard went after her. Just before he left the gallery, he saw Dolly laying face down in a dew-pond, the hedges rooted out, the sky full of fumes and the water stagnant.

Selina stopped hurrying as she reached the bridge over the oily channel of this part of Bristol docks. She looked down at the sheen of its surface, moving and melding with a garish yellow glow from a nearby warehouse window. She heard the footsteps behind her and felt someone grab her arm and turn her to face them,

"Selina," Richard said. His other hand pulled out the bottle and, quicker than she could see, threw it away over her shoulder, falling as a dull blue star for an instant before it hit the water. Selina did not even turn back to see what made the syrupy entrance into the sediment-laden water. Richard watched it sink in a slow swaying motion. Its light like some luminous sea creature hurrying to escape this place.

"Come in and see your painting," Richard said.

"I can't. I do not know why I came," Selina said.

"Because you had to. It is beautiful. He has taken away all the things fools like me tried to put there." Richard had seen that clearly. And felt in a small way that some of his own guilt was washed away with it. "Now you must come back, please. I know William has been looking out for you."

"Richard, it was good to see you guys together. Don't let me spoil things," Selina touched his hand.

"My brother seems very sad," Richard said hoping just maybe she might forgive him one day. And trying to deny the other feeling that he was getting from her. "I'm sure your appearance will make his night, and yours, complete. Don't be a coward now."

Richard escorted her back in. He saw Madeline react exactly how they could have all predicted. Herbie smiled and nodded as his wife threw his hand away from hers as if it were suddenly contaminated. William was being introduced to two men and cornered by the gallery owner. Richard watched the look that came to his brother's face. "Don't need to be an artist to recognize that one Bill Bob," he said to himself and without any jealousy, as unbelievably he saw Annie take Selina's arm and lead her in front of her own painting. Secretly, he was hoping she might have wanted to take a look at the one of him first. "Silly bugger," he whispered going to look at it one more time alone.

William was loading the three paintings into the hire van. Even though Caradoc insisted on pricing them, they were never really for sale. Everything else, apart from those on loan was sold. The gallery wanted some more and there were new commissions on offer. The agent was desperate to sign him. And William couldn't have cared less. Selina had managed no more than a stiff and formal greeting. And then left before he could escape all the attention and find a chance to talk to her. Even with the genuine happiness he felt at his reunion with Richard could not shake the sadness and gloom from him now. She did not even manage to say goodbye.

"I even recognized her with her clothes on," the young man quipped as William loaded Selina's painting last. The two girl assistants joined in with his laughter.

"I'm just fucking surprised a little tosser like you would recognize any woman: kit on or off. Now piss off back to the other still life's inside." He drove off quickly before his anger turned into something more tangible than words.

Back in his studio William made his mind up. He guessed that Herbie and Madeline might still be awake, waiting for his safe return, maybe even hoping that he would call in for a night cap so that they could toast his triumph. He had definitely seen Herbie's chest swell each time another 'sold tag' appeared. Or to discuss the first family meal they were planning back at the farmhouse for next week. William did not care. He walked straight past. Then along the village road. The large full length portrait of Selina resting against the side of his body, her breast warm against his face, her black hair above his.

Her house lights were on as he entered her drive so he kept to the shadows. William placed the painting to the side of her doorway. He rang her doorbell and ran off like some schoolboy playing tricks again. Back in his studio, William turned all of the lights off except for two small glow bulbs lighting the stairs. And waited. By the morning he would know. Was his gift a goodbye card or a letter of invitation ?

Much later the sound of footsteps on the stairs was soft. The sound of her coat slipping off and falling to the floor softer still.

~

Herbie, old 'Hawkeye' spotted them. He slipped out of the bedroom into the tower that ran up the side of his barn. He kept a powerful pair of binoculars here and liked to watch out over the farm from its various windows. Of course it was still too dark to use them now, but what he was looking for was near enough to see unaided.

It was the early dawn of the Friday before the planned family meal on Sunday. Herbie imagined the table laid and the food in front of them. Richard letting him sit at the head of the table Madeline next to him. He heard his grandchildren getting excited. Annie trying to show Madeline how capable she was. Then his two sons in their old places. Only, not this time, he knew; and had known since the show. He squeezed his head out of the window into the cold night air and watched William and Selina loading the van.

They were crafty. Making certain, he noted, to get a dark one, and to have pushed it silently in from the road. The sound of it passing the barn a mere whisper of friction across the cobbles. Maybe, to most, just another barn owl ghosting onto its prey. But not to Herbie.

He saw the last of the stuff go into the back of the van and its door eased shut. Then William take Selina in his arms and stand for a long while kissing her passionately. Herbie wanted for one moment to wake Madeline and let her witness their leaving. And how they actually looked together. Not how she would see them in the morning's light. It would, he realized, be pointless and mean nothing to her within a few days at the most.

William went back into the studio and came out carrying two large paintings. They were wrapped in what looked like newspaper and he leant them gently by the side of the entrance. Herbie could see a label hanging from each of them. He guessed they gave the names of the new owners, but no other message: except one. The only one his son could really give them. William turned the key in the large door.

"Take the key," Herbie whispered into the funnel-shaped stone of the window: a slit designed once to let arrows fly out and find no easy return. "Take the key," he fired another of his mental bolts as William carefully tied the key to one of the paintings. Then with a rush they were in the van, the engine started, the lights came on and they were gone.

Herbie went back into his bedroom. He would not go back to bed or attempt any more sleep. He never did. Once, Herbie recalled, trying to explain to William why he still insisted on rising so early, now he was *supposed* to have retired. "If after you awake, you lay there and drift back off, you can have the strangest dreams. Weird notions. Disturbing things to stay in your mind for ages."

"Great," William's enthusiastic reply at the time.

Herbie looked at Madeline sleeping. He would get the blame for this. Endlessly, over and over. It would be added to her list of things he'd already taken from her. He tried not to imagine how many times she would tell him that she should have driven away with *her* artistic lover. How *he* stopped her. Herbie smiled and left her to her dreams.

He went down to the kitchen and waited for the first ray of sunlight to enter. Herbie had made a spot on this wall - the same as back at the farmhouse - so that he could sit and judge how high the sun was rising. When it reached that mark, he knew summer had returned. And the season of cold and darkness was over. Today, and for a long time yet, it would be well short of that.

FLAME BOOKS

Flame Books is an ethical publisher who supports new writers and, through online sales, also supports various creative projects. If you have enjoyed this book then visit our website soon - www.flamebooks.com - for more original and exciting contemporary literature.

COVER ARTWORK

The cover artwork has been created especially for The Bestowing Sun by artist Louise Yeandle. Louise, born in Winchester, studied at the Arts Institute at Bournemouth and Winchester School of Art. She is a painter who seeks to create disquieting atmospheres in her work. Her lurid paintings challenge traditional notions of landscape painting.